WITCH QUEEN BOOK SIX

WITCH QUEEN

A.D. STARRLING

COPYRIGHT

Witch Queen (Witch Queen 6)
Copyright © AD Starrling 2024. All rights reserved.
Registered with the US Copyright Service.
Second paperback edition: 2024
ISBN: 978-1-912834-44-0

www.ADStarrling.com
shop.adstarrling.com

Edited by Right Ink On The Wall

DISCOVER AD STARRLING'S SEVENTEEN UNIVERSE AND MORE

Seventeen Series

OTHER SERIES BASED IN THE SEVENTEEN UNIVERSE
Legion
Witch Queen

MILITARY ROMANTIC SUSPENSE
Division Eight

MISCELLANEOUS
Void - A Sci-fi Horror Short Story
The Other Side of the Wall - A Horror Short Story

PROLOGUE

Memories came to Rose Blake in bright, distorted flashes drenched in blood and the stench of Hell.

A red moon dominating an obsidian sky devoid of stars. A rooftop littered with the corpses of those she had tried to defend. The agonizing pain that tore through her chest when a demon ripped open her flesh and bones with his claws.

But it wasn't the fiend who had mortally wounded her that captured her mind and soul in her infinite dance toward death. Instead, it was the woman she considered her best friend and sister who stole her breath and broke her heart.

The power Mae Jin had wielded that night as she tried desperately to save Rose had made the very air tremble and the city shake. And the anguish and despair painted across her beautiful face when she'd realized she had failed would forever be imprinted in Rose's darkest recollections.

Her last living memory was of falling, her body

numb and weightless, the devil who had brought the forces of the Underworld to the city and wreaked havoc upon their lives wrapping her in his suffocating black wings.

But death had not brought her peace.

Instead, it had turned her reality into a nightmare from which she feared she would never find salvation.

Most of the time, she floated in what felt like eternal darkness, deaf and blind, her consciousness barely there.

But there were moments when she was roused. When visions of what was happening in the world of the living played across her inner mind like a macabre show. In most of them, the devil who had killed her engaged Mae in some kind of violent battle that often left her bloodied and bruised.

It took Rose a while to realize what had happened to her mortal remains. But however much she howled and raged at the fiend who had possessed her physical form and performed the most unspeakable acts with the hands that had once healed the living, Rose knew no one could hear her.

Until someone did.

Rose...

Rose tore her wretched gaze from the fading sight of Barquiel fighting Mae once more. She looked around the endless void surrounding her, wondering if the voice she had just heard call her name was yet another figment of her imagination.

It came again, startling her.

Prepare yourself...Rose...

Rose tensed. She had not imagined it after all.

Is this one of Barquiel's tricks?

She swallowed and fisted her hands. Considering she was somewhere between the land of the dead and the living, she didn't have anything to lose if she responded to the voice.

Rose lifted her chin defiantly. "Who are you?"

I am...Ran...Soyun...

Rose startled. She knew that name from Barquiel's memories. Ran Soyun was the first witch who ever walked the Earth and the wife of her killer's mortal enemy, the demon Azazel. She was also the mother of Na Ri, Mae's original incarnation.

"How—how come I can hear you?!"

We don't have much time, Rose...

Rose flinched as Mae's voice reached her, the fury it contained staining the darkness around her with a palpable aura of rage.

"CHAOS SEAL!"

A fracture appeared in the gloom. It was small and thin but so shockingly bright it dispelled the shadows around Rose, revealing a faint crimson haze.

Barquiel's scream tore through the void.

The crack expanded a fraction. Rose froze.

Something pulsed beneath it. Something that echoed the beat of her once human heart.

"What is that?" she mumbled.

The answer, when it came, stole away the breath she shared with the demon who had possessed her.

That is a fragment of your soul, Rose. The soul Barquiel subjugated and destroyed when he took over your body...

Rose's throat tightened as she stared at the miracle before her, Ran Soyun's voice sounding faintly inside her skull.

"Why—why did he keep a part of my soul?!"

He needed a piece of it to take over your mortal coil. Your consciousness should have disappeared when your soul shattered, but it didn't. That is how strong that fragment is. Ran Soyun's voice hardened. *Are you ready to fight for what is left of your soul, Rose Blake?*

Hope flared inside Rose for the first time in ages. She clenched her jaw.

"Tell me what I have to do."

CHAPTER ONE

Nikolai Stanisic stood on a rooftop terrace overlooking Manhattan. He gently rubbed the faded photograph in his hand with a thumb.

It was the picture Mae Jin had found in the palace that once served as the headquarters of the Dark Council, the prison he and his mother had been confined to for years.

The setting sun cast an orange glow on his mother's pale face where she sat holding him on her lap. His chest grew tight with a wealth of emotions.

Nikolai still remembered Gabriela Stanisic begging one of the few palace attendants who had been tolerant of her presence to take the photograph on the day he'd turned ten. They'd had but an hour in which to enjoy a hastily arranged secret birthday party, one which only his mother and himself had attended.

She had been summoned to Vedran Borojevic's private chambers shortly afterward, only to return late at night, her face ashen and the fresh bruises the

Sorcerer King had inflicted upon her body showing above the neckline of her long-sleeved dress.

By then, Nikolai had been old enough to realize just how his father treated his mother. Even if he hadn't been, his half-brother Oscar had relished recounting the ways in which their father regularly degraded her.

The rage that had burned in his young heart when he'd grasped the horrors she suffered to keep the two of them alive in that pit of black-hearted snakes was something he still carried to this day.

A haze of Hellfire Magic ignited around him despite his best intentions. Even though Nikolai knew it would not harm anything he cherished, he hastily suppressed his powers, worried they would accidentally scorch the precious memento he clasped.

Alastair rustled his wings and made a worried sound on his shoulder.

"I know." Nikolai stroked the familiar, remorse a bitter aftertaste in his mouth. "I need to do something about these feelings."

His breath shuddered out of him. *Before they destroy me.*

The resentment and fury festering inside him since he'd woken up from the Illusion Sorcery cast upon him had only grown with the passage of time. He still found it hard to swallow all the horrible things he had done to Mae and her bonds in that church in Concord. How he had allowed his father to absorb his and Alastair's powers and use them against the woman he loved and their friends.

In the aftermath of the battle that had seen Mae free

his and Alastair's minds from their dark shackles and Hellreaver meet his shocking end, Nikolai had focused all of his energy on bringing solace to the witch he had betrayed.

He knew Mae had forgiven him for what he did to her. He just wasn't ready to acquit himself of his sins yet. Especially since the Hellfire Magic Vedran now possessed gave him a distinctive advantage over them. He now had in his hands the one artifact that could lead him to the soul of the first Sorcerer King: the *Book of Light* that he had destroyed Hellreaver to obtain.

Dietrich Farago, the Immortal scientist who had worked for Barquiel and Vedran, had theorized that there was a very high chance Fire Magic could open the book. And Hellfire Magic was the most powerful of all Fire Magic.

The rooftop door opened behind Nikolai, distracting him from his grim thoughts. He slipped the photograph into the pocket of his jeans.

Mae Jin crossed the terrace and joined him, Brimstone padding silently beside her. "There you are."

Alastair fluttered down onto the fox's head.

Mae stopped next to Nikolai and looked at the scenery spread out before them. "Pretty, isn't it?"

"If you don't mind the stink of the river," he murmured.

Mae rolled her eyes. She turned, propped her elbows on the metal railing, and studied him inquisitively.

"Wanna talk about it?"

Nikolai stiffened a little. "Talk about what?"

Mae pursed her lips. "Stop trying to pretend nothing's wrong. I know something's eating at you." Her expression sobered. "Considering everything you and I have been through, it's hardly surprising."

Nikolai clenched his jaw. "It's not your problem to fix."

Mae furrowed her brow. "I think you'll find that it is. You are my consort, after all."

Nikolai's breath caught. With everything that had happened in the past few weeks, he kept forgetting the most staggering development of all. Mae had officially chosen him to stand by her side.

That realization warmed his belly and sent heat coiling through his veins.

"Oh." Nikolai arched an eyebrow, his tone dropping an octave as he twisted to face her. "So, does being your consort mean I have zero privacy now?"

Mae blinked at his gravelly voice. The color that bled into her cheeks and the way her breathing accelerated told Nikolai she wasn't immune to the attraction sparking between them.

"You are mine." She caressed his jawline boldly before dancing her fingers down the column of his throat and his chest, her eyes bright with resolve. "Your mind. Your heart. Your body. Your soul. I will claim your everything, sorcerer."

Nikolai's pulse spiked. *Shit.*

He moved, his arms closing tightly around the woman who had bewitched him, his mouth descending upon hers. She responded with a fierceness that made his blood sing, her hands rising to clasp his nape and her body pressing against his like she couldn't bear the distance between them.

The moan that left her throat ignited the fire smoldering inside him. He skimmed his hands down her back to her butt.

A blast of incubus energy rolled across the rooftop, startling them.

"I knew it!" Vlad Vissarion snarled from where he stood framed in the doorway, his tiger familiar at his side.

Nikolai and Mae reluctantly disentangled themselves.

Vlad glared accusingly at the witch. "I told you to fetch him for dinner, not violate his lips! And you!" The incubus's slit-like gaze switched to Nikolai. "How about you do me the decency of not making out with her on my property?!"

"Technically, we're not on *your* property at the moment," Nikolai pointed out.

"Really?" Mae said out the corner of her mouth. "You want to go there?"

"I own the damn building, shit-for-brains," Vlad ground out.

Nikolai smiled. "You mean the *Black Devils* own it."

"Wow," Mae mumbled.

The incubus's eyes flashed crimson. "She may have chosen you as her consort, but that doesn't mean I can't kick your ass, sorcerer boy."

Nikolai lowered his brows. "I'd like to see you try."

"Enough." Mae sighed. "Let's go in and eat. Tarang looks like he's about to faint from the lack of calories."

The familiar had rolled onto his back and was doing his best starved tiger impression. He yowled in agreement.

Nikolai and Vlad grumbled under their breath and followed her down the stairs and into the incubus's glitzy penthouse. Unease twisted Nikolai's stomach as he observed the casual way Mae and Vlad set the dining table.

He'd reluctantly agreed to move into the incubus's apartment after he and Mae had left her family home in Flushing. After all, no one could deny her wish to keep Brimstone and Tarang together. The tiger had proven to be a source of comfort to the demon fox following Hellreaver's destruction.

Still, Nikolai couldn't completely quell his misgivings about their circumstances. Nor could he deny the ugly truth that had been gnawing at him since they'd showed up at Vlad's place.

If I'm being honest with myself, he deserves the role of Mae's consort more than I do. They both have demonic blood running through their veins. Whereas I am the son of her enemy and the man who betrayed her.

"Nikolai?"

He blinked.

Mae was studying him with a trace of concern. "You haven't touched your food."

Nikolai suppressed a wry smile. Mae had already cleared her plate and was on her second serving.

"Sorry, my mind was on…other matters."

He picked up his knife and fork, sliced a chunk of carrot for Alastair, and dug into his steak. Irritation shot through him at the way the meat melted in his mouth.

He squinted at Vlad. *This asshole even cooks perfectly.*

Vlad narrowed his eyes. "What's that look for?"

"You'll make a good wife," Nikolai admitted reluctantly.

An expression of utter disgust dawned on the incubus's face. He shuddered. "Please, the way you said that is giving me chills."

Nikolai scowled and stabbed his steak viciously.

"Hey, watch the china!" Vlad growled.

Mae's mouth flattened into a thin line. "Has anyone heard from Cortes? He hasn't answered my last few messages. I can't get in touch with Anya either."

Enrique Cortes and Anya Mendes had left for South America a week ago to talk to their respective covens and for Cortes to have a one-on-one with the *Bacatá Cartel* boss. As the future head of the Medellin coven and Anya's fiancé, the sorcerer's presence in the world of magic needed to be permanent. For that to happen, he needed to cut his ties with the criminal underworld.

According to Vlad, there was only one way for someone like Cortes to leave a cartel. And that was in a coffin.

"They've been in the *Bacatá Cartel* compound for the last two days," the incubus admitted reluctantly.

Surprise jolted Nikolai. "They?"

Mae sucked in air. "You mean, Anya went with him? Why?!"

Realization struck.

"Oh," Nikolai muttered. "So, if things don't pan out

the way they want, she'll cast her Illusion Sorcery on the cartel and they'll walk out of there unharmed?"

"Bingo." Vlad made a face. "Better than us waking up to the news that the most powerful criminal gang in South America's gone up in flames overnight. You can say what you want about the *Bacatá Cartel,* but they keep a tight leash on the psychopathic cabals in that part of the world."

"Still, how could Cortes take her there?" Mae protested.

"I know you think Anya is some kind of fragile flower, but she has a pretty strong backbone," Vlad said. "She did survive the Dark Council's torture."

"You're right." Mae wrinkled her nose thoughtfully. "And she said some pretty nasty things in that warehouse when the Dark Council attacked us."

"Yeah, trash talk still doesn't suit her though," Vlad muttered.

Nikolai's cell pinged with an incoming message. He checked the screen and frowned before leveling a wary look at Mae.

"Bryony wants to see us."

CHAPTER TWO

THE NEXT MORNING SAW THEM PULLING UP OPPOSITE the address Abraham Whitworth had given them. Mae stepped out of the Jeep with Nikolai and stared at the imposing facade of the seven-story, redbrick and limestone mansion taking up half a block on 5th Avenue.

"This is the temporary headquarters of the coven?" she said leadenly.

"It's Bryony's ancestral home."

Mae startled. "Really?"

A smile tilted Nikolai's lips as they crossed the road, late autumn leaves dancing colorfully around them on a mild breeze. "Don't tell me you thought she lived in the apartment at the coven?"

"I totally did."

The sorcerer chuckled. Relief lightened Mae's chest at the sound.

Over half a month had passed since their return from Europe. Most of that time had been spent grieving what they had lost during their last battle with the Dark Council.

But the time for mourning was over.

There may not have been any signs of the Sorcerer King, Barquiel, or even the missing Oscar Beneventi as of late, but no one in the world of magic was foolish enough to believe that they were truly gone. The magic councils and the covens allied with them all over the world remained on high alert, aware their enemy could strike at their heart at any given moment.

Mae greeted the guards manning the entrance distractedly as she and Nikolai entered the building.

We need to put in motion the plan I came up with if we are to have a fighting chance against Vedran and Barquiel.

Nikolai was not only crucial in any future fight against Vedran. He was the most powerful white magic user on Earth and had been able to follow traces of Ran Soyun's magic to where Barquiel had hidden her in Hell. Mae was convinced that once they met up with Azazel, the sorcerer and the demon's combined abilities would allow them to track down her stolen soul and body.

She shot a faint frown at Nikolai. *And for that plan to work, he needs to be on top of his game.*

She could see the darkness gnawing at him in his eyes and the troubled expression he often wore when he thought she wasn't watching him. Mae suspected the sorcerer still had not absolved himself of what he had done to her and her bonds after he fell under Anya Mendes's Illusion Sorcery. And she feared the wrathful emotions he harbored toward his father and brother would influence his future actions in such a way that they would put him in danger once more.

She had already lost him once. Mae's nails dug into her palms.

I refuse to lose him again.

Warmth thrummed across her bond with Brimstone.

The fox nudged her leg. *Are you alright, my witch?*

Yes. I will be.

Hellreaver's pendant lay against her chest under her T-shirt, his broken pieces temporarily fused with their magic. His silent presence was a cold reminder of their defeat at Vedran's hands.

Brimstone's gaze found Nikolai. *He is strong. Stronger than he was before he fell under the Illusion Sorcery. You must trust in him, my witch. His heart may be tainted with rage but he will stand by your side whatever comes.*

Guilt knotted Mae's shoulders at his solemn words.

Or you could just take two consorts, Brimstone continued blithely. *In case something happens to one of them. Even if it doesn't, I hear from a reliable source that threesomes are all the rage these days.*

Mae's footsteps faltered. "What reliable source?"

Nikolai aimed a puzzled glance her way.

The tiger told me some pretty saucy stories about the incubus. Brimstone sniffed. *That guy could charm the pants off Satanael himself.*

A group of witches and sorcerers came out of a corridor to their right. They slowed when they spotted Mae and Nikolai, admiration and awe etched across their faces. Heads bobbed sheepishly in greeting as they scurried across the foyer.

Stories of the epic battle in Europe had spread through the covens like wildfire.

Mae smiled and waited until they were out of earshot before fixing Brimstone with a glare. "Is that why the two of you were snickering in the corner of the room the other day while we were watching a movie?!"

Alastair eyed the demon fox disapprovingly.

Suspicion clouded Nikolai's face. "What did he say?"

"Nothing you want to know."

She was still watching Brimstone with a pinched expression when a familiar voice rang across the vestibule.

"Mae!"

Oh, look. Brimstone's eyes shrank to amused slits. *Here comes consort number three.*

Mae's eyes widened. "Roman?!"

A handsome young man with blond hair and tawny eyes was crossing the marble floor, a jade and sapphire chameleon clinging to his shoulder. Roman Volkov seemed oblivious to the admiring glances he was drawing from the coven members in the foyer as he closed the distance to them.

Mae stared. *The Vissarion bloodline is really something, huh?*

And you have two of them willing to be notches in your bedpost, my witch, Brimstone contributed with a grin.

"Could you not put it that way?!" she muttered under her breath.

Shocked gasps sounded from several onlookers when Roman took Mae in his arms and hugged her tightly. She rocked back on her heels and hesitated before returning his heartfelt embrace.

Filomena hissed out a friendly greeting.

Mae suspected from the avid stares locked on them like laser beams that this too would spread through the covens like wildfire. She swallowed a resigned sigh and sneaked a peek at Nikolai.

The sorcerer's expression was turning thunderous.

Roman ignored Nikolai. He straightened and beamed at Mae.

"I'm really happy to see you." His smile faded. "And I'm sorry about Hellreaver."

A dull ache stabbed through Mae's chest. "Thank you. How did your training go?"

"It's been a good experience." A fireball the size of an apple whooshed into life above Roman's finger, the flames tight and precise. "Filo and I have finer control of our magic. We can even do wordless incantations. And accessing ley lines is becoming easier." He raised a mocking eyebrow at Nikolai. "I bet he can't do wordless spells, like *us*."

Mae masked a wince.

"No, but I *can* kick your ass all the way to Prague, kid," Nikolai growled.

"Now, now, stop trying to wind him up," someone drawled.

A figure appeared behind Roman. Nadia Hadid ambled leisurely toward them, her desert fox Horus draped around her neck like an expensive fur stole.

The High Priestess of the Council of the Sun was wearing a lazy expression that failed to hide the sharp intelligence in her hawk-like eyes.

"I didn't know you were in New York," Mae told the witch.

Nadia shrugged. "The High Council called all of us in for the meeting, so I decided to chaperone young Roman here."

"I don't need a chaperone," Roman protested.

Nikolai sneered. "You're still under age, brat."

"We're having a meeting?" Mae said warily while Roman glowered at Nikolai.

"Budimir Volkov and Ludmila Vissarion will have my hide if anything happens to you," Nadia reminded Roman thinly. "I might be a powerful witch, but those two's constant nagging is enough to drive anyone into an early grave." She waved an irritated hand at Mae. "And of course there's a meeting. Why did you think Bryony called you guys here?"

"There you are," someone interrupted brusquely before Mae could respond.

They turned.

Abraham was standing on the first landing of the grand staircase dominating the foyer.

"Come on, it's already started," the aide said, beckoning briskly.

"No one mentioned anything about a meeting," Mae said, sullen.

"What do you have against meetings?" Nadia asked.

"Something bad always happens when there are meetings."

"She's not wrong," Nikolai muttered.

"Ah." Nadia grimaced. "I'd forgotten about that acid-inducing Philadelphia incident for a moment."

Abraham sighed heavily at Mae's disgruntled expression. "We have sandwiches and cake. There's even food for the fox."

Mae and Brimstone brightened.

It was as they were climbing the stairs to the upper levels of the mansion that Mae noticed the buzz of activity around them. Almost all the rooms had been taken over by the New York coven. Even the sweeping hallways they passed were jampacked with workstations and filing cabinets.

She scanned the defensive magic she sensed throughout the building. It extended to a fifty-foot radius around the entire block and down into the bowels of the structure. She frowned faintly.

We should augment their barrier, she told Brimstone. *The coven headquarters on Madison Avenue had ancient runes built into its foundations. Barquiel still managed to smash those in minutes.*

The demon fox's eyes flared crimson. *I hope that damn demon is suffering wherever he is.*

Heat flushed through Mae at the thought of the Archduke of Hell who had hurt Na Ri and her kin. It still sickened them that he'd coveted Ran Soyun for all these years.

Bryony's study took up most of the northwest corner of the third floor. The New York coven High Priestess was in the middle of a full-blown argument when they entered the palatial chamber.

"I'm not going to stop her from doing what she wants, Karin!"

Bryony slammed her tea cup on her saucer and glared at the witch seated opposite her.

Karin Everheart scowled. "We can't just let her waltz into Hell. What if something happens to her?"

"Karin has a point," Derrick Adlington murmured, absentmindedly stroking the hawk perched on his knee.

"We all know what a trouble magnet Mae Jin is," Gerard Mosele added with a grunt. "Ten bucks says she gets into a fight with an even bigger numbskull the minute she steps foot in the Underworld."

"They sure trust you, huh?" Nadia told Mae drily.

Mae pursed her lips as the witches and sorcerers in the room finally registered their presence.

Roman twisted around and gaped at Mae, eyes bulging. "Wait. You're trying to go *where?!*"

CHAPTER THREE

Marlena Kosek smiled brightly and rose to greet her nephew. "Nikolai."

"Hey." Nikolai hugged his aunt and kissed her cheek. "You should have told me you were in town."

"I flew in this morning." The High Priestess of the Council of the Moon glanced at Bryony. "It seemed urgent."

"Hi," Simon Roth greeted them awkwardly.

The new head of the Atlanta coven was doing his best not to fidget in his seat where he sat beside Isabelle West. Rumor had it the pair were currently an item.

"I was only gone a goddamn minute," Abraham muttered under his breath as he crossed the floor and joined Raven Quinn on a couch.

"I'm sorry." The witch apologized to her boyfriend with an irate sigh. "I wanted to keep the peace, but that would have involved some pretty powerful destructive magic and I know how much Bryony cherishes those Ming Dynasty vases on the sideboard."

Bryony cut her eyes to the L.A. coven High Priestess before studying Mae with a frown. "You're late."

"Traffic was a bitch," Mae said thinly. "Also, no one said there was a meeting."

Brimstone zoomed over to a serving cart holding half a dozen steaming dishes. Bryony's cat familiar Penley slinked off the desk and joined the fox.

Nikolai maintained a diplomatic expression as he and Mae headed over to a sofa. A stilted silence ensued. It was broken by a loud grumble.

Everyone looked at Mae.

She sniffed. "It's been two hours since breakfast."

Bryony sighed. "Why don't you eat something before we talk?"

Mae helped herself to two sandwiches and a slice of chocolate cake from the tiered trays on the coffee table.

"So, are you really planning to go to Hell?" Karin asked sharply after she'd finished inhaling her food.

"Yes. Once Alicia gets Astarte's approval."

Mae hid her unease behind a resolute expression. The truth was, she hadn't heard from the Soul Reaper queen since she left for Hell over a week ago to seek Astarte's permission for her to travel to the Underworld with Nikolai and Vlad.

Astarte was the Goddess who headed the alliance of powerful fallen angels opposed to Satanael's wicked plans for mankind. Once Artemus Steele's sworn enemy, she was now one of his most ardent allies.

Well, I have a backup plan in case she says no anyway.

Mae was eyeing another slice of chocolate cake when she became conscious of the High Council's brooding stares. Guilt stabbed through her at their worried expressions.

She could understand their concerns. The only ones who seemed resigned to her decision were Bryony, Raven, Marlena, and Nadia.

Gerard sighed heavily. "How about you give Hellreaver to the Soul Reaper queen and let her ask this Armaros guy to fix him instead?"

The eleventh leader of the Grigori and once Heaven's most talented blacksmith, Armaros had forged Hellreaver at Azazel's bequest when Na Ri was born.

Mae frowned. "This isn't just about getting Hellreaver fixed. I also want Armaros to take a look at the skeleton key that was meant to open the *Book of Light*." She raised a hand when Gerard tried to interrupt. "I know what you're going to say, but I'm still certain it serves a purpose we haven't fathomed yet. Call it a witch's instincts." She clenched her jaw. "And I *have* to find my father. Azazel needs to know what took place in Europe and the secret Nikolai uncovered when he followed Barquiel to Hell."

"And if Astarte says no?" Lines furrowed Derrick's brow. "What will you do then?"

"Then I'll ask Artemus Steele to take me to Hell instead."

Bryony sucked in air at this bombshell statement. Abraham stared at her like she'd lost her mind.

"You will?" Nikolai mumbled.

"Who the heck is Artemus Steele?!" Roman hissed at Nadia.

Mae avoided Nikolai's stunned gaze. She hadn't told him or Vlad about her backup plan. "That guy knows the layout of the place and Armaros's location. Besides, I'm pretty sure he'll want to help."

She toyed with the bracelet on her wrist.

It was the one Serena Blake had given her a month ago. Forged by Artemus Steele and infused with the divine energy he had inherited from his parents, it had allowed Mae to resist Vedran's attempts to enslave her and her bonds.

"Artemus wasn't the one who opened a doorway to the Underworld," Bryony informed her in clipped tones. "It was Sebastian Lancaster who created the rift that allowed them to enter Hell." She lowered her brows. "And he's far more sensible than that idiot. Sebastian won't cave in to your demands so easily."

Mae's stomach plummeted. "The Sphinx opened the rift?"

"Yes."

"We have a Sphinx?" Roman mumbled.

"We even have a Phoenix," Raven said.

Mae chewed her lip. *Dammit. This Sebastian guy sounds even more uptight than this lot.*

"Anyway, the reason I called all of you here is because you need to see something," Bryony said.

Her tone had Mae stiffening. Brimstone glanced over curiously from where he was demolishing his third dish of beef.

Abraham went to Bryony's desk and brought an envelope over. He took out the contents and spread them on the coffee table, his lips pressed into a grim line.

It was a series of photographs.

Isabelle made a horrified sound. She covered her mouth with a trembling hand, the color draining from her face. Simon clasped her shoulder, his own expression turning strained.

"Look familiar?" Bryony asked in a brittle voice.

"Shit," Nikolai ground out.

Tension knotted Mae's shoulders. Brimstone joined her.

The bodies in the pictures had the same appearance as Isabelle's butler and housekeeper when they were found buried in shallow graves on her property, after she was kidnapped and held hostage by the Dark Council. Except there were dozens of corpses piled haphazardly atop one another on the scorched ground.

Mae's pulse raced as she tried to understand what they were looking at. Bryony's next words sent a chill down her spine.

"They are Dark Council members," the older witch stated in a flat voice. "And they all died from injuries consistent with black magic."

Mae's eyes rounded. "What?!"

"We found the first…group twelve hours ago," Abraham said sourly. "We've discovered three more since then." A muscle ticked in the sorcerer's jawline. "The crazy part is these witches and sorcerers aren't even from around here, yet we keep finding their bodies in our territory."

"The only silver lining to this incident is that it hasn't made the news headlines yet." Bryony looked her age all of a sudden. "The bodies are turning up in areas of New York under the strict jurisdiction of our coven," she explained wearily in the face of their stares. "I've had to inform the mayor of our findings and Jared is doing his best to keep things under wraps so no one in the NYPD leaks information to the press, but I don't know how much longer we can keep this from the eyes of the ordinary public."

"Why would they kill their own?" Nadia said stiffly in the fraught silence.

"Maybe it's some kind of message," a pale-faced Roman hazarded, his gaze locked on the macabre images.

Nikolai went as still as stone at his words.

"I think Roman is right," he mumbled. He traced one of the figures in a photograph with a finger. "This wasn't a normal fire. It looks like Hellfire Magic was used on them."

Alastair rustled his wings restlessly on his shoulder.

Ice formed in Mae's veins. "So, this is Vedran's work?!"

Nikolai met her anxious gaze and bobbed his head.

"But how?" Derrick leveled a hard stare at Mae. "Wouldn't you have picked up on the Sorcerer King's presence if he was in the city?"

Mae shared a wary glance with Nikolai. "Not if he's using *Void*."

"The only way to cancel that spell is with pure white magic from a ley line," Nikolai elaborated.

"If he was in New York, he would have come after Mae," Raven said dismissively. She lowered her brows. "More importantly, why is he killing his own sorcerers and witches?"

Brimstone nosed at the photographs. *He must be in need of their magic, my witch. It is the only logical explanation for him to sacrifice his army.*

A sour taste filled the back of Mae's mouth.

"Mae?" Nikolai asked worriedly.

"Brim thinks he's after their magic."

Another thought struck her then. Her stomach grew heavy with dread and guilt.

Could it be that our attacks injured his core? And he needs his subordinates' powers to heal himself?

"Oh fuck," Nikolai said hoarsely.

The color had leached from the sorcerer's skin, leaving him ashen. His crow familiar made a worried sound.

"What is it?" Mae said tensely.

"I think I know how he's killing them," Nikolai replied numbly. "And he doesn't even have to be in New York to do it."

"What?!" Karin gasped.

Blood pounded dully in Mae's skull as the truth Nikolai had just grasped emerged from her subconscious.

"The spell your father put on them," she mumbled. "The one I erased from your core." A dizzy feeling swept over Mae. "*That's* how he's killing them?!"

"It has to be," Nikolai murmured, his knuckles white.

Derrick cursed.

"How utterly evil," Marlena mumbled.

Mae swallowed. "He must need the black magic he put inside their cores to recover from the wounds Nikolai and I inflicted on him during our last battle."

Abraham drummed his fingers on his armrest. "It still doesn't explain how or why he's choosing to leave those men and women's bodies here though."

"His black magic can open rifts." Nikolai cut his eyes to Mae, his expression haunted. "As to why—"

He paused, his face darkening with disquiet.

"It *is* a message," Mae stated flatly. She scrutinized the photographs on the table. "He's telling us we're next."

CHAPTER FOUR

"Dammit!" Bryony cursed. "Does that mean he's managed to find the soul of the first Sorcerer King?"

"I doubt it," Mae said grimly. "If he had, he would have come after us."

The study door opened before anyone else could speak. Violet and Miles Nolan came in ahead of Ephra Erwin. The Houston coven High Priestess appeared physically drained.

Violet rocked to a stop when she clocked their bleak expressions.

"What happened?" The witch grimaced. "Did someone die?"

"Yeah," Roman muttered.

Violet recoiled. "Really?! It was a rhetorical question."

Ephra's expression grew stilted when she saw the pictures on the coffee table.

"I see you told them about the bodies," she murmured to Bryony.

"Where were you?" Mae asked Violet and Miles curiously. "And why does Ephra look like she needs a tonic?"

Ephra gave her a jaundiced glance as she plopped down on the couch next to Karin. Karin passed her a sandwich.

Violet and Miles exchanged a guarded look. "We were keeping watch while she tried to do something about that lynx."

Mae tensed.

A muscle jumped in Nikolai's jawline. "How is Drabek?"

Ephra sighed. "Not great. She doesn't eat and she barely sleeps. And her fur is shedding." She glanced at Mae. "At this rate, it might be kinder to put her down."

Mae's insides twisted.

Oscar's familiar had been driven mad by the *Subjugate* spell Nikolai had used on her and her sorcerer in Europe. Being abandoned by Oscar had only made things worse.

Though Nikolai had trapped them inside a *Contain* spell, he'd discovered in the aftermath of their battle with the Dark Council that his brother had escaped it somehow. No one knew if Oscar had left voluntarily or been dragged away by Vedran against his will. Still, Mae was certain Oscar had been forced to leave his familiar. Despite the evil deeds he had committed, the sorcerer had clearly loved the lynx.

Now that Drabek's soul was free of black magic, the creature's true nature had finally resurfaced. And she wasn't the vicious animal she'd always appeared to be. Even in her madness, she never tried to harm anyone.

Brimstone nudged her knee with his head. *I know her circumstances trouble you, my witch. But it could not be helped.*

Mae clenched her fists. She couldn't help the sorrow and pity she felt for the lynx's wretched fate.

"Where's Gyuri?" Bryony asked.

"She's still down there," Ephra said. "She's having a break before she tries to calm her again."

Mae frowned. "Gyuri?"

"Mrs. Son-Ha," Bryony clarified.

Mae blinked. "Mrs. Son-Ha is here?!"

Koreatown's number one gossip and busybody had turned out to be a powerful Shaman who'd been gifted a divine artifact by the archangel Camael. She'd used it to protect Mae, Nikolai, Vlad, and their friends when Anya Mendes's Illusion Sorcery had turned the world of magic against them.

"We asked her over to thank her after you left for Europe," Bryony explained. "It was the least we could do."

"She and Bryony hit it off," Abraham grunted. "The two of them are like peas in a pod."

Bryony narrowed her eyes slightly at that. "Being referred to as a pea in a pod hardly suits a lady of my age and station."

Raven smirked. "Better than a shrew in a castle."

Violet swallowed a snort. Marlena did her best to pacify Bryony while the witch glared at Raven.

"What's all this?" Miles said.

He indicated the photographs on the coffee table uneasily. Abraham brought the cousins up to date on the latest developments.

"Shit," Miles mumbled, ashen faced.

His boa constrictor Millie tightened anxiously around his waist.

Violet frowned. "Does this mean the Sorcerer King will continue to taunt Mae with corpses until he's ready to fight her?"

No one knew the answer to that.

"Say what you want about the guy, but he's an expert at psychological warfare," Gerard said darkly.

A knock came at the study door. Abraham rose to get it.

It was a witch. She glanced awkwardly at them before whispering something in his ear. The aide thanked her and closed the door, his expression troubled.

"What's wrong?" Bryony asked.

Abraham's gaze moved to Mae. "Mrs. Son-Ha is asking for you."

NIKOLAI'S PULSE QUICKENED AS THEY APPROACHED THE door that led to the basement. He could hear the high-pitched sound of a distressed animal in the distance.

Abraham led them down a flight of stairs and along a shadowy corridor. They came in sight of the cell at the end.

Mrs. Son-Ha sat on a low stool outside it, her dog

Dexter on her lap. She was eating a rice cake and sipping a cup of green tea. Her Chihuahua whined as he gazed at the creature pacing the floor of the prison restlessly.

Nikolai's throat constricted. Alastair croaked softly.

Drabek was but a shadow of her former self. The lynx looked gaunt, her ribs protruding through her thinning fur. Her ragged claws left trails of blood on the ground as she cried and yowled, her orange eyes radiating grief and loss.

"How did she get injured?" Mae asked in a voice devoid of emotion.

Nikolai glanced at her. He didn't have to be a genius to know the sight of Oscar's familiar was hurting her as much as it was him. Her nails were digging so hard into her palms he was surprised she hadn't cut herself.

Mae flinched when he took hold of her hand. She swallowed and gave him a grateful look.

"She clawed at the floor until her nails wore down," Mrs. Son-Ha said quietly. She sighed. "I think that's enough rest for these old bones." She put her cup on the tray beside her, got down off the stool, and reached a hand through the bars. "Come here, cat."

To Nikolai's surprise, Drabek slinked over to her. The lynx stopped and lowered her head obediently so Mrs. Son-Ha could touch her face.

Mrs. Son-Ha's pupils flashed white.

The hairs rose on Nikolai's arms. Mae stiffened beside him. The power emanating from the old woman felt different from magic.

"There's an element of divine energy in it," Mae murmured, surprised.

Nikolai stared at the pale light shimmering around Mrs. Son-Ha's fingers. *Is that because she deals with the dead?*

Drabek slowly relaxed under her touch. She plopped down on her belly, her expression a little glazed. Dexter pushed his head between the bars and licked her nose.

The lynx made a soft sound and closed her eyes. She lay on her side, her body loosening as she succumbed to sleep.

Mrs. Son-Ha gently stroked her head.

"It would be best to put her out of her misery soon," the Shaman said in a cold voice that was in sharp contrast to the kindness she was showing the animal.

She fixed Mae with a hard stare.

The old woman's features softened a fraction at her distraught expression.

"Unless you undo this spell and reconnect her core to her sorcerer, she will be driven to death by her madness," the old woman stated with a finality that made Nikolai's stomach twist. "And she will suffer immensely before that time comes."

He swallowed. "I—I will do it."

Mrs. Son-Ha shook her head. "You shouldn't. You won't be able to live with yourself if you kill your brother's bond."

"So, you're saying it has to be me?" Mae asked in a brittle voice.

"Yes." Mrs. Son-Ha rose with some difficulty and

pressed a hand on Mae's shoulder. "This is also your duty as the Witch Queen."

Her words haunted the silence between Mae and Nikolai during their drive back to Vlad's apartment. Nikolai's fingers clenched on the steering wheel as he replayed their final conversation with Bryony.

"I want you to examine one of the bodies we found," the witch had asked Mae. "You're the only one who can confirm whether your theory is correct."

Mae had reluctantly agreed. Since the hospital in the basement of the main headquarters of the coven was out of action, she would have to sneak the corpse into the mortuary at Grandview General to carry out the autopsy.

"Steve would kill me if he knew what I'm about to do," Mae murmured as they drove into the underground garage beneath Vlad's apartment building.

"He still can't get the higher-ups to grant you an extension on your leave?" Nikolai said.

"No." She grimaced. "At this rate, I'll be without a job soon."

Nikolai refrained from telling her that the combined wealth of all the covens meant she could live out the rest of her life in gold-plated luxury and eat all the cake she wanted. He knew how she felt about using money she hadn't earned for herself.

She must get it from her parents.

They'd just gotten into the lift to Vlad's penthouse when Mae startled.

"Oh."

Nikolai frowned. "What's wrong?"

"I just felt Cortes and Anya's cores in the building." Mae's expression grew puzzled. "That's strange. They weren't there a second ago."

She stiffened the next instant. The hairs rose on Nikolai's arms. He could sense something in the distance. Something sinister.

A vile pressure thickened the air, drawing a gasp from them both. The cabin trembled.

Nikolai's eyes widened. *That's*—

Crimson lit up Mae's pupils. "There are hellbeasts in the building!"

Brimstone's hackles lifted.

Nikolai's pulse quickened as he reached for his magic. His spear manifested in his hand, brimming with the pale light of his Moon and White Magic.

CHAPTER FIVE

A FOUL STENCH FLOODED MAE'S NOSTRILS WHEN THEY emerged on the landing outside Vlad's apartment. Relief shot through her.

She couldn't sense the incubus or his familiar.

A violent burst of magic brushed against her cores just as Nikolai reached for the door handle, its taste as familiar as her own. She grabbed the sorcerer's arm and yanked him aside a second before the door exploded outward and crashed into the opposite wall.

The giant hellboar that had smashed into it left a bloodied trail as it slid to the floor, golden sparks sizzling inside the six-inch crater in its chest. The red light in the monster's eyes faded.

Mae's stomach roiled when the creature's dead form collapsed into inky threads that vanished with a hiss of corruption.

"What the hell?!" Nikolai mumbled.

A scream came from inside the apartment. "Enrique, *no!*"

The chilling power of Anya's Illusion Sorcery drenched the air.

Mae scowled. "Let's go!"

The inside of Vlad's penthouse looked like a bomb had gone off. Broken glass and debris crunched beneath their feet as they closed in on the sounds of the battle. Mae's heart lurched when they came in sight of the living area.

Cortes stood in the middle of the floor, his eyes and those of his bird familiar Popo blazing with a fierce light as he braced against the bull-like monster towering over them. The sword in his right hand sparked against the beast's wicked horns while blood dripped from a nasty wound on his flank and soaked into his suit.

The muscles and tendons in his left arm bulged where he hung on grimly to the whip he was using to stop a hellwolf from shredding Anya to pieces, the bright cord raising the sickening stink of burning flesh as it scorched the creature's hind leg.

The wolf snarled and snapped its jaws inches from the witch, heedless of the pain, claws scraping deep grooves in the floor.

Blue flames flickered around Anya and her Harpy Eagle Sable, their magic focused on the dozen hellbeasts that had surrounded her and Cortes. The witch's left cheek and forehead bore shallow cuts and she was favoring her right leg. Though most of the creatures had frozen in their tracks under the spell Anya had unleashed, the hellbull and the hellwolf seemed immune to it.

Magic surged through Mae's veins. Half a dozen *Devour* spells burst into life above her hands. She blinked.

Black and ivory flickered within *Devour,* the threads intertwining with the crimson light of her demonic power.

Fire resonated across her bond with Brimstone, distracting her. The demon fox shook himself out into his nine-tailed form, the red aura that surrounded him making the air tremble.

It too was tainted with darkness and light.

Mae's throat tightened on a sudden wave of dread. *Is that white magic and—black magic combined?!*

Na Ri's presence rose inside her. *Focus, Mae!*

Mae clenched her jaw. *She's right. I'll worry about that later!*

She hurled the *Devour* spheres at the hellbull just as Nikolai cast *Hell Flare* upon the wolf. The monsters screeched under their attack. The sounds pierced Mae's ears and shattered what remained of the windows.

Brimstone brought the hellbull to the ground. He pressed a powerful paw against its chest, sank his fangs into its neck, and ripped it open with a savage growl. A crimson tide gushed out of the monster's torn vessels, the ripples washing against Cortes's expensive shoes before they bubbled down into obsidian threads that dispersed into nothingness.

The corpse of the hellwolf similarly disappeared inside the deadly firestorm that had engulfed it, the spear stuck in its heart clattering onto the floor.

Mae and Nikolai exchanged a tense glance.

There was no doubt about it. Whatever this was, it stank of Vedran's magic.

"Thanks!" Cortes panted.

Popo flapped his wings gratefully on the sorcerer's shoulder.

They turned to face the monsters Anya had immobilized.

"Let's clean this up," Mae said coldly.

It took them a handful of minutes to dispose of the remaining creatures. Anya sagged when the last one vanished in a fading pool of corruption. The pale fire in her pupils faded. She crumpled to the ground, violent shudders racking her body. Sable crooned worriedly in the witch's lap.

Cortes fell to his knees beside them, unheeding of his wound. "Anya!"

"I'm okay," she mumbled numbly as he took her in his arms.

She gripped his shirt and pressed her face into his chest. Tears seeped from under her eyelids as she squeezed them shut.

Mae whirled around at the sound of breaking glass, her fingers spasming as she automatically sought Hellreaver. The fight drained out of her. She straightened.

Vlad and Tarang were crossing the floor, demonic power flickering around them and the black swords the incubus held. A muscle jumped in Vlad's cheek as he observed the damage to his apartment.

"What the hell happened?!"

"WE WERE AMBUSHED AFTER WE LEFT THE CARTEL compound," Cortes said in a hard voice.

Nadia frowned, Sun Magic gleaming around her fingertips where she sat on the couch beside the sorcerer and healed his wounds. Roman watched on worriedly.

He'd accompanied the High Priestess when Nikolai had called the coven to ask for her help.

"There, all done." Nadia lifted her hands off Cortes and turned to Anya. "You're next."

Vlad passed Cortes a glass of whiskey. The Colombian accepted it gratefully.

"You mean, those hellbeasts just turned up at your location?" Nikolai said sharply.

"Yes." Anya winced when Nadia touched her leg. "We have no idea how they found us or what their intentions were." A cynical laugh left her. "Apart from killing us, that is."

Sable flew over from where she'd been perching on Tarang with Popo and nudged her witch's arm with her large head. Anya released a shaky breath and stroked the Harpy Eagle gently.

Cortes gave Mae a troubled look. "I think they were after my magic."

Anya's eyes rounded. "What?"

A cold sweat broke out on Mae's brow. She held the sorcerer's gaze, the photographs of the bodies the New York coven had found flashing through her mind.

From Nikolai's harrowed expression, he'd just had the same thought.

"That hellwolf tried to tear my stomach open, like it wanted to reach my core." Cortes pressed a hand to his belly. "*Soul Shield* resisted the attack."

"It was clever of you to suggest putting that spell inside us, oh former queen of my heart," Popo said effusively.

Cortes narrowed his eyes at his familiar.

Mae chewed her lip. She'd placed *Soul Shield* around everyone's core upon their return to the States. With Vedran and Barquiel still at large, both wounded and desperate, she'd feared what they might attempt to do to those she cared about.

Seems it was the right call, after all.

Indeed, Na Ri concurred.

"But—how did you end up here?" Vlad said, indicating his penthouse.

The members of the *Black Devils* clean-up crew he'd called were clearing up the wreckage and replacing the broken glass and damaged floorboards. Mae shivered as she recalled the cold efficiency with which they'd cleaned her apartment when she and Nikolai had been attacked by ghouls a few months back.

"I don't know." Cortes furrowed his brow. "One minute I was standing on the road with Anya and we were fighting those monsters, the next moment there was a flash of golden light all around us. When I opened my eyes, we were here."

"A black-magic portal brought those monsters to

the apartment seconds after we got here," Anya said bitterly.

Nikolai scowled. A sour taste filled Mae's mouth.

So, we were right. This was Vedran's scheme.

Something that Cortes had just said made her draw a sharp breath.

"Wait." Mae's pulse quickened. "You said you saw a flash of golden light?!"

Cortes frowned. "Yes."

My witch? Brimstone murmured quizzically.

Mae focused on Cortes's core. It was Na Ri who felt it first.

Wonder filled her first incarnation's voice. *His magic. It's...different.*

"Did your body feel strange when it happened?" Mae asked Cortes tensely.

He stared. "Now that you mention it, yes. My stomach felt hot."

Anya's fraught gaze swung between Cortes and Mae. "What's wrong?"

Mae rose and went over to Cortes, her heart thudding dully against her ribs. "I'm going to examine your core."

Cortes grimaced. He was no doubt recalling the time she had analyzed his magic so she could incorporate it in the spell she'd created to counter Anya's Illusion Sorcery.

Anya's voice trembled. "Is something wrong with Enrique?"

The sorcerer had told the witch about his past and how Mae and Nikolai had fixed his once broken core.

"I'm not sure yet," Mae replied guardedly.

Cortes braced himself when she pressed her hand against his stomach. He blinked.

"Oh. It doesn't hurt."

Mae closed her eyes and directed her attention toward the source of his magic. Her breath stuttered a few seconds later.

We were right! Na Ri exclaimed. *His magic has evolved.*

CHAPTER SIX

THE COMPLEX, GOLDEN RUNES THAT ENVELOPED Cortes's core no longer danced chaotically behind the white-magic-infused barrier that was *Soul Shield*. Instead of imploding and regenerating frenziedly, they slithered smoothly in and out of view, like cogs in a well-oiled machine. And there were even more of them than before.

What is that, my witch? Brimstone asked curiously.

Intertwined amidst the glittering runes were faint crimson threads.

Mae's stomach sank. *Is that our magic?!*

Yes, Na Ri replied.

Mae swallowed. *Is that why Cortes didn't feel any discomfort this time around?*

Probably.

Mae realized her first incarnation did not seem particularly concerned by what they could see. *This isn't going to mess with his core, is it?*

No, Na Ri replied. *Our power is actually augmenting*

his Arcane Magic. It won't harm him. But...it might bestow new abilities upon him. She grew pensive as she studied the bright, golden runes. *I wonder if the same thing would happen if we touched the others' cores.*

Mae grimaced internally. *How about we not experiment on our friends?*

Nikolai's voice reached them. "Mae?"

Mae opened her eyes. He was studying her with a worried frown.

"What's the verdict?" Cortes said stiffly.

Mae hesitated.

"I don't know how to tell you this, but your magic is changing," she told the Colombian with a contrite look.

Cortes paled. Popo came over and perched on his shoulder, his claws sinking anxiously into his jacket.

"Changing?" Vlad lowered his brows. "Changing how?"

Mae scratched her cheek awkwardly. "It, er, looks like some of my power fused with his core when I was analyzing his Arcane Magic, that time at the warehouse."

"What?" Cortes said leadenly in the hush that followed.

"Your magic is inside him?!" Nikolai gasped.

Anya's face fell. "But—you said examining his core wouldn't hurt him!"

"It hasn't," Mae reassured her hurriedly. "In fact, Na Ri believes it will make him stronger and give him new skills."

"You and my Enrique made a magic baby," Popo croaked in an awed voice.

Everyone fixed the bird with a glare.

Cortes glanced at Anya's pale face before narrowing his eyes at his familiar in a way that said he was contemplating murder.

"Can you please not say it like that?" Nikolai ground out.

"Yeah," Vlad snapped.

"What kind of new skills?" Roman shrugged at their irritated stares. "Mae said he's got new skills. I'm curious to know what they are."

Na Ri startled inside Mae.

Mae blinked. *What is it?*

I recognize a rune, Na Ri said excitedly. *I think I saw our father attempt to create it, once.*

Surprise jolted Mae. *You did?*

Yes. It's right—there.

Na Ri touched the rune. A dazzling, golden light flared into life around Mae. She squinted.

The world lurched.

Mae gasped, stumbled, and fell flat on her face beside Cortes. Humid heat washed over them, bringing with it the rich smell of vegetation. They were lying on the side of a road, in the middle of a tropical jungle. The burnt carcass of a car sat on the asphalt some dozen feet from them.

A hellbeast was feasting on the remains of the dead man lying beside it. Several others sniffed at the undergrowth a short distance away.

Popo squawked and flapped his wings, alarmed.

The hellbeasts' heads snapped around. Their pupils

constricted when Mae and Cortes fell in their line of sight.

"What the hell just happened?!" Cortes said numbly.

Mae's heart raced as they climbed to their feet. "I think you…just warped space!"

They shared a dazed stare.

"You mean—I *teleported* us here?!" Cortes croaked.

The hellbeasts bounded toward them with vicious snarls.

Mae pressed a hand to Cortes's back. "Think of Anya!"

Light exploded around them.

Cold air slammed into Mae, along with a sudden feeling of weightlessness. Her eyes rounded.

They were a thousand feet in the air above New York.

"I meant her exact location!" she yelled at Cortes as they started to fall.

"Yeah, well, it's not as if I'm an expert at this freaking thing!" he shouted back.

Popo grabbed Cortes's jacket with his claws and flapped his wings desperately. "I shall save you, my Enrique!"

"That's not gonna work, bird brain!" Cortes snarled.

Mae unleashed *Levitate*. Relief flooded Cortes's face when he found himself inside the crimson sphere. Popo flew agitatedly around their heads as they bobbed in midair.

"You think anyone saw us?" Mae mumbled.

Cortes stared past her shoulder.

"You mean, like that news helicopter?" he said flatly.

Mae whirled around. "Dammit!"

The pilot of the aircraft gaped at them, the machine hovering some hundred feet away. The man beside him recovered and swung his camera clumsily up onto his shoulder.

"Vlad's apartment!" Mae grabbed Cortes's arm. "Focus on it!"

The world tilted violently inside a flash of incandescent radiance. They reappeared some ten feet above Vlad's living room floor, pinwheeled wildly, and landed face down.

"Ugh," Mae mumbled. She lifted her head and scanned Cortes's face. "Are you okay?"

"I will be once you get your knee off my crotch," Cortes groaned.

"We're back! We're back!" Popo screeched.

"Mae!"

Nikolai and Vlad rushed to her side, Roman in their footsteps.

My witch! Brimstone reached her first and jumped into her arms. His voice quivered, his dread echoing across their bond. *Where did you go?!*

"I'm sorry." Mae hugged him, remorse tightening her chest. "I didn't know that was going to happen."

Anya sat frozen and ashen faced on the couch. "Enrique?"

"What in God's name did you guys just do?" Nadia asked hoarsely.

Nikolai and Vlad pulled Mae to her feet while Roman helped Cortes up.

Mae and Cortes traded a hesitant look. Mae dipped her head.

Cortes swallowed. "I teleported us back to where those beasts attacked us."

Nadia's eyes bulged. "You did what?!"

The others gaped.

Na Ri sounded sheepish when she spoke inside Mae's head. *I have figured out the name of the space warp spell. It's called* Distort. She faltered. *Our father tried in vain to create something similar, once. It seems the missing ingredient was Arcane Magic.*

Mae frowned. *But aren't portals equally effective?*

Portals are like tunnels in space. It can take minutes to cross one. This spell is a hundred times more efficient.

Vlad recovered first. "By teleport, you mean you—crossed space instantly?"

"Yes," Cortes admitted reluctantly.

"How?" Nikolai asked, just as dubiously as the incubus.

Cortes arched an eyebrow at Mae. "Care to explain? Because I still haven't got a clue how all of that just happened."

"Your core has new runes."

Cortes's eyes widened.

"You have a new space warp spell in your repertory," Mae continued. "It's called *Distort*. All you have to do is think of where you want to be, invoke that spell, and you'll be there in a heartbeat."

Cortes stared at her dazedly for a moment before furrowing his brow. "But...I wasn't thinking of anything when I teleported us from here."

"Oh." Mae wrinkled her nose. "Yeah, that was Na Ri's fault. She, er, touched the spell. It looks like it automatically engaged and took us to your last location."

Cortes's mouth flattened.

"She apologizes," Mae muttered.

"Wait." Roman was frowning. "So, the first time the spell engaged and they came here, is that because Cortes was thinking of Vlad?"

Everyone gazed at Roman before appraising Vlad and Cortes with fresh stares. Vlad glowered at the Fire Magic sorcerer.

Roman shrugged. "Look, man, I'm just saying it like I see it."

Cortes sighed. "I wasn't thinking of him. I wanted Mae's help. I knew she was staying here."

Popo rubbed his beak awkwardly with a wing. "Are you certain, my Enrique? It isn't because you still harbor amorous feelings toward—*mmmph! Mmmph?!*"

Cortes had gagged the bird. "How about you stay quiet for a while?"

Nikolai's eyes shrank to slits. Alastair gave Popo a haughty look.

Vlad blew out a heavy sigh and ran his hand through his hair. "With all the craziness that just happened, I didn't get a chance to ask how things went with the cartel."

"Oh." Cortes's expression turned strained. He cut his eyes to Anya. "We…persuaded them to let me go."

They all observed Anya with various degrees of

doubt. A defiant light dawned on the witch's face. She sniffed.

"She threatened them, didn't she?" Mae said.

"Totally," Cortes admitted flatly.

Nadia waved a hand at Mae and Nikolai. "You should tell them about the bodies."

Vlad's gaze turned probing. "What bodies?"

Nadia's phone pinged before anyone could answer. She checked the message and eyed Mae awkwardly.

"Bryony wants to know why there's a blurry video of what looks like you and Cortes floating in midair above New York circulating on a local news channel."

Mae paled. "She's gonna kill me."

"Not if your mother kills you first," Nikolai muttered.

CHAPTER SEVEN

Demonic power surged through Barquiel's veins as he attempted to tear open the prison he was trapped in with his bare hands. It had been days since he'd smashed his broadsword to pieces attempting to shatter its walls.

The demon grunted, his claws scraping in vain against the solid blackness. An enraged sound finally left him. He shot back and glared at his cage, his chest heaving with his breaths and anger flushing through his body.

He couldn't believe how weak he felt.

Mae Jin's face rose before him. Barquiel gnashed his teeth.

It's that damn bitch and her spell! I'm going to kill her when I get out of here!

Even the black magic Vedran had gifted him had been all but consumed by *Reverse*. In all his centuries as an Archduke of Hell, the demon had never felt as impotent as he did now.

No. He sagged, his talons sinking into his palms. *There was another time when I was this helpless.* Barquiel closed his eyes and shuddered. *It was when I had to watch her die.*

What the demon missed more than anything right now was not his freedom, nor the authority granted him by his title, nor even the monstrous army he had once commanded. Not being able to see the woman he loved was a far worse fate.

"Ran Soyun," he whispered brokenly.

A cold sensation trickled down his spine. Barquiel stiffened.

Dread, a sensation that was alien to him, was filling his veins. *Is it because I can no longer sense my troops?*

It had been several days since he'd lost all trace of the demonic creatures he'd been gathering in the Underworld to do his bidding. He frowned.

Still, that is hardly a reason to be feeling such a cowardly emo—

A sharp sensation pierced the demon's body with his next breath. Barquiel clutched his stomach, startled. Something had just twisted deep inside him.

He gasped when it came again.

His body transformed into that of the human he had possessed before morphing back into his demonic appearance just as quickly.

Barquiel stared wide-eyed at his trembling fingers. *What's happening? Why am I losing control over my form?!*

A voice sounded faintly in his ears. Barquiel twisted, his frantic gaze scanning his surroundings where he floated in the void.

"Who are you?" he barked after a moment. "Show yourself!"

The voice came again. It was followed by a heat that threatened to scorch his very being. Barquiel grunted and doubled over, stunned. He froze when the words dancing on the edge of his hearing finally became perceptible.

I'm coming for you, asshole! Rose Blake growled in his mind.

Barquiel recoiled. *What?! But—how?! There shouldn't be anything left of her consciousness!*

Only a fragment of Rose Blake's soul remained inside the body he had taken over. It should have been impossible for her mind to survive the destruction he had wreaked upon her consciousness.

The voice faded, along with the fire licking at his insides.

"Impossible," Barquiel mumbled, his throat tight. "It —it must have been a figment of my imagination."

But however much the demon tried to deny what he'd heard and felt, he wasn't able to convince himself that it had been fake. Because there remained a lingering heat deep inside the body he had stolen and the taste of a fury that wasn't his.

"THIS IS CREEPY," ROMAN SAID NERVOUSLY.

Filomena clung to his shoulder and tested the air warily with her tongue.

"Nobody asked you to come, choirboy," Nikolai said coldly.

"I wanted to see Mae's workplace." Roman scowled. "What's it to you, douchebag?"

Vlad said something rude under his breath.

Mae gritted her teeth. "How about everyone shut up before security catches wind of us?"

Would you like me to teach them a lesson, my witch? Brimstone asked enthusiastically.

Mae rolled her eyes. *Do I look like I want that kind of trouble right now?*

Their footsteps echoed quietly on the linoleum floor inside the morgue at Grandview General. A body bag floated ahead within *Levitate*. It contained the remains of one of the Dark Council witches the New York coven had discovered the night before. Mae frowned.

Their mission to find Vedran had gotten even more urgent in the last couple of hours. Abraham had contacted Nikolai on their way to the hospital.

It wasn't just Dark Council members who were going missing from every city they used to haunt. Witches and sorcerers belonging to smaller covens all around the world had vanished too, their disappearance only recently coming to light after the High Council issued an international announcement about their recent findings.

It's like Philadelphia all over again.

Brimstone glanced at her. *He already possesses the* Book of Light. *I hardly think he has the same use for them now as Barquiel and Oscar did at that time.*

Mae feared what Vedran intended to do with the missing victims was far worse than having ghouls possess their mortal coil.

Pipes rattled overhead. Roman flinched.

Nikolai gave him a contemptuous look.

They had waited until after midnight to break into the hospital. To Mae's utter lack of surprise, it had been child's play to get in the basement.

Well, it isn't as if this place is a bank vault.

Except for the dead people, Brimstone observed. *There's a lot you can do with magic and dead people. For example, you can—*

How about we change the subject. Mae shuddered. *Maybe I should reinforce this place with some defensive spells.*

She unlocked an autopsy lab with her passkey, crossed the office, and led the way into the inner room. The ventilation system hummed quietly in the cool darkness.

Mae flicked on the overhead lights and guided the body to an examination table. She was slipping on personal protective gear when she became aware of a battery of curious stares.

Mae lowered her face shield and eyed the three men watching her through the transparent, polycarbonate plate. "What?"

"It's weird seeing you in work mode," Vlad admitted.

Nikolai's expression turned brooding. "That outfit looks good on you."

Heat warmed Mae's cheeks. Roman and Vlad curled a lip at the sorcerer.

"How about you keep your flirting to a minimum?" the incubus said icily.

A loud clatter made them jump.

Tarang blinked when he found himself the target of a score of spell bombs. His tail had brushed against an instrument tray on the counter and sent it crashing onto the floor while he'd been exploring the lab.

The tiger slinked over to Vlad and sat sheepishly beside him.

Mae eyed the door. "I hope no one heard that."

"The dead did," Roman said.

They fixed him with a leaden stare.

"Come on, I'm trying to lighten the mood," he protested.

Mae sighed and opened the body bag.

The putrid smell of scorched, rotting flesh flooded the air. Roman gagged.

She narrowed her eyes when she got her first good look at the corpse. The black magic that had killed the woman had hastened the decomposition process by several days. The body was heavily bloated, livor mortis evident in the few patches of skin that had been spared by Vedran's Hellfire Magic.

Roman turned slightly green when Mae picked up a scalpel and incised the victim's chest with a practiced move.

It didn't take her long to remove and examine the witch's internal organs. They were free of disease and well preserved despite her charred remains. Even her coronary arteries looked perfect.

I wonder if she was a healer.

She cut open the witch's skull next and extracted the brain. It too turned out to be a perfect specimen.

"Found anything?" Vlad said.

"Apart from the fact that she was as healthy as a horse, no." Mae chewed her lip. "I'm going to examine her core."

She placed her hand a couple of inches above the cadaver's abdomen and focused. It took but a moment for the dead witch's core to appear in her mind's eye.

It was pitch black and shriveled.

A low growl left Brimstone at the sight shared through their bond.

Mae clenched her jaw. *We were right.*

"Mae?" Nikolai said warily.

She met the sorcerer's gaze. "Her core has been sucked dry of magic, like we suspected. I'm going to use *Soul Conjure* and see if I can find a clue to where Vedran might be."

Nikolai frowned.

"Are you sure that's safe?" Vlad said tensely.

"We haven't got anything else to go on right now."

Mae silently incanted the spell.

Roman paled and stumbled back a step as the corpse shuddered and arched off the table. "What the—?!"

His eyes bulged at the sight of the pale, flickering, distorted orb that drifted upward from the woman's body.

"This your first time seeing *Soul Conjure?*" Vlad asked Roman.

The young man gulped. "Yeah."

A tortured scream left the manifestation and reverberated across the autopsy lab. Mae flinched. Vlad and Nikolai unleashed their weapons. A sphere of sizzling Fire Magic blossomed in Roman's right hand.

"It's alright," Mae reassured them hastily.

My witch, Brimstone warned, looming over her in his demonic nine-tailed-fox form.

"I'll be careful. I promise."

Her heart raced as she reached out and gently clasped the dead witch's soul. She drew a sharp breath.

Images flashed across her vision, the witch's memories playing before her mind's eye like a flickering movie. She saw the woman as a child playing in a garden full of flowers, then as a weary, angry adult swearing her allegiance to the Sorcerer King, full of resentment for a world that had rejected her.

Mae's stomach knotted when she witnessed the moment Vedran placed his dark spell inside the witch. It had slowly robbed her of all empathy and positive emotions, turning her into an unfeeling monster who did his evil bidding without batting an eyelid.

Is that why the Dark Council members all act the same? Because of their master's black magic? She shuddered. *It's a miracle Nikolai managed to remain sound of mind with that inside him.*

Na Ri hesitated. *I believe his white magic protected him.*

The witch's final moments came to her. Skin and flesh consumed by the dark power seeded within her and the storm of Hellfire Magic that had engulfed her body, her shriek of agony and those of her dying companions echoed in a vast, shadowy place from which there would be no escape.

Mae was trying to make out details of the location through the flames and smoke when a voice sounded faintly in her mind.

Help...me...

CHAPTER EIGHT

The hairs lifted on the back of Mae's neck.

The voice did not belong to the dead witch.

Mae, Na Ri said guardedly.

Brimstone stepped closer to her, his hackles rising warily.

Help me...please...Witch...Queen...

Mae's breath caught as black threads flickered to life around the witch's soul orb.

Magic blasted around Nikolai. "What is that?!"

"Get away from it, Mae!" Vlad snarled.

She ignored them, her chest tightening at the agony emanating from the new apparition. It was the remains of another soul. One drowning in sorrow and despair.

*That's—*Na Ri paused, her tone wretched.

"*My witch,*" Brimstone whined.

His head drooped.

Mae could tell they'd made out what they were looking at and were just as troubled as she was. They'd glimpsed it once before, in the castle where they had fought Vedran and lost Hellreaver.

It was the tainted soul of Vedran's familiar. The one he had killed so he could turn them into a weapon that would allow him to wield his most formidable spells.

The familiar's true form manifested for a fleeting moment.

Mae's throat constricted.

It was a beautiful wolf. One as black as night, whose soul had once been as pure as snow.

My name...is...Balkin...You...must...kill me...my queen...

The breath Mae had been holding shuddered out of her.

Despite his suffering, the wolf was calm and as noble as a king.

"What's going on, Mae?" Roman asked in a strained voice. "What is that thing?"

"It's what's left of Vedran's familiar."

Nikolai recoiled. Roman sucked in air. Vlad's knuckles whitened on his swords.

The dark threads that made up Balkin's soul faded, leaving behind the remnant of the witch's pale orb. Mae blinked away the tears that had sprung to her eyes. She could no longer sense the tortured presence of the Sorcerer King's familiar.

"My witch," Brimstone murmured.

"I know."

Mae steeled herself. She still had a job to do. Heat danced through her veins, heralding the demonic power that soon engulfed the pale sphere in her hands.

"Be at peace," she whispered.

The dead witch's gratitude washed through her as her soul vanished from the world of the living with a last, bright flicker. A hush descended inside the autopsy lab.

Vlad broke it. "What was that about?"

Instead of replying, Mae frowned at Nikolai. "Did you know?"

Nikolai swallowed. "I heard rumors when I was a child. But I was never certain of their accuracy." He hesitated before meeting her stare squarely. "My father has never had a familiar for as long as I can remember."

Mae finally answered the question burning in Vlad and Roman's eyes. "That was the soul of Vedran's wolf familiar. He killed him so he could use him as a weapon."

Vlad cursed. Roman paled, his fingers automatically finding Filomena.

"He was a very dignified creature, my witch," Brimstone observed sadly.

Mae fisted her hands. "Yes, he was."

What a pity that his bond was that wretched man, Na Ri murmured.

"Did you manage to see something that might help us find that bastard?" Vlad said in a hard voice.

"No." Mae observed Nikolai with a frown. "But one thing is for certain. Your father's familiar wants no part of this."

A muscle jumped in Nikolai's jawline.

Mae knew he loathed that the man responsible for his mother's death was related to him by blood.

"Did you meet him before?" Roman said. "That

familiar. You and Brimstone didn't seem surprised when you saw him."

"He was there the night we fought Vedran."

"*We caught a glimpse of him in the black sword the Sorcerer King manifested,*" Brimstone explained somberly at their shocked expressions. "*The one that destroyed Hellreaver.*"

Resolve tightened Roman's face. "Is that a weakness we can exploit?"

A wave of lassitude washed over Mae. "I hope so."

She sighed and rubbed her forehead.

After a couple of quiet weeks, events were moving at breakneck speed once more. The dark truths the Sorcerer King and Barquiel had long hidden were coming to light one by one. She could feel her final battle with them looming in their imminent future.

If I lose, a lot of people will be in danger.

The prophecy Bryony had mentioned when they first met rose in her mind for the first time in a while.

On the day the world becomes shrouded in shadows, a woman with white and dark magic will bring about an age of justice and the fall of a false God.

A wry grimace twisted her lips. *No pressure then.*

She unleashed *Devour* and destroyed the witch's physical remains.

"Come on, let's get out of here."

They were halfway to the exit when corruption saturated the air with a suddenness that made them freeze. A brutal pressure bore down on them, rooting their feet to the ground. Brimstone snarled and shifted back into his nine-tailed form.

The stench of black magic imbued the room a second before a dark portal whooshed to life near the ceiling.

Mae's pulse spiked when she sensed Vedran's presence on the other side of the rift. *"Soul Guard! Augment!"*

The spells she and Na Ri had refined to defend all those who fell under their protection fortified *Soul Shield* inside the men framing her.

Heat surged through her veins, the power she called forth from her cores thrumming across her bond with Brimstone. A red aura detonated around them on a violent tide that made glass tinkle and metal vibrate.

She startled.

Vlad and Roman's eyes widened at the sight of the thick, black threads woven through the paleness of Ran Soyun's magic and her own demonic energy.

Dread chilled Mae to the bone. She finally tasted a power that was at once alien and familiar. *I was right. This is black magic!*

Nikolai's expression hardened. "So I didn't imagine it before. That's Vedran's magic, isn't it?!"

Mae opened and closed her mouth soundlessly. She could hardly deny the truth before their eyes.

Brimstone towered over her, his pupils ablaze. *"You are wrong, sorcerer. It is my witch's right to wield all magic. That power was never the Sorcerer King's to begin with."*

Surprise jolted Mae at her familiar's words.

He is correct, Na Ri said. *Black magic is part of our heritage.* Her first incarnation's tone turned steely. *Our enemy is almost here.*

Mae's gaze snapped to the portal. "We don't have time for this! Get ready!"

The creatures that fell from the hellish doorway before it closed cracked the floor when they landed. Vlad swore.

"Mother of God," Roman mumbled shakily.

Mae's throat grew dry as her head tilted up and up. "Brim, what the heck are those?!"

The trio of monsters smashed the ceiling with their heads as they straightened, massive forms casting shadows over the room.

"They are giants!" the demon fox spat.

Mae's hands itched for Hellreaver's presence as the creatures lowered their gazes and fixed her with obsidian stares. It was moments like these when she and Brimstone felt his absence the most.

The giants' attention shifted to Roman and Nikolai.

Na Ri gasped. *Vedran is after their cores!*

Mae's heart lurched. The monsters blurred.

"CONTAIN!"

Crimson bloomed around Nikolai and Roman as they prepared to defend themselves, their movements sluggish compared to those of the giants. The monsters' clubs smashed against the red globe in an explosion of black-magic-tinged sparks.

Contain held.

Mae swallowed. *Damn! I can't believe how fast they are considering their size!*

The biggest monster dropped his weapon and slammed his hands palm down upon the barrier. A sour taste filled Mae's mouth as Vedran's dark powers bloomed on his fingertips and swarmed the surface of her demonic shield.

"Vlad! I'll target their heads! You go for their legs!"

The incubus dipped his chin, his expression an ice-cold mask. Tarang released a deadly growl beside him.

"Let us out!" Roman yelled angrily from behind *Contain.*

"Mae!" Nikolai shouted, his face contorted in frustration and fury.

"Those monsters were sent by Vedran to kill you and absorb your cores!" Mae scowled. "Stay put for now!"

Roman jerked back at her words. Nikolai clenched his jaw so tight she feared he would crack a tooth.

The other giants turned their attention to her and Vlad while their companion unleashed Vedran's corrupt magic upon *Contain.*

Power hummed around Mae. "Here they come!"

Brimstone's quivering tails sent debris flying around the lab as he snatched the first creature's weapon out of his grasp with his jaws and lobbed it across the room. The fox carved deep grooves in the giant's face with his claws, taking out his left eye.

Tarang jumped on the monster's leg and took a chunk out of his thigh before he could land a blow on Brimstone with his fist.

Mae shot out of the way of the second giant's club, missed his knuckles by a hairbreadth as he spun and swung for her face, and concentrated her magic into her hands and feet. Crimson, black, and white merged until they covered her flesh in layers of pure magic.

She somersaulted into the air, landed on the creature's arm as it straightened, and ran straight up toward its head, her movements lightning fast. A shadow swallowed her, the monster's hand closing in to swat her away, his speed just as blistering.

Mae's stomach dropped. *Shit!*

The beast grunted and sagged a second before it could strike her. She glanced down.

Vlad had carved through the creature's left Achilles tendon with his blades.

It was all the time she needed.

Mae leapt off the giant's shoulder, twisted her body as she arced above his head, and brought her fists up when gravity took over. Scarlet lightning wreathed with black and ivory currents crackled around her fingers.

A roar left her throat. She struck the beast in the temple with a double hammer punch before spinning in midair and delivering a roundhouse kick to the same spot. Bone shattered under the storm of indomitable power she wielded.

The monster's pupils crossed. He staggered sideways and fell, eyes rolling back in his head. Glass exploded and metal crumpled as he crashed into a row of cabinets. He sagged, his body limp in death.

A heavy thud sounded behind Mae. She landed lightly on the ground and looked over her shoulder, her heart slamming against her ribs.

Vlad had slashed through the other giant's heel tendons and brought the monster to his knees. Brimstone and Tarang pounced and finished him off before he could defend himself, their fangs glinting with redness while they tore his jugular open.

Vlad joined her. "Did you really just knock out a giant with your bare fists?"

He eyed the translucent power wrapped around her hands warily.

"Let's just say I found a new way to use my magic," Mae said darkly.

CHAPTER NINE

They regrouped with Brimstone and Tarang and turned to the last giant. The monster seemed oblivious to their presence, his attention focused on destroying *Contain* with Vedran's magic. Mae narrowed her eyes.

The spell was starting to wear thin.

Looks like it has a five-minute limit in the face of that bastard's magic.

It will be stronger with the power of three, Na Ri reassured her.

Her first incarnation made a suggestion that made Mae blink.

"We should try and keep that one alive."

Vlad lowered his brows. "Why?"

"Because Na Ri thinks he might prove to be our ticket to Vedran's location." The savage aura around Mae thickened. "Can you guys distract him for a couple of minutes?"

Vlad nodded.

"*Of course, my witch,*" Brimstone snarled.

Tarang bared his teeth on a threatening growl.

Mae rose inside *Levitate* while they charged the giant. The monster ignored their attacks, Vlad's blades and Brimstone and Tarang's claws and fangs barely scratching his flesh.

Damnit! Is that one made of rock?!

An angry sound rumbled out of Brimstone.

Goosebumps broke out on Mae's arms with her next breath. A fire was building deep inside her belly. She pressed a hand to her stomach before cutting her eyes jerkily to her familiar. It was coming from their bond.

Scarlet boiled in Brimstone's eyes. His body swelled an instant before he opened his jaws. Mae's eyes rounded at the sight of the incandescent, rotating sphere of crimson and black magic that exploded into life inside his mouth. It grew exponentially.

"Holy—" she mumbled.

"—fuck," Vlad said hoarsely.

Na Ri startled. *Oh. I never thought he would be able to manifest our father's* Wrath *in this realm!*

Mae swallowed. "Wrath?! Also, since when can Brimstone do *spells?!*"

The giant finally sensed danger. His pupils flared at the sight of the spinning orb growing inside the demon fox's mouth.

He dove to the side just as Brimstone fired the spell.

Wrath missed the monster by a whisker, glanced off *Contain,* and punched a hole straight through the wall.

The resulting explosion shook the building and filled the room with dust and debris.

Mae coughed and covered her mouth and nose with an arm, her pulse racing. Car alarms sounded faintly. The air slowly cleared.

She joined Vlad as he peered around the edge of the sizzling, ten-foot-wide, jagged opening. A mess of fused concrete and glowing hot metal was visible within it.

The spell hadn't just smashed straight through the autopsy lab and the outer wall of the hospital. It had carved a tunnel inside its foundations and beneath the main road. Water gushed from broken pipes and cooled the sizzling, exposed steelwork of some kind of structure in the distance.

"Isn't that the underground parking lot where I left the Bentley?" the incubus asked leadenly.

Mae turned and squinted at Brimstone. "How about you warn us next time you want to use that spell?"

The demon fox avoided her accusing stare.

Everyone tensed as the giant stirred.

Magic flashed through Mae's veins. Black static tinged with crimson danced around her body.

"Ice Fortress!"

The spell formed instantly, trapping the monster in a thick, glittering prison laced with the white runes of Ran Soyun's magic. He fell backward slowly, his face frozen in an expression of surprise. The building trembled when he landed on the floor.

Mae scaled his body and slammed her hand on the ice above his stomach. *"Sever!"*

The giant shuddered. A tiny crack appeared in *Ice Fortress*.

Mae gritted her teeth. Vedran's magic was countering her attempt to break his hold on the monster's soul.

"Oh yeah? Let's see you resist this, asshole!" she growled. "*REVERSE!*"

For a moment, nothing happened. The corruption wrapped around the creature's soul orb finally trembled before exploding into inky tendrils that vanished with a hiss. The giant stilled.

Mae jumped to the ground and retracted *Ice Fortress*.

Vlad stiffened. "Should you really—?!"

"It's okay. He won't hurt us."

The giant stirred and sat up groggily, his movements sluggish. He looked around with a confused expression, only to blanch when he saw the bodies of his fallen comrades. His eyes bulged at the sight of Brimstone.

The monster whimpered in fear and crawled hastily onto his hands and knees before bowing his head to the ground before the demon fox, his body trembling.

Mae and Vlad stared.

"Is there something you want to tell us, Brim?"

Brimstone sniffed. "*He is only showing respect to a superior creature. My word used to be law among the giants in the Underworld.*"

Vlad made a face. "So, you were a one-fox gang leader, huh?"

Yelling and banging reached them.

Nikolai and Roman were pounding on the inside of *Contain*, their expressions seething.

"You should just keep them in there," Vlad suggested sourly as Mae hastily ended the spell.

Nikolai stormed across the lab. "I can't believe you did that!"

Mae grimaced. "Look, it was—"

"How could you, Mae?!" Roman interrupted angrily. "We're strong enough to fight by your—!"

He froze and sucked in air, horrified.

Nikolai had taken Mae in his arms and was kissing her passionately. She responded with equal vigor.

"You scared the life out of me," the sorcerer mumbled against her lips when he finally ended their torrid kiss.

Remorse knotted Mae's belly as she gazed into his eyes. "I'm sorry. I—I just couldn't risk letting him take you again."

She shuddered. A pained expression came over Nikolai. He hugged her tightly.

"How about you let her go?" Roman said sullenly.

"What's it to you, kid?" Nikolai sneered over Mae's head.

Roman turned to Vlad. "Help me out."

"This isn't some back-alley tussle," the incubus said coolly. "She's made her choice."

Nikolai stared. Mae blinked. It was the first time Vlad had openly admitted to the sorcerer securing his position as her consort in public.

"That doesn't mean she can't choose a second one though," Roman argued.

Mae sighed. *He's just as stubborn as Budimir and Ludmila.*

Vlad arched an eyebrow. "If so, then that makes you my direct competition, doesn't it?"

Roman swallowed before squaring his shoulders and glaring at the incubus. "Oh yeah? Bring it, old man."

Crimson bloomed in Vlad's eyes. "Don't make me put you over my knee and spank you, brat."

Mae disentangled herself from Nikolai. "How about everybody calm down?"

It was at this point that hospital security showed up.

"I can explain."

Jared Dickson watched her woodenly before indicating the monster crouching meekly in a corner of what remained of the autopsy lab. "Explain that."

Mae scratched her head awkwardly. "It's a giant from the Underworld. Vedran sent him here."

Vlad shrugged. "We didn't really have a choice but to fight."

"Yeah," Roman murmured.

Jared cocked a thumb at the Fire Magic sorcerer. "Who's this?"

"Budimir Volkov's grandson," Mae admitted nervously. "You know, the guy I told you we met in Prague."

Nikolai maintained a tactful silence.

Jared's brows met in an almighty scowl.

Mae fidgeted. "Have you heard from Alicia?"

"Don't change the subject!" the Immortal detective snapped.

One of the other cops wandered over. "The chief just called. He's asking us to arrange autopsies for these," he glanced at one of the dead giants and shivered, "—creatures."

Steve Hodge tensed where he'd been clearing up some of the mess in the lab and pretending not to listen in on their conversation. Mae's boss had taken the appearance of a monster from Hell in his stride when he'd come in to assess the damage to the pathology department. Compared to the demon who had tried to disembowel him on the night Mae's powers had first awakened, the giant looked like a cuddly teddy bear.

"I don't think that's going to help," Jared said sourly. "And not a word about this to anyone," he warned his associate. "The last thing this city needs is another alarmist report." His eyes shrank to slits. "Whoever leaked that story to the press is going to wish they'd never been born."

The Immortal cracked his knuckles. The cop flinched. Hodge swallowed.

The bodies the New York coven had discovered in the last twenty-four hours had finally made the news. Though the piece had broken out in the middle of the night, Mae was pretty certain the photographs that had been disclosed to the media would be all over the headlines by morning.

She swallowed a weary sigh. *Mom's gonna go apeshit when she finds out it involves the coven.*

She won't be pleased when she discovers what you intend to do next either, Brimstone observed.

Mae chewed her lip. With Alicia still MIA and Vedran's efforts to consume powerful magic cores accelerating, she had no choice but to adopt plan C.

Let's hope he agrees to do it.

CHAPTER TEN

"You want me to do what?" Cortes said dully.

Anya sat with her jaw open beside the sorcerer.

They were at the makeshift headquarters of the New York coven. Dawn was just breaking across the city, along with news about the dead bodies that had been discovered in several locations across the state.

Abraham recovered from his shock first. "Are you nuts?!"

Told you they'd react like this, Brimstone said smugly, chomping down his breakfast.

Mae cut her eyes to the fox. "How about you focus on that bacon sandwich?" She turned to the others. "Look, hear me out—"

"There's nothing to discuss, Mae," Bryony interrupted grimly. "It's one thing agreeing to let Alicia escort you to Hell. It's a whole other ballgame asking a human to take her place."

Anya and Roman nodded vigorously. Vlad and

Nikolai remained silent. Judging from their expressions, they still harbored misgivings on the subject.

"The fact that we haven't heard from Alicia could mean there's a reason she can't return to Earth right now," Abraham said stiffly.

Mae curled her hands into fists. "Then, that's even more grounds to go find out what's keeping her. Whatever it is might have to do with Barquiel's disappearance."

Cortes ran a hand through his hair in the fraught silence that followed. "It's not like I don't know what you're getting at, Mae." His voice churned with frustration. "But I only just found out I can use that teleportation spell. There's no way I can master it in a couple of days." The Colombian's tone hardened. "Besides, you're forgetting something crucial. I've never been to Hell. How am I supposed to get us there in the first place?"

Mae chewed her lip. That was the part of her plan she didn't quite have an answer for yet.

"Brimstone is from there," Miles said.

Everyone stared at the sorcerer.

He shrugged as he tickled his boa constrictor under the chin. "If Mae uses her power to channel his memories to Enrique's core, they should be able to teleport there."

Millie's eyes shrank to happy slits.

Mae's heart lurched. *Oh. I didn't think of that.*

It could work, Na Ri mused. *And I have my own memories too.*

"You're not helping, Miles," Bryony groaned.

"He's right." Violet furrowed her brow. "Mae needs Hellreaver if she's going to face Vedran and Barquiel head on. And meeting Azazel sounds like the right thing to do."

Bryony's face tightened. "Did *she* tell you that?"

Mae knew the High Priestess was referring to the Seer in Chicago.

"No," Violet replied in clipped tones. "But she didn't ask me to stop her either."

Bryony's shoulders slumped. She pinched the bridge of her nose. "I can't believe I'm actually thinking of agreeing to this harebrained plan."

Hope fluttered through Mae.

The New York coven High Priestess sighed and met her expectant gaze. "Do you remember the prophecy I told you about? All of it will be pointless if you die in Hell."

Mae hesitated. "The dark magic part of it came true, so I think the rest is still valid."

Tension thickened the air when an inky sphere covered with sizzling, black static bloomed above her palm.

Her scalp prickled. It scared her how quickly she'd grasped how to manipulate this new part of her powers. *It's almost like we were born to wield it.*

We were, Na Ri reminded her quietly.

Mae retracted her new magic.

Bryony stared at the fading wisps, her face pale. "How exactly did you manage to harness black magic?"

It was Vlad who replied.

"I believe the trigger was the barrier she absorbed when we went to Budapest," the incubus explained moodily. "The one that was shielding the Dark Council's original headquarters. Vedran erected it."

Roman swallowed. "So, she—*ate* his magic and can now use it?!"

Everyone gave Mae a worried look.

She grimaced. "Eating it sounds gross."

Bryony indicated Cortes. "You still have to convince him."

The sorcerer was frowning heavily at Mae.

"We should go, my Enrique."

Mae blinked.

Popo fluttered onto Cortes's lap and studied his sorcerer solemnly, his eyes bright. "We are the only ones who can help our queen right now. And our fates very much depend on her success in overcoming our foes."

Mae's pulse raced. She had never heard Popo sound so serious.

A muscle jumped in Cortes's cheek as he watched his familiar.

Anya shuddered and closed her eyes briefly before fixing her boyfriend with a steady look. "As much as it pains me to say this, Popo is right. If it helps Mae defeat our enemy, then I won't stop you." The witch's gaze shifted to Mae. Her voice turned steely. "You better make sure he comes back alive and with all his body parts intact."

Mae swallowed and dipped her head, her mouth dry.

Vlad grimaced. "So, we're really doing this, huh?" The incubus rubbed the back of his neck. "I guess I'll go say farewell to my uncle."

"You should visit with your family," Nikolai told Mae.

"I will. I have something to take care of first."

A low rumble reached them. They turned and stared at the back of the ballroom.

The giant flinched where he was kneeling quietly in a corner. He'd managed to squeeze his body inside the building through the terrace doors. He lifted a hesitant hand and mumbled something shyly.

Mae glanced at Brimstone.

He says he needs to pee, the fox translated.

"What's the matter?" Bryony asked suspiciously at her awkward expression.

Mae looked hopefully outside the window. "He needs the rest room."

Bryony followed her gaze to a flowerbed in the garden.

"He's not relieving himself in my petunias!" the witch snapped.

IT WAS LATE BY THE TIME THEY ENTERED THE residential area where the Jins lived. Nikolai maneuvered the SUV down the road, parked in the driveway, and turned to Mae.

"Was that really the right thing to do?"

She met his troubled gaze steadily. "I believe so."

The something Mae had wanted to take care of before leaving the coven headquarters had been Drabek.

The heaviness that had weighed on Nikolai's heart since he'd first witnessed the distressing state *Subjugate* had left his brother's familiar in had almost choked his breath when they'd descended into the basement with Abraham and made their way to the cell where the lynx was being kept prisoner.

Drabek had lifted her head weakly off the bed of straw she'd been lying on when Mae had opened the cell door and wandered inside. She'd greeted the witch with a feeble swing of her tail, her eyes dull with pain.

Mae had sat on the ground and lifted the familiar's head onto her lap so she could stroke her. Brimstone had lain down beside them and licked the lynx's gaunt face, his crimson gaze full of sorrow.

Nikolai had fisted his hands where he'd stood in the doorway of the prison.

"Are you really going to do this? Are you—" he'd stopped and swallowed, "are you going to kill her?"

He hadn't been able to stop his voice from shaking.

"It will feel like death," Mae said quietly. "But she will still be alive."

Nikolai had frozen at her words.

Abraham had inhaled sharply. "What do you mean? What are you—?!"

Mae's magic had filled the cell with a warm, crimson light as she'd invoked the last spells Nikolai had imagined she would use. Just as she had with Sable, she had summoned *Soul Conjure* to isolate the lynx's soul and invoked *Purge* to rid her damaged core of the source of her agony.

The lynx had stiffened for a timeless moment before going limp in her hold, her breathing slow and steady as she fell into a deep slumber that skirted the fine line between life and death, her soul orb floating silently above her body inside Mae's *Contain*.

"Why?!" Abraham had mumbled numbly.

The look on Mae's face when she'd finally lifted her head and met their strained gazes had made Nikolai's heart ache.

"What kind of Witch Queen would I be if I killed an innocent creature like her?" she'd said tremulously, her cheeks streaked with tears. "She only became a monster because of Vedran's black magic."

Nikolai had gone to her then and silently taken her in his arms while she'd cried, Abraham watching on with a remorseful expression.

Mae's voice jolted him back to the present. "I know it's stupid of me to think this, but I want her to see Oscar again, even if it is for the final time."

Nikolai's stomach clenched. He knew she was thinking of Hellreaver and how abrupt their parting had been.

The tiny spark of hope he'd harbored deep inside ever since they'd witnessed the dramatic change in Drabek's nature grew a little more.

Could the same thing have happened to Oscar?

He knew Vlad would call him a fool for wanting to

reconcile with the man who had killed his mother and his half-brothers and sisters. But still, he would regret it forever more if he didn't try one last time. Because the Oscar he thought he knew might never have been the real Oscar at all.

"It's a foolish wish indeed." He took Mae in his arms and kissed her hair. "And it makes me love you even more."

They stayed like that for a while before going inside the house to spend their last evening on Earth with Mae's family and her mother's new beau, Mr. Fusanaga. Vlad, Cortes, and Anya came over a while later, their expressions just about managing to conceal their growing dread.

Dinner was as high-spirited an affair as it always was in the Jin household, with Ye-Seul shocking everyone by announcing she was considering getting engaged to her ballroom dancing partner. Mr. Fusanaga had to pat Mae's choking mother on the back before Yoo-Mi sharply pointed out to Ye-Seul that she and Mr. Choi were getting on in age and the excitement of a wedding might be the final straw that put them six feet under.

"Oh, we're not planning on having a honeymoon if that's what you're worried about," Ye-Seul said with a wave of a wrinkled hand. "My woman bits are not what they used to be. And Mr. Choi's look like a mummified corn dog and a couple of raisins that are well past their sell-by-date."

Mr. Fusanaga's eyes glazed over a little. Cortes spluttered on the wine he'd just sipped.

Vlad leaned sideways.

"I thought things had calmed down a bit since she started going out with that Choi guy?" he hissed out the corner of his mouth to Noah Tegner, the Jins' bodyguard and Ryu's boyfriend.

"They talked about sex toys last night," the sorcerer revealed glumly. He shuddered. "There were pictures."

It wasn't until Nikolai was returning from using the rest room a while later that he was ambushed by Yoo-Mi.

"So, you're really going to Hell?"

Nikolai did his best to mask his surprise. "I—"

"There's no use lying." Mae's mother narrowed her eyes. "Mrs. Son-Ha told me."

It was Nikolai's turn to frown. "Bryony should make that woman sign an NDA."

"She was only thinking of my best interests." Yoo-Mi sniffed. "It's not that I mind Mae not telling me. After all, she has a lot on her plate."

The fight drained out of Nikolai. "Most mothers would be upset if their kid suggested a trip to the Underworld."

"Yes, well, I'm not most mothers." Yoo-Mi's expression became pinched. "If it hadn't been for Mae, Ye-Seul and Ryu would have died at the hands of the demon who possessed Rose." Resolve hardened her face. "I can't say I'm completely thrilled by what my daughter is about to do, but I won't stop her either. So, do me a favor, will you?"

Nikolai met her stare steadily. "Whatever you need."

Yoo-Mi smiled. "I knew she made the right choice

when she picked you." To Nikolai's surprise, she patted his cheek lightly. "Make sure you help my daughter kick those bad guys' asses. Especially that Bark person."

"You mean Barquiel?"

"Yeah, that guy."

CHAPTER ELEVEN

Oscar flinched, Vedran's enraged roar piercing his ears.

"That bitch!"

The Sorcerer King clawed at his face, skin and flesh coming away in his hands as he mutilated his own body with his black magic.

The wounds healed almost as soon as they formed.

So, his plan failed.

Relief shot through Oscar as he watched Vedran pace the floor, his father's wrath and bitterness rendering the air so suffocating he found it difficult to breathe.

"I will rip her cores from her body and make her eat her own heart!" the Sorcerer King snarled. "How dare she get in my way again?!"

Oscar stiffened. A sphere of sinister power blossomed next to Vedran. He hurled it with a furious bellow.

The black magic orb took out half the face of the

unlucky hellbeast who happened to be standing in its path and carved a hole through the chest of a monster behind it. The creatures fell, their dark blood spilling across the ground as they convulsed. Their comrades crowded around them and began feasting on their twitching bodies.

Bile flooded the back of Oscar's throat at the sight of their gore-festooned talons and teeth.

It felt like an eternity since he'd become trapped in this hell with the Sorcerer King and what was left of his army. Though Oscar had heard Barquiel mention *Void*, he'd never experienced it before. It was like being stuck in a black hole, senses blinded and all awareness of time and space lost to the infinite emptiness.

His scalp prickled when his father turned his insane gaze on him.

"How is your new familiar?"

Oscar swallowed and looked down at the creature beside him. It was a lynx, like Drabek. Except it was dead, its body animated by the black magic buried inside its corpse.

Even Vedran's powers could not hide its caved-in skull or missing eye.

It took Oscar all he had to keep his voice from trembling when he met his father's stare. "I don't think it's going to work out."

Vedran scowled. He raised a hand.

Oscar masked a shudder. The lynx's corpse disintegrated into nothingness, flesh and bones consumed instantly by the sizzling, stygian and crimson flames that engulfed it from the inside out.

Though the Sorcerer King had been weakened by the last battle he had fought with the Witch Queen, the Hellfire Magic he had stolen from Nikolai was still powerful.

"Come, let us find you another familiar," Vedran commanded.

Oscar dragged his feet as he followed his father, conscious of the watchful stares of the army of fiendish creatures who lurked silently in the shadows. He shivered.

It wasn't just demons, hellbeasts, devils, and ghouls Vedran now held sway over by virtue of being able to wield Azazel's Hellfire Magic. What skulked in the gloom was ten times more vile. It was an army born of an alchemy of twisted souls and bodies, fused together by black magic and the evil will of a man who wished to be a God. Had Dietrich Farago still been around, he would have shuddered at how badly they'd been put together.

Oscar's old self would have relished the devastating power he would have been in line to inherit as the next Sorcerer King. But he was no longer his old self. Not since Nikolai had used *Subjugate* on him and shattered his bond with Drabek. Because it wasn't just his bond with his familiar that had cracked that fateful night.

The darkness that had long swallowed his soul and mind and turned him into a villain capable of the most foul and despicable deeds had started to wane.

It felt akin to waking from a timeless nightmare, one where he'd stained his hands with blood over and over again to satisfy the whims of a man whose appetite for death seemed boundless.

For the first time in a long time, Oscar was beginning to see the Sorcerer King for who he truly was. A monster who thirsted for ultimate power. Immortality and dominion over all living creatures on Earth.

Oscar's chest tightened. He knew he would never be able to absolve himself of all the sins he had committed while under the influence of his father's sickening magic, however much he wished to atone for them.

Something rose in the murk ahead of them, distracting him from his wretched thoughts. His pulse quickened as they approached it.

It was a mound some fifty feet high and nearly twice as wide.

It was made of the bodies of the familiars and Dark Council members Vedran had killed so as to absorb their magic. Though he could not leave *Void* for the time being, the Sorcerer King had made use of his portals to send his demonic henchmen to track down all those who'd once sworn allegiance to him.

Metal glinted inside Vedran's cloak as he used his powers to sift through the corpses, in search of yet another familiar to bond Oscar with.

Oscar avoided staring at the *Book of Light*.

The damage Mae and Nikolai had inflicted on the Sorcerer King's core during their last encounter meant he still hadn't managed to manipulate the artifact to find the *Book of Shadows*. Oscar knew this state of affairs would not last long. Not given the rate at which his father was consuming the magic of others.

The Sorcerer King hadn't let the *Book of Light* out his sight since they'd become trapped in here. He was so paranoid about it he'd even killed a couple of devils he'd thought were looking at it.

Even if I somehow manage to get my hands on that thing, there's nowhere I could hide it in this infernal prison.

Vedran stiffened. Oscar peered curiously past him.

He had uncovered the body of a black wolf.

Seconds ticked by while the Sorcerer King gazed at it unblinkingly.

"No," he mumbled to himself. "That won't do at all, Balkin."

Oscar frowned. *Who's Balkin?*

Vedran finally unearthed an animal he deemed compatible with his remaining heir. Ice filled Oscar's veins.

It was a fox. One that looked eerily like Mae's demon familiar.

"This one is perfect," Vedran crooned.

Oscar gritted his teeth. The Sorcerer King animated the corpse and used his black magic to force an unnatural bond between his son's damaged core and that of the undead creature. Oscar's nails sank into his palms as he resisted, just as he had done with the last three familiars his father had wanted to impose on him.

Drabek was still alive. He could feel it in his bones.

Oscar had become certain of two things in the time he'd been confined in *Void*.

His father had gone mad and would kill him and absorb his magic if he managed to make his core whole again, just as he intended to kill Nikolai and Mae and consume their powers.

And his brother would never forgive him for his crimes against Gabriela Stanisic and their siblings.

Still, Oscar wanted nothing more than to help Nikolai achieve his dream of defeating Vedran. Because if the Sorcerer King won, the world was doomed to enter a dark era from which there would be no escape.

His thoughts turned to the woman his brother had chosen to side with. *Hurry up, Witch Queen. You're the only one who can stop him now.*

CHAPTER TWELVE

Tension knotted Mae's stomach as Violet and
Miles drew a circle on the ground.

They were inside the basement of the condemned
New York coven headquarters, on Madison Avenue.
Though the building remained unstable, the magic
built into its foundations still made it the most secure
place in the city from which to attempt to teleport to
Hell.

Light stabbed through the scaffolding enclosing the
high-rise above them, the beams painting pale lines on
the runes surrounding Mae, Nikolai, Vlad, and Cortes.

It was early Sunday morning and the city was just
waking up. The unnamed victims whose remains were
yet to be identified occupied the headlines of all the
news channels. Rumors of mass abductions and ritual
killings abounded on the internet and social media.
Bryony and Abraham had spent most of yesterday
fielding calls from concerned covens around the
country and abroad.

Magic hummed through the air as the powerful witches and sorcerers who'd gathered in the gloom-filled space prepared to pour their powers into the divine barrier Violet and Miles planned to erect.

"Any last words of wisdom before we do this?" Mae asked Violet.

Violet hesitated. "Artemus did give me a piece of advice to pass on to you. I wasn't sure if he was being serious though."

Mae brightened. "He did? What'd he say?"

Violet made a face. "He said to treat Hell like an amusement park."

Mae gave her a leaden look.

"I told you he might be pulling your leg," Violet muttered.

Vlad scowled. "Does that guy have a screw loose?"

"There's a reason we call him an idiot." Violet sighed at their expressions. "I suspect he meant it. He said the best way to survive Hell is not to get bogged down by the tiny details and to focus on why you're going there in the first place."

Mae swallowed. Artemus Steele had forced his way into the Underworld to save his brother. Now that the time had come to put her own crazy plan in motion, she was feeling nervous. The disquiet churning her stomach had as much to do with the fact that she was going to be visiting a place only a handful of living humans had ever been to, as it had with the doubts she still harbored about the success of her mission.

It was a stab in the dark to hope that Armaros

might be able to fix Hellreaver or that she would be able to locate Azazel's whereabouts.

Do not fret, my witch, Brimstone said. *Armaros was the best blacksmith in all of Heaven before he fell to Hell. And I am certain my master will feel your presence when you enter that realm.* The fox wagged his tail. *The Underworld can be quite an entertaining place once you get past the lava pits and the rivers of fire where the souls of the damned writhe in eternal suffering.*

Mae grimaced. "You're not helping, Brim."

"What did he say?" Nikolai asked guardedly.

"You don't wanna know."

"By the way, be careful if you meet a purple helldragon called Vozgan," Violet warned. "That guy has a tendency to want to eat any human he meets first and ask questions later."

"Is that the helldragon who fought the undead chicken?" Cortes said flatly.

Violet blinked. "How'd you know?"

"Wait," Roman whispered to Nadia. "There are *helldragons?!*"

Miles straightened where he'd been putting the finishing touches to the spell. "Alright, I think we're done."

"You really sure about this?" Karin said in a brittle voice as Miles and Violet took up position at opposing cardinal points. "There's still time to change your mind. After all, this might be a one-way ticket to the Underworld for all of you."

Mae met her anxious gaze steadily. "My father is

down there, as is my mother. Besides, I'm sure you'll be glad to have me out of your hair for a while."

"Oh." Karin squinted. "You mean, we're supposed to enjoy performing the bulk of your duties while you go traipsing about on a ridiculous adventure?"

Mae sighed. "I'm not sure traipsing is the correct term for what we're about to do."

Derrick muttered something under his breath. Gerard rolled his eyes.

Anya walked over to Cortes, clasped his face, and tugged his head down for a heated kiss.

"Those two should get a room," Raven muttered after a full minute had passed. Her vine snake hissed where he'd coiled around her shoulders.

"Yeah," Roman mumbled, his ears reddening.

Anya finally peeled her lips from Cortes's, her face flushed.

"Come back to me," she breathed shakily.

He took her hand and kissed her palm, his expression fierce. "I will. I promise."

"Good luck," Marlena said quietly.

Nadia grinned and gave them a thumbs up. "Break a leg."

Ephra cut her eyes to the Sun Magic High Priestess.

"I really wish you'd let me come with you," Roman said dejectedly.

Mae made a face. "Ludmila will burn the city down if I do that. And Budimir will probably light the torch for her." She looked at Bryony and Abraham. "Hold the fort while I'm gone, will you?"

Bryony frowned. "We will. Say hello to Astarte for me."

"Don't do anything too crazy," Abraham murmured.

Magic exploded around Violet and Miles as they incanted *Shield*. The maelstrom of purple and gold flowed along the outer edge of the circle before rising to fuse into a dome that surrounded Mae and the three men.

The witch and the sorcerer stabbed their weapons into the edge of the barrier and brought forth the divine energy they had inherited by virtue of their alliance with their friends in Chicago.

A shimmering, translucent layer covered the shield. Bryony and everyone else poured their powers into it.

"Whenever you're ready!" Violet shouted above the violent hum of magic filling the underground space.

Brightness bloomed in Nikolai and Alastair's eyes. A scarlet haze enveloped Vlad and Tarang. Gold flared on Cortes's skin and in his and Popo's pupils.

Mae took a deep breath and called forth the power that was hers and hers alone to wield. The basement trembled as a tempest of crimson laced with black and white flashed into life around her and Brimstone.

She placed a hand on Cortes's stomach. He met her resolute gaze, clenched his jaw, and dipped his head.

Mae's heart thumped as she drew on her bond with Brimstone. She focused his mind into her connection with Cortes's core, Na Ri bolstering the link with her own memories.

A moment passed.

The sorcerer drew a sharp breath.

"I—I can see it!" he mumbled dazedly, his eyes growing unfocused. "I can see their memories of Hell!"

"Now!" Mae ground out.

She invoked *Levitate* and *Contain* just as Vlad and Nikolai pressed their hands to her back.

Arcane Magic pulsed from Cortes and Popo.

"*DISTORT!*" the sorcerer barked.

The world twisted dizzyingly around them. The basement vanished. There was a blistering sensation of speed.

They emerged on the edge of a battlefield filled with the war cries of a thousand demons and hellbeasts.

CHAPTER THIRTEEN

Vlad's heart thundered violently in his chest as he stared at the hellish landscape before them from where they bobbed inside Mae's spells.

They were in an immense valley ringed by dark, towering peaks. Rivers of lava spouted from their summits in violent eruptions, filling the air with clouds of smoke and acrid sulfur. The yellow haze hid the distant sky and blanketed the dark forests covering the flanks of the mountains.

His stunned gaze switched to the two armies fighting one another viciously in the cradle of the valley. The ground trembled as giant beasts clashed horns and tusks and claws, the demons sitting astride them bellowing orders to their troops while they tore into the winged enemies surrounding them with their weapons.

"What kind of amusement park did Artemus Steele go to when he was a kid?" Nikolai said hoarsely.

Vlad had to agree. It was a scene from another

world. A nightmarish one where monsters ruled and only the strongest and most vicious among them survived.

Tarang made a soft sound and pressed closer to him. Vlad touched the tiger's head and swallowed past the lump in his throat.

It was becoming clear that one side was defending the city that rose in the midst of the otherwise barren terrain.

Mae scanned the battleground with a guarded look. She seemed much calmer than Vlad felt.

Then again, Na Ri was born in the Underworld.

"Brim, do you know what's happening?" Mae asked the fox tensely.

Brimstone transformed, *Contain* enlarging to accommodate his growing size. They stared.

"Is it me or is he bigger than usual?" Cortes said.

Popo's gaze dropped. "Whoa, look at the size of his—!"

"*My demonic powers are stronger in this realm,*" Brimstone interrupted, towering over them, "*hence my true physical manifestation.*" He looked at Mae. "*You, my witch, are infinitely stronger here than you are on Earth.*" His crimson gaze switched to Vlad. "*And so are you, son of Ilmon.*"

Vlad's throat tightened. "Is that why I'm feeling strange?" He touched his belly. "Like there's some kind of fire in me?!"

A hot feeling had ignited within him since they'd materialized in the Underworld. It was expanding at a speed that made his insides churn. In its wake came a sense of potency he'd never experienced before.

His bond with Tarang thrummed with the same formidable energy.

"You should both stop resisting it." The nine-tailed fox nudged Tarang gently with his snout before straightening and looking out across the battlefield. *"As for what we are witnessing, it appears we have found the reason for the Soul Reaper queen's disappearance."*

They followed his gaze. Mae sucked in air.

Alicia Calvarro carved the heads off a score of ten-foot-tall demons where she fought not far from a bridge that led to the gates of the city. Her black cloak fluttered around her skeletal form and her giant scythe dripped with the blood of the enemies she had felled.

A chill danced down Vlad's spine when he spotted the allies who fought alongside the Reaper queen. They were hard to miss.

Each ruby-eyed, demonic figurehead was as big and as powerful looking as Barquiel. The enormous monsters they rode stamped on lesser fiends and beasts, the helldragons among them decimating entire hordes of the enemy as they spewed jets of black-tinged flames from their wicked jaws.

But the figure that captured his attention was a female demon with inky wings and an enormous spear whose shaft was made of dozens of hissing, black vipers the width of his arm. She moved like a Goddess of death across the battle ground, her lone figure blurring and her weapon and fists and feet raining damnation on all those she struck.

"Is that Astarte?!" Mae gasped.

"Yes. That is Astaroth, the Great Duke of Hell. She was the Goddess Astarte before she fell from Heaven. The ones fighting alongside her are Leaders of the Grigori. They too were once powerful Heavenly beings." Brimstone's eyes flashed. *"It seems we are to be called to battle sooner than we anticipated, my witch. We must assist—"*

A shadow engulfed them. They looked up.

Bile burned the back of Vlad's throat.

A pair of snarling helldragons was plummeting toward them.

Mae cursed and hastily maneuvered *Contain*.

The falling beasts missed them by inches, the monsters' passage sucking the magic sphere into a powerful downdraft before Mae stabilized it.

The helldragons carved a giant depression in the ground when they crash-landed.

The smaller, purple beast slipped out from under its enemy's body and batted it with a thick, horned tail. The green helldragon screeched as the barbs raked its face and left eye. The purple beast sank its teeth into its foe's wing with a mighty growl and ripped a jagged tear in the upper pinion.

The green helldragon opened its jaws on a fireball that seared Vlad's vision. He blinked in time to see the purple helldragon jump aside nimbly and charge the enemy.

It headbutted the green helldragon violently in the chest and sent it stumbling and rolling to the ground. The green helldragon shook its head dazedly before climbing unsteadily to its feet. A fireball struck it straight in the face. The wounded party whirled around and took flight, one wing drooping.

"And there's more where that came from, scumbag!" the purple helldragon shouted after its enemy.

"Shit," Cortes mumbled. "It can talk?!"

Popo released a worried squawk.

"What I want to know is who taught him to say scumbag," Nikolai commented dully.

The helldragon noticed their presence for the first time.

Vlad's knuckles whitened on his diamond-edged swords as it lowered its head and squinted at them.

Cortes cut his eyes to Mae. "Didn't Violet warn us about a purple helldragon called Vozgan?"

"Oh." The helldragon blinked, surprised etched across his face. "You know Vi?"

"Yes." Mae lifted her chin. "We are friends of Violet and Artemus Steele."

The helldragon brightened. "You're pals with Art too?"

"Seriously, why is he talking like that?" Nikolai hissed to Cortes. "It's freaking me out!"

Cortes shrugged. "At this point, I'm willing to believe anything."

Mae hesitated. "So, you're Vozgan?"

The helldragon straightened to his full height and thrust his chest out. "I am indeed the Almighty Vozgan."

Vlad pursed his lips. He was willing to bet the dragon had added that title to his name himself. From

Mae's narrow-eyed expression, she was thinking the same thing.

Vozgan watched them broodingly.

"What?" Mae said uneasily.

"It's a shame. I was just thinking it was time for a snack."

He licked his chops. A sliver of drool fell from his jaw and splattered onto *Contain*.

It would have drenched them had it not been for the spell.

The aura that detonated around Brimstone startled Vlad and made the dragon's tail stiffen.

"*How impertinent of you, dragon!*" the demon fox snarled.

The air outside the barrier whined despite the spell containing most of the power the familiar had unleashed. Rocks and dirt lifted off the ground.

Vozgan studied the violent storm of magic and demonic energy bubbling around Brimstone uneasily. "Sheesh. It was just an observation." He turned toward the battlefield. "*Hey, Dad?*" the helldragon bellowed. "*There are some humans here!*"

A black beast of a helldragon raised his horned head in the middle of the combat zone and spat out the body of the helltigress he had just impaled with his teeth. "*That's impossible, son!*"

"Well, there's a bunch of them right here and they say they know Artemus and Violet," Vozgan whined.

He pointed a claw at *Contain*.

Alicia's gaze found them through the warring

armies. Her expression turned horrified, which was saying something for a skeleton.

Mae waved weakly.

Crimson bloomed in Alicia's orbits. "What the hell are you guys doing here?!"

Her voice boomed across the battleground and resonated in their ears.

"Sound sure carries well in this place," Nikolai muttered.

Astarte slowed at the sound of the Reaper queen's snarl and stared in their direction. She scowled. "Wait. Don't tell me that's—?!"

A dark helldragon dove toward her, claws extended to tear her apart. Astarte flashed out of the path of its talons and kicked it in the face.

"I'm trying to have a conversation here, asshat!" she hissed.

The dragon went flying backward into a hellmammoth and took it to the ground, crushing some hundred demons and smaller hellbeasts in the process.

Vlad flinched when Astarte's scarlet gaze pierced them where they floated inside Mae's spell.

"I see that we're going to need to have a nice, long chat when this is over."

The Goddess cracked her knuckles in a way that made it clear that words were not the only things that would be exchanged in said heart-to-heart.

"Are we sure she's on our side?" Cortes said dubiously. "She looks like she wants to kill us."

Popo fidgeted nervously on his shoulder. "I can sense her murderous intent from here, my Enrique."

Vozgan scratched his snout with a claw. "Father said Aunt Astarte had a nasty temper even when she was in Heaven."

A surprised "Ooof!" left the helldragon as a hellmammoth slammed into his flank.

Tension knotted Vlad's shoulders. Dozens of demons and hellbeasts had surrounded them.

"Well, what are you waiting for, you fools?!" Astarte shouted from the other side of the battleground. "Use your damn magic and fight them!"

"Anyone else get the feeling she's going to be a major pain in our ass?" Cortes said leadenly.

CHAPTER FOURTEEN

MAE'S PULSE RACED AS SHE STUDIED THE DEMONIC
horde fixing them with ravenous stares. Her
heightened senses and the power bubbling inside her
raised the hairs on the back of her neck.

"I guess we should do as she says."

Cortes unleashed his sword and whip and gave her
a dark look. "I can't believe we almost got eaten by a
dragon the second we arrived in Hell."

"I said I was sorry!" Vozgan protested where he was
clashing horns with the hellmammoth.

"You know you're the one who brought us to this
exact location, right?" Vlad pointed out to the sorcerer.

Cortes scowled.

Nikolai watched a demon wipe drool from its chin.

"I bet we look like meat on a stick to them," he said
flatly.

Alastair squawked uneasily on his shoulder.

Mae sighed. "On the count of three?"

A haze of Hellfire Magic licked Nikolai's frame and

flashed in his crow familiar's eyes. The veneer of incubus energy coating Vlad's flesh and Tarang's fur thickened. Cortes dipped his head.

Mae drew on her cores as she brought her barrier down. The demons and hellbeasts charged the instant *Contain* vanished.

"Wind Fury!"

The blaze that filled her veins when the spell left her lips made the air lock in her throat. A veritable tempest of crimson and black detonated around her.

Cortes cursed as he was pushed back some dozen feet. Nikolai stabbed his spear into the ground and hung on grimly to the weapon.

Only Vlad and Tarang were able to withstand the full force of the spell, their pupils bright with the unholy energy bubbling inside their own cores.

Mae's scalp prickled as she tasted the potent forces coursing through every cell in her body. It wasn't just her demonic energy that was being amplified by her current location. So too were her white and black magic. And just as Brimstone had said, the spell she'd invoked was bigger and more vicious than anything she'd ever manifested on Earth.

Wind Fury swept demons and beasts up into its vortex, the deadly currents cutting their flesh until their blood misted the inside of the spinning funnel.

Brimstone's quivering tails crackled with demonic energy and black magic. His chest swelled as he inhaled.

The *Wrath* he unleashed felled three giant hellbeasts

and a swathe of demons before blasting a fifty-foot-wide hole in a hill a quarter of a mile away.

Incubus energy swamped the air as Vlad and Tarang faced off against a score of ten-foot-tall monsters, their attacks so blistering Mae could barely keep up with their movements. The demons went flying into the air, bodies landing in a mess of broken limbs and caved-in chests and torn flesh.

Hellfire Magic engulfed the pack of hellbeasts leaping for Nikolai and Alastair. The sorcerer finished them off with a barrage of white magic spell bombs and a blast of *Hell Flare*.

Cortes fixed the two helltigresses prowling around him with a deadly stare, Popo's wings and eyes blazing brightly on his shoulder. The beasts sprang on murderous roars, fangs and claws glinting.

Arcane Magic and steel split the skin and flesh of the first one as the sorcerer dropped to the ground and sliced its belly open from underneath. It collapsed heavily in the dirt, blood and guts spilling from its fatal wound.

A strangled sound left the second monster when Cortes's whip found its throat. The crack its neck made when the sorcerer snapped it echoed in Mae's ears.

It didn't take long to dispose of the fiends and beasts that had ambushed them. More came over from the main battlefield, bloodlust brightening their pupils.

Vozgan returned from where he'd felled the hellmammoth.

"You guys are strong," the helldragon said brightly. "We should have a mock battle." He sobered at the sight of the approaching enemy. "But after we get rid of them."

The energy pouring out of Mae's cores made her very bones tremble. Her magic was flourishing with every minute she spent in this realm. Brimstone and Na Ri were experiencing the same thing, their souls welcoming the demonic strength their birthplace granted them.

"Let me try something."

Her tone caused Nikolai to cast a worried look at her.

She stepped forward, heat surging through her bond with Brimstone, fusing their cores. A black aura bloomed around her. She raised a hand toward where the sky should be, the taste of magic making her tongue tingle.

"Eclipse!"

The spell that formed at the summit of the valley bathed the battlefield and the very mountains in twilight. A deafening silence rolled out across the landscape as every living thing stopped and stared at the phenomenon.

"Shit," Cortes mumbled, sword and whip hanging limply in his grasp.

"Well, I think you just demonstrated to everyone here that you really are Azazel's daughter," Vlad told Mae flatly.

She met his crimson gaze and swallowed, the incubus energy in his pupils vibrating along the same wavelength as her own demonic strength. Brimstone towered over her, his and Na Ri's presence bolstering her magic.

Even Astarte startled at the negative pressure that erupted from *Eclipse* when it fully manifested its devastating ability. Hellbeasts and demons panicked and shrieked as they were dragged across the ground and swept up toward the gigantic black hole.

Mae raised a shield around those who fought alongside the Goddess and Alicia, her growing powers and Na Ri's soul allowing her to differentiate between friend and foe in a heartbeat. Brimstone's tails quivered savagely as he poured his magic into the spell.

It took less than a minute for *Eclipse* to rid the battlefield of most of the enemy. Some managed to escape through tunnels in the mountains and burrows in the ground. The rest were cut down by Astarte and her alliance.

Mae shuddered and retracted her magic. She could only imagine the damage she could inflict on Earth if she ever unleashed *Eclipse* the way she'd just done in Hell. A wave of dizziness washed over her. She swayed.

Nikolai steadied her with a hand on her shoulder.

"Are you okay?" the sorcerer said quietly.

Mae met his concerned gaze, her chest tight. "I'm not sure." She looked blindly at her fingers, doubt assailing her for the first time in months. "This power is insane. Surely, no one should be allowed to wield something like this."

Cortes exchanged a guarded glance with Vlad. Vozgan stared, puzzled.

Do not fret, Mae, Na Ri murmured. *We will need that*

spell when we join our allies in the final battle against Satanael.

Mae's heart lurched at the reminder of what she'd learned when she'd first manifested her magic. That they were destined to join the army humanity would need to defend itself at the End of Days.

"Na Ri is right, my witch." Brimstone lowered his giant head and almost sent her tumbling to the ground when he nuzzled her affectionately with his snout. *"You must not fear your abilities. The daughters of Azazel and Ran Soyun would never abuse the powers gifted to them."*

"He's right, Mae," Vlad said.

Cortes nodded.

Nikolai straightened. "Here they come."

Astarte and the demon commanders were making their way over, their armored boots raising dust as their armies parted deferentially ahead of them. The ground quaked in their wake, Vozgan's black helldragon father and the colossal hellbeasts they'd ridden in battle following them.

The Goddess and the demons looked even more daunting up close, the power they emitted distorting the air around their monstrous physiques.

Nikolai stepped in front of Mae, his expression devoid of fear.

Astarte raised an eyebrow. "You sure are courageous, sorcerer. But I suspect your witch does not need your protection." Her expression softened a little when she looked up at Brimstone. "It is good to see you again, Sotsuna."

Brimstone bowed his head. *"The pleasure is mine, Goddess."*

"Sotsuna?" Cortes whispered to Nikolai.

"That was the name given to him by Na Ri," he murmured.

Astarte stopped a short distance from them. Her brow furrowed. She turned and scrutinized a spot some fifty feet to Mae's left.

Vlad drew a sharp breath. His head moved mechanically to follow the Goddess's line of sight. Surprise jolted Mae.

A powerful tide of incubus energy was washing across the valley.

A portal opened where Astarte and Vlad stared. The figure that stepped out of it made the incubus freeze and Mae's eyes round.

It was a magnificent, handsome demon with alabaster skin, artfully curved black horns, and crimson points flaring in the center of his inky eyes. A scarlet robe hung upon his dark armor, adding to his majestic presence.

"What are you doing here, Ilmon? You know it's dangerous for us to travel through rifts right now." Astarte's tone hardened. "You're meant to be guarding Armaros's keep."

One of the demon commanders beside the Goddess waved a hand irritably. "Dial down the incubus charm, will you? My troops look like they're going to keel over from lust."

The demon soldiers and beasts behind him

flinched, faces flushed as they stole covetous glances at the new arrival.

Ilmon only had eyes for Vlad. He hesitated before slowly making his way over.

Vlad swallowed heavily and stood his ground. Tarang's tail started swinging as he stared at the approaching figure. He let out a friendly huff.

Ilmon stopped opposite Vlad, his scarlet gaze roaming his face hungrily.

"Are you really Ilmon?" Vlad said thickly.

Ilmon nodded. His chin quivered. A strangled sound left him.

He rushed over, took a stunned Vlad in his arms, and hugged him tightly.

"My little—my little *malyshka!*" the king of Incubi and Succubae mumbled weakly.

"*Malyshka?*" Mae hissed to Nikolai and Cortes.

"It's a Russian endearment," Nikolai replied.

The sorcerer looked like he was trying hard not to curl a lip at the display of affection taking place before them.

Alicia approached.

"Hey, is that really Ilmon's kid?!" a demon commander asked the Reaper queen in a stage whisper.

"Yeah." Alicia swung her scythe onto her shoulder and cut her eyes to Astarte. "You should stop him. You know what happens when he gets emotional."

"Why? What happens?" Cortes asked warily.

"He once flooded a city with his tears when he broke up with a girlfriend," Astarte said absentmindedly.

Everyone except the Goddess stared at the tears rolling down Ilmon's cheeks and the puddle forming by his feet. Cortes inched away from the Incubus king.

Mae chewed her lip. Vlad's darkening expression indicated he was giving serious thought to dinging his father's ear.

A demon commander started making gagging noises. The guy next to him looked pleadingly at the sulfurous clouds high above the valley and muttered, "Just kill me," under his breath.

"Stop him before he turns this place into a lake!" another demon snapped at Astarte.

"Come now." Astarte sighed heavily before going over to gently pat the Incubus king's shoulder. "You're embarrassing yourself in front of your son."

"I don't care," Ilmon blubbered. "My little rabbit is finally home!"

He squeezed Vlad so hard the incubus choked.

"Christ," Nikolai muttered with a disgusted expression.

Several demons sucked in air and eyed the sorcerer disapprovingly. A few made the sign of an inverted cross, like he'd said something blasphemous.

Alicia pinched the bridge of her skull when Ilmon's sniveling intensified.

Astarte scowled. "For Hell's sake, comport yourself like the king that you are!"

CHAPTER FIFTEEN

THE WIND WHIPPED AT MAE'S HAIR AND CHILLED HER face where she clung to Vannog's back. Vozgan's father was flying across an immense valley shrouded with mist, his giant wings eating the miles in seconds. The yellow haze swirling above the top of the dark forest they passed churned violently in his wake.

Mae shivered and hugged Brimstone to her chest, Nikolai a comforting, warm presence at her back.

It felt strange being cold in the Underworld. Then again, the place was nothing like any of them had imagined when they'd made the fateful decision to come here.

Instead of a realm of fire and ash filled with the screams of damned souls, Hell looked like a world from the Jurassic era stuck inside the bowels of the planet. It was a veritable maze of cavernous spaces big enough to house mountains and the largest human cities. As for its valleys, forests, deserts, oceans, lakes, and rivers, they dwarfed anything that could be found on Earth.

Artemus was right. Mae's stomach roiled as she looked over Vannog's flank toward a distant river of lava. *This dimension is too vast and overwhelming for a mere human to comprehend.*

You soon get used to it, Na Ri reassured her.

Nikolai tightened his hold around her waist when another shudder racked her body, his body heat seeping into her flesh.

They had spent a few hours resting in Arakiel's palace after the battle outside his city had ended. The Second Leader of the Grigori turned out to be the cantankerous demon commander who'd looked like he wanted to barf at Ilmon's show of affection toward his son.

As for the Incubus king, he had left shortly after meeting Vlad, but not before promising that they would soon reunite.

Mae had wondered if Barquiel was behind the army Astarte and her allies had fought, but the Goddess had told her otherwise. And her explanation had been nothing if not sobering.

"Satanael is consolidating his troops by forcibly absorbing demonic settlements," the Goddess had explained with a troubled expression. "Most of these places are remote and well beyond his usual scope of operation. He's left them alone for many a millennia." She drummed her fingers on the armrest of her chair. "It seems his council has advised him that now is the time to start growing his forces again."

"I bet you it was that son of a dung beetle, Oriens," Arakiel sneered.

The demon commander beside him gracefully overlooked his interjection.

"This will only lead to more territorial conflicts," Tamiel observed. The Fifth Leader of the Grigori was a demon with wise eyes and a calm demeanor. "We haven't seen the end of these skirmishes yet."

"Surely, if those demons and beasts are against being ruled by—" Cortes had faltered.

"Satanael," Zakiel, the Fifteenth Leader of the Grigori, had added helpfully.

The sorcerer had shuddered. "Yeah, that guy." He'd studied Astarte and the demon commanders with a faint frown. "Aren't they technically on your side?"

"Not necessarily," Ramiel, the Sixth Leader of the Grigori, had replied in Astarte's stead. "They were willing to slaughter the demons and beasts under Arakiel's protection to lay claim to his city. Not all those in Hell are capable of upholding alliances."

Vlad had grimaced. "So, there are different factions even among the demons who oppose Satanael?"

"Yes." Astarte had sighed. "There are as many cabals as there are breeds of helllizard."

Mae, Nikolai, Vlad, and Cortes had stared at the Goddess.

"There are many types of helllizard," Chazaquiel had expounded.

The Eighth Leader of the Grigori had begun naming them before mumbling to a stop in the face of Astarte's pointed look.

"Come." Astarte had risen to her feet and turned to Mae. "The hour is late. If we want to get to Hell Deep by nightfall, we should leave now. Alicia and Ilmon are likely already at Armaros's keep."

"Should I try teleporting us there?" Cortes had suggested. "All I need is someone's memory of the place and Mae's magic to translate it to my core."

The Goddess and the demon commanders had stared at the sorcerer like he'd suggested they perform a frightful sex act.

"Wait." Arakiel had cocked a thumb at Cortes, his tone full of suspicion. "This guy can teleport?!"

Cortes made a face. "Let's just say I gained some new spells after Mae...touched my core."

This time, the Goddess and the Leaders of the Grigori had fixed Mae with various pearl-clutching expressions of disapproval.

"There were extenuating circumstances," she'd said defensively.

Astarte had lowered her brows. "So, *that's* how you guys got here? A space warping spell?!"

Mae had avoided her stare and maintained a tactful silence.

Astarte's shoulders had slumped.

Tamiel had gently patted the Goddess's shoulder. "She is her father's daughter, after all."

Mae had brightened. "Oh. Did Azazel do something similar?"

"Don't sound so damn proud about it!" Arakiel had snapped.

Mae had hesitated. "Alicia told us something

recently. That a demon who looked like Azazel was spotted near this domain. Is that true?"

"It is," Arakiel had grunted. "But I could find no trace of him when I went looking so I am uncertain if it was truly Azazel."

Astarte's voice broke through Mae's reverie. "We're almost there."

Mae squinted when they emerged from some clouds. All she could see up ahead was a whole lot of gray.

Nikolai's fingers clenched on her waist. "Isn't that a mountain?!"

"Shit!" Vlad cursed.

"We're going to crash!" Cortes yelled.

"No, we're not," Vannog huffed haughtily, smoke billowing from his enormous nostrils.

Astarte smirked at them over her shoulder. "Enjoy the ride, kids."

She rolled off the helldragon and dropped from view.

Mae's stomach flip-flopped as Vannog dove after her. Alastair squawked. Popo shrieked. Tarang yowled.

Astarte whooped excitedly where she flew beside the helldragon, her hand skimming his flank.

The floor of the valley rose to meet them at a speed that made Mae's eyes water. Leaves and branches exploded off trees in the powerful downdraft caused by Vannog's wings as he pulled up sharply and skimmed the top of a forest.

This is fun! Brimstone chuffed, face wobbling with the G-force.

Mae was starting to think the ride had affected her familiar's brain.

Vannog sailed over a lake where giant, shadowy beasts swam beneath the surface, folded his wings, and darted inside an opening in the base of the mountain.

Astarte reappeared and alighted nimbly on the back of the dragon's neck as he glided through a huge tunnel that burrowed beneath the land. She cackled when she saw their ashen expressions in the gloom.

"Ah." The Goddess wiped a tear of mirth from her eye. "I should have brought a cellphone to the Underworld just so I could take a snapshot of your faces right now." She chuckled. "Artemus is going to crack a rib laughing when I tell him about this."

A full body snigger shook her frame.

Mae scowled. Nikolai peeled Alastair's wings from his face and spat out a feather, similarly annoyed. Vlad was cajoling Tarang out from under his jacket.

"I told you guys she was going to be a pain in our ass," Cortes muttered darkly, carefully unhooking Popo's claws from where the parrot clung grimly to his chest.

Vannog navigated a maze of burrows that twisted and dipped and rose beneath some twenty miles of mountains, the tips of his wings at times brushing the rock walls. The gloom finally dwindled when he approached an exit. He emerged into a canyon carved by a turbulent river and looped smoothly around the edge of a bluff.

Mae's breath caught when the helldragon shot out onto a vast plain where golden fields swayed in a gentle breeze. Her wide-eyed gaze danced over the wheat crops covering the immense prairie and around the ring of towering, mist-wreathed mountains enclosing the valley they were crossing.

Evergreen forests draped the flanks of the peaks, along with colorful meadows full of flowers and pastures where hellbeasts grazed. Waterfalls glinted here and there against dark rock faces, liquid silver cascading down vertiginous ridges to meet the river that meandered through the valley.

"How is this possible?!" Nikolai shouted, stunned. "This place is just like somewhere you'd find on Earth!"

Astarte twisted around and leveled a steady look at Mae. "It is a blessing granted to us by your father's magic."

Mae's stomach knotted as she gazed at the demon Goddess. "My father did this?!"

"Yes." Astarte faced forward again. "This place used to be like the other valleys we passed not long ago. Dark and bleak, with only dead forests and dry, cracked land. It's come back to life in the past couple of months. We believe it's because Azazel found out you were still alive."

Mae's fingers clenched on Brimstone. The fox keened softly and raised his head to lick her chin.

"There are a handful of places like this in Hell Deep that Azazel helped create," Astarte said. "The most beautiful of them was the kingdom he built for Ran Soyun."

Mae stiffened. "Is that still—?"

"No." Astarte's tone hardened. "The war the first

Sorcerer King and Barquiel brought to that dominion devastated it beyond repair. I doubt even Azazel would be able to resurrect the realm he once inhabited with his wife and child."

A lump formed in Mae's throat as Na Ri's sorrow fluttered through her heart.

A city appeared up ahead. A pale citadel crowned the low hill within its towering walls.

"Are those—bones?!" Vlad gasped.

The castle gleamed in the low light, the human remains making up its facade radiating a sickening light.

"Before you get all misty-eyed, those bones are from humans who died in wars on Earth," Astarte grunted.

"Yeah, that doesn't make me feel any better," Cortes muttered.

Mae scanned the landscape nervously while Vannog closed in on the city. She could feel the presence of many demons in the mountains and forests, as well as some thousand creatures who reeked of incubus energy.

The way Vlad frowned as he followed her gaze told her he'd sensed them too.

"Do not fear," Astarte said. "They are the army Armaros and Ilmon put together to defend this place should Hell's Council ever dare to invade."

CHAPTER SIXTEEN

VANNOG SHOT OVER A DRAWBRIDGE SPANNING THE RIVER encircling the keep. The guards on the walls shouted and waved as the helldragon flew over the city gates.

"Welcome back, Lord Dragon!"

Mae's pulse quickened at the sight of the demonic metropolis beyond the fortifications.

It was laid out like a human city, with several wide thoroughfares crisscrossing the streets to form blocks. Most of the buildings and homes were constructed of stone and wood. The smell of roasting meats carried from chimneys and open windows.

I wonder if a city in medieval Europe would have looked like this.

I would think so, Na Ri said. *The designs on which Father based the keeps of Hell Deep eventually appeared on Earth in the Middle Ages. I suspect it was the Immortals who refined them.*

Mae drew a sharp breath as they passed an industrial district home to a maze of narrow lanes and canals crowded with factories, smithies, and workshops, most of which spouted acrid fumes from their smokestacks.

Wait. So, you're saying dad came up with the blueprints for Earth's cities?!

Yes.

Mae was still reeling over this morsel of information when Vannog flashed across a waterway and took them over an area of the city where the houses were bigger and more elaborate, their walls made of bricks and bones.

Nikolai tensed behind her.

Mae's chest tightened as she studied the palace straddling the knoll ahead. The moment of truth would soon be upon them. And she wasn't sure what she would do if Armaros told her Hellreaver could not be fixed.

Vannog crossed a drawbridge and the outer walls of the castle before spiraling down toward an immense, sunken courtyard made of black granite. His claws raised sparks when he landed, his enormous wings casting long shadows on the ground before he folded them against his body.

Mae's pulse quickened at the sight of a large forge where hot coals simmered. *Brim, is that where—?*

Yes.

Mae swallowed and touched the pendant beneath her shirt.

Movement drew her eyes. A group of demons had rushed out into the palace forecourt and was hurrying toward them.

"Lord Dragon, you are finally back." Relief flooded the face of the head demon, a creature who was nearly as wide as he was tall and who towered above the rest. He cut his eyes to a pair of fiends behind him. "Inform the kitchens at once. We must prepare a feast for our noble beast."

"You know, it's not like we starved him on this mission," Astarte said wryly. "He devoured twenty hellboars all by himself just last night."

"Twenty hellboars are nothing but an entrée, woman," Vannog rumbled.

The head demon drew a sharp breath at the sight of Astarte. He lowered himself to one knee and bowed his head. "My apologies, Goddess. I did not see you there."

The servants behind him followed suit.

"At ease." Astarte landed lightly beside the head demon as he straightened. "I am glad the city is safe, Us'gorith."

"It is by your grace, Goddess." Us'gorith peered curiously at Mae and the others as they climbed awkwardly down Vannog's body. "I see you have brought some unusual guests again." His eyes flared when he got his first good look at them. "Oh. The woman carries Lord Azazel's scent." His surprised gaze found Vlad. "And this one smells like an incubus."

Astarte made introductions. "This is Mae Jin, Azazel's daughter. And that guy is Vlad Vissarion, Ilmon's son. Those two are white magic and Arcane Magic wielders." She waved a hand at Nikolai and Cortes curtly before indicating the head demon. "Everyone, this is Us'gorith. He is Armaros's chief steward and the main reason this city hasn't fallen to ruin."

Mae and the three men murmured guarded greetings. Us'gorith's jaw had dropped open. Shocked whispers rippled through the attendants behind him.

The head demon recovered first. "I shall make preparations for your stay." He caught sight of Brimstone and squinted. "Why do I feel like I've seen that fox somewhere before?"

Brimstone jumped out of Mae's hold and shook himself out into his nine-tailed form.

He towered over the demons, his voice booming across the courtyard. *"Hello, old friend."*

Us'gorith gasped, his face brightening. "Lord Sotsuna! You have returned!"

Brimstone lowered his giant head and poked the head demon gently with his snout. *"You can call me Brimstone. It is the new name given to me by my witch."*

He wrapped a tail around Mae.

"Where's Armaros?" Astarte asked Us'gorith curiously while the other fiends crowded happily around the nine-tailed fox. "I thought that damn fool would be glued to his forge as always."

The head demon's expression turned strained. "He is…currently entertaining his majesties King Ilmon and Queen Thod."

Astarte's expression soured. "So, Ilmon and Alicia are bitching about their lives over drinks and he's keeping them company?"

"I cannot lie to you, Goddess," Us'gorith murmured.

"I pray that you intervene before an unfortunate incident occurs."

A loud curse made them all jump. Mae looked up warily. It had come from an upper window of the palace. More swearing followed.

"*Not my thousand-year-old wine!*" The voice grew thunderous with rage. "Ilmon, you bastard! How could you?!"

The sound of breaking glass ensued. Us'gorith paled.

"Looks like I'm too late," Astarte muttered.

VLAD STARED AT THE STUFFED HEAD OF A HELLMAMMOTH mounted on the wall of the wide hallway they navigated. It wasn't the only monster Armaros had chosen to display on the walls of his palace.

Cortes eyed a colorful tapestry hanging between a hellbear mounted on a stand and a halberd that could probably fell a helldragon. "This place sure is… different."

The decor was a mix of the grisly and a kind of gaudiness usually associated with the nouveau riche. It was as far removed from the austere and elegant furnishings of Arakiel's palace as an art shack on the beach was from the Louvre.

"It didn't used to be this garish." Astarte grimaced. "Let's just say a certain purveyor of antique goods and his English friend persuaded a gullible demon to invest in a few period pieces."

She waved a hand at a vase Vlad was pretty sure he'd seen in a museum.

Mae wrinkled her nose. "So Artemus and Sebastian hoodwinked Armaros into buying their stuff?"

Us'gorith lowered his brows. "This is but a fraction of what those two scoundrels tried to pawn off upon my liege."

"What kind of idiots must they be to try and deceive a demon commander?" Cortes muttered.

Astarte rolled her eyes. "The kind whose father is an archangel and one who harbors the soul and will of a prickly divine beast."

Noisy revelry rose from the room they were approaching. Us'gorith opened the door and went in ahead of them. To his credit, the demon didn't even flinch when a scythe hummed past his face and stabbed into the wall to his right.

"Oops," the Queen of Soul Reapers mumbled. "Sorry. We were playing darts."

She swayed a little where she stood behind a couch covered in the hide of a helltigress, her flushed cheeks and glazed eyes indicating that she was well on her way to getting stone drunk.

"I think you will find that the darts are in your other hand, my queen," Us'gorith observed with the stoic expression of a demon who'd dealt with this shit a thousand times before and had the receipts to prove it.

"Wanna come work for me?" Astarte asked the head demon kindly while Alicia inspected the bone darts in her left hand with a cross-eyed look.

"I best not, Goddess." Us'gorith's mouth grew

pinched. "I went on a trip once and the city almost burned down."

"Oh." Astarte grimaced. "Was that the time your lord organized a fire-breathing contest?"

"Yes." Us'gorith's shoulders slumped. "In a city made of wood construct." He shuddered and covered his face with his hands as he revisited the horrors of that particular incident. "He even got the helldragons to participate."

Vlad listened distractedly while Astarte murmured words of consolation.

The chamber they'd entered was a reception room, not that anyone could tell right now with how messy the place was. Empty mugs, glassware, beer kegs, and bottles crowded the floor and the surfaces of the furniture. The air reeked of so much potent alcohol he was surprised the fire crackling in the hearth hadn't ignited the fumes.

His pulse quickened at the sight of the pair of demons engaged in a tussle on one of the couches.

The stout one with the bulging muscles and curved horns tipped with Hellfire was desperately trying to wrench a bottle out of Ilmon's hand.

"Why," he grunted and groaned, "are you so ridiculously strong?!"

Vlad presumed the demon was Armaros. To his surprise, his father, who was slumped against the backrest, didn't even look like he was trying that hard to hold on to the bottle.

He swallowed. *Father. I never thought the day would come when I would be in a position to actually use that word.*

In all honesty, I have long considered Yuliy to have fulfilled that role. He fisted his hands, his chest hot with an emotion he could not deny. *It seems there is space left in my heart for—*

"When is my little rabbit going to get here?" Ilmon moped while Armaros huffed and grunted, neck cording as he desperately tried to peel one of the Incubus king's fingers from the bottle. Ilmon straightened and looked blearily at Us'gorith's lord. "Did I tell you how pretty my rabbit is? His hair is like ringlets of spun gold and his eyes exude a beauty that could outmatch the brightest sun in their resplendence. Why, just one of my little rabbit's cheekbones could launch a thousand sailboats into the Styx."

Vlad scowled.

"You should put that on your resumé," Nikolai said with a straight face.

Cortes's lips twitched.

Vlad was about to flip the two sorcerers the middle finger when Ilmon finally noticed them. The incubus energy that bloomed across the room and blasted through the castle had Astarte groaning and Us'gorith flushing.

Ilmon let go of the bottle and jumped to his feet, his eyes bright. "My little rabbit! You're here."

Armaros stumbled backward and cursed, almost dropping his prize. He beamed at the bottle before pressing it to his cheek and murmuring sweet nothings to it.

"Your liege is disgusting," Astarte told Us'gorith coolly.

Ilmon crossed the room, his arms wide open and his expression pure mush. "Come, give your papa a kiss, my sweet little rabbit!"

He puckered his lips.

"I swear to God, I will cut you if you touch me!" Vlad snapped.

Alicia let out a belch that smelled like something that could strip paint. "Pardon me."

CHAPTER SEVENTEEN

Barquiel panted and wheezed, his entire body trembling from the effort it had taken to finally break out of *Chaos Seal*. He looked over his shoulder at the crack in the spell he'd climbed out of.

The dark dimension where he'd been trapped for days was visible inside it.

He swallowed. *Curse Azazel for teaching her that awful magic!*

The demon scanned his surroundings cautiously. One thing to be grateful for was that *Chaos Seal* hadn't brought him to the same place where Azazel once contained Hellfire Magic.

He didn't recognize the deserted cave around him, but it had to be somewhere in Hell. He only had to smell the hot sulfur filling his lungs and feel the heat beneath his boots to know that a river of lava was close by.

A sharp pang stabbed his insides, catching him off

guard. Barquiel clutched his stomach with a grunt and nearly doubled over.

Fear brought a sour taste to his mouth. It was happening more often now. He waited for the fire scorching his soul to abate, sweat dripping off his chin and splashing onto the warm stone with faint hisses.

Dammit all to Hell!

He couldn't understand why Rose Blake's soul fragment had gained a life of its own, nor how she was able to hurt him so.

Barquiel clenched his jaw, silently raging at his recent misfortunes and the malediction that was cast upon him when he was driven out of Heaven. One that meant he could not easily cast aside the body he had taken over.

He had to find Ran Soyun. Before what was left of Rose Blake won the battle being fought inside him.

Barquiel straightened and pressed a hand against the rock face to steady himself before heading slowly into the gloom.

MAE'S STOMACH CHURNED AS SHE WATCHED ARMAROS inspect the skeleton key she'd handed to him. A rabble of voices rose around them.

They were in a dining hall that took up half the basement of the castle. Brimstone and Vannog poked their heads into the extensive kitchen next to it, picking and choosing their menu for the night. The demons tending to the dozens of roasting pits and the multitude of bubbling vats didn't seem to mind their presence, some even making shy suggestions.

"Hmm." Armaros rubbed his chin, squinting at the indentations Hellreaver had made on the shank and the bit. "I see why this thing didn't work." He placed the key on the table. "Fixing it is pretty straightforward. But it was Azazel who imbued it with the necessary magic to make it do what it's supposed to do." The demon gave Mae a shrewd look. "Seeing as you're his daughter, I hope you will be able to do the same."

Mae's pulse quickened. She held his gaze. "And Hellreaver?" She unhooked the pentagram pendant from around her neck and laid it carefully on the table. "Can he be fixed?"

An expectant silence fell around the table. Armaros picked up the cracked pieces she had fused together using her and Brimstone's magic. The demon was quiet for some time, his brow furrowed while he ran his fingers expertly over the metal.

He raised his eyes to meet Mae's. "It might be easier to forge you a new one."

Mae's throat tightened. "It wouldn't be the same. It," she stopped and swallowed convulsively, "—*he* wouldn't be Hellreaver."

Nikolai placed a hand atop her trembling fist.

"Can you fix the weapon or not, Armaros?" Astarte asked in an exasperated voice.

"Of course I can," Armaros grunted. "I will need her magic to repair him though."

A giddy feeling swept over Mae. "Oh."

She blinked back tears and slumped in her chair.

Brimstone shifted into his smaller form, returned to her side with a whimper, and leapt onto her lap.

Nikolai scowled at Armaros while Mae hugged the fox to her chest. "Why didn't you say that in the first place?"

"I was testing her resolve."

Alicia sighed. "She traveled to the Underworld to try and get him fixed. I don't think there's anything wrong with her resolve, you boor."

"Azazel begged me to make this weapon for months," Armaros protested. "I can't just cave in to his daughter's demand in a day."

"We don't have months, or even weeks," Nikolai snapped. "My father may soon come into possession of the first Sorcerer King's soul. If that happens, the world of magic will be screwed."

Mae touched his arm lightly.

Armaros furrowed his brow. "Why should I care what happens to the world of magic?"

"Because we need that magic when we fight Satanael," Astarte said. "Never mind what will happen to your precious city and all the others who have benefited from Azazel's grace if he falls into a depression again."

"Has the alcohol you've been guzzling finally addled your brain?" Alicia asked Armaros sourly.

Armaros glowered at the Reaper queen. "I don't want to hear that from the woman who's drunk half my wine cellar."

They'd just started bickering when an enormous casserole slammed heavily on the table between them, making them jump and spilling the juices of the fragrant meat and vegetables sizzling inside it.

"I believe it's time for everyone to calm down and eat," Us'gorith stated thinly.

He took off his helllizard oven mitts and marched stiffly back into the kitchen.

"I think you guys pissed him off," Cortes remarked.

"You'll be lucky if he doesn't poison your food," Astarte muttered to Armaros.

More dishes arrived until a veritable feast covered the table.

An ominous rumble erupted across the dining hall. Its echoes bounced off the walls and drew worried stares from the demons dining at the next table.

Everyone looked at Mae.

"Sorry," she mumbled, her cheeks heating up. "Breakfast was a long time ago."

Nikolai finally relaxed. "I'm glad to see your appetite is okay."

Cortes picked up a chunk of bread and broke it into pieces to feed Popo. "I think it would take more than this to kill her appetite."

"What's wrong?" Mae asked, clocking his morose expression.

"I was thinking that we can now officially claim to have dined in Hell," Cortes said glumly. He looked around. "What's keeping Vlad?"

Astarte helped herself to a bowl of hellboar stew. "I suspect he and his father have a lot of catching up to do."

WINDOWS GLOWED IN THE CITY BENEATH THE CASTLE, soft points of light that brightened the gathering gloom. Vlad's gaze rose from the myriad trails of smoke swirling from hundreds of chimneys to the distant roof of the cavern which housed the valley and mountains surrounding the keep. Now that night was falling, he could see millions of sleeping glowworms covering the dark rock face.

He was wondering how big the creatures were, considering he could almost make out their bodies, when incubus energy fluttered against his skin.

"Pretty, isn't it?" a voice said behind him.

He tensed as Ilmon joined him on the terrace. Tarang made a soft welcoming sound, his tail sweeping the ground. Vlad frowned at the tiger.

Traitor.

Tarang ignored him, his eyes shrinking to happy slits as the Incubus king scratched him under the chin.

Ilmon smiled at the tiger. "Your uncle found a great familiar for you."

Surprise quickened Vlad's pulse. He stared at Ilmon. "How did you know that?"

"I always had someone watching you. Ever since you were born."

A melancholic look dawned on Ilmon's beautiful face. Heat flushed through Vlad's body. He ground his teeth.

"You have no right to be sad! Not after what you did to my mother! Not after," he stopped and took a shaky breath, angry at himself for the tears welling in his eyes, "—not after you seduced her and abandoned her!"

Ilmon's gaze grew hooded. "Is that what you believe happened?"

Vlad tilted his chin, his jaw so tight his face ached. "Do you deny it?"

Tarang huffed worriedly, his blue gaze swinging between them.

Ilmon looked out across the valley.

"Fate is a cruel mistress," he said quietly. "That's what I thought when I met Katarina." He cut his eyes to Vlad briefly. "I know you will find this hard to believe, but it was your mother who seduced me."

Vlad recoiled. "What?!"

"She was the strongest Fire Magic witch your world had seen in centuries, nay, millennia. Her powers were so potent an attraction that I, who had lived in the Underworld for thousands of years, could not help but visit the human realm to see with my own eyes who could harbor such immense power within their mortal coil."

A hundred questions stormed Vlad's mind. He swallowed past the lump in his throat and asked the one that mattered the most.

"Did you…love my mother?"

Ilmon's expression turned brooding. "I am an incubus. It is in my nature to seduce women." He faltered. "But I can honestly say that she was the first to touch my cold, demon heart in a long, long time."

A stilted silence fell between them.

"Then why did you abandon her?" Vlad asked miserably.

"Because she asked me to leave once I fulfilled the promise I made to her."

Vlad grew as still as stone then. "What promise?"

A muscle jumped in Ilmon's jawline. He gripped the balustrade overlooking the courtyard, his knuckles white.

"Your mother knew she was dying when I met her. And she wanted something only I could give her." The Incubus king's tone turned harrowed. "She wanted it more than she'd ever wanted anything in the whole wide world."

The truth struck Vlad like lightning and made his chest tighten until he could barely breathe.

"A baby?" he said numbly. "She wanted a baby?!"

"Yes. She knew it was within my power to grant her that wish. That my incubus energy and her Fire Magic together would keep her alive long enough to carry and birth a child. Katarina was an incredibly shrewd witch." Ilmon's voice shook slightly. "I begged her to let me stay at her side until the end. But she would not have it so. She told me she did not want me to see her in that state." The Incubus king squeezed his eyes shut. "She wanted me to remember her still looking beautiful and healthy."

Vlad's knees buckled. Blood pounded dully in his ears as he gazed blindly at the demon who had sired him.

Everything—everything I thought I knew about my past was wrong!

He sat down heavily on the ground, his body shaking uncontrollably. Tarang made an anxious sound and plopped down next to him.

Ilmon lowered himself beside them.

"All this time." Vlad swallowed heavily and met his father's eyes. He could see the kindness and immutable love shining in the incubus's patient gaze. "All this time, I hated you." A harsh bark of laughter left him. "Hell, I didn't even know who you were until a few months ago."

Ilmon hesitated before putting an arm gingerly around his shoulders. "Yuliy did a grand job raising you. You've become a fine man indeed, my son. I am sure Katarina is smiling upon us both from Heaven."

They stayed like that for a while, Tarang's tail curled around them.

"Vlad?" Ilmon said.

"Yeah?"

Ilmon's eyes twinkled with hope. "About that kiss—"

"No."

The Incubus king sighed at his mutinous expression. "Alright, then how about I teach you how to take your incubus powers to the next level? It will help in your battle with that Sorcerer King."

Vlad stared. "There's a next level?"

Tarang cocked his head inquisitively.

Ilmon smiled. "There are many levels."

CHAPTER EIGHTEEN

Nikolai could feel the heat from Armaros's forge even where he and Astarte sat beside Vannog and Vozgan on the other side of the courtyard. Father and son were having a mid-morning snooze, their snores rattling the windows facing the castle forecourt. The purple helldragon had arrived that morning with fresh news.

The last of the army that had attacked Arakiel's city had finally been disposed of.

Nikolai had wanted to ask Astarte if chasing the remaining troops was worth the effort, but he'd never questioned her in the end. It was not his place to doubt the will of a Goddess, nor the decisions of demon commanders who once occupied the highest seats in Heaven.

Tension coiled through him as he watched Mae and Brimstone where they framed Armaros. Demonic energy woven with black and white magic throbbed off them as they infused the pendant the demon was painstakingly melting with their powers while it returned to its liquid state.

They'd been at it for two hours already and had barely liquefied a fraction of Hellreaver's dormant form.

"She's quite something, isn't she?" Astarte murmured.

Nikolai's chest tightened a little. "Yeah, she is."

The Goddess smiled faintly. "Spoken like a man truly smitten." She fixed him with a curious stare. "What would you have done if she'd picked the incubus instead of you?"

Nikolai's insides twisted at the question. It had kept him awake more nights than he cared to admit. He hesitated.

"I…would have accepted her choice."

Vannog opened a lazy eye.

"Really?" Astarte said.

Nikolai frowned at their dubious stares. "What, you think me incapable of bowing out of a fight gracefully?"

"Yes," Astarte said bluntly. "You seem like the kind of guy who'd toast your competition alive with Hellfire Magic before you ever admitted defeat."

Nikolai's frown deepened.

Vannog scratched his cheek with a giant claw. "Your father *is* that dastardly Sorcerer King, after all."

"I would prefer it if you did not remind me," Nikolai said coldly.

"We cannot choose who sires us." Astarte's gaze found Mae. "Nor who will steal our heart." A faraway look came over the Goddess. "Protect that which you cherish, sorcerer."

Nikolai could not help but suspect a hidden meaning behind her words. From the worried glance Vannog gave Astarte, it seemed he was right.

The Goddess's next words made him stiffen.

"That Hellfire Magic should have consumed you when you first touched it. That you are able to withstand its destructive powers means it has accepted you for some reason."

Nikolai's pulse accelerated under her guarded stare. "What do you mean?"

"What I mean is that not just anyone can handle a power akin to Heaven's Fire."

Nikolai swallowed. He'd forgotten that Azazel had based Hellfire Magic on Heaven's Fire. Cold fingers danced down his spine as he recalled an ugly truth.

"Vedran absorbed that magic from my core. He can control it too."

"I wouldn't be so sure about that." A dark smile curved Astarte's mouth. "Those who mess with powers they don't fully grasp soon find out how dangerous they truly are."

Alastair rustled his wings nervously and inched closer to Nikolai.

He was still wondering what the Goddess meant when Cortes returned from his tour of the city with Us'gorith. Popo was clinging limply to the sorcerer's shoulder.

"What's the matter with him?" Nikolai asked.

"He almost got eaten by a kid," Cortes muttered.

"I apologize again, treasured guest," Us'gorith said, contrite.

Some fiends approached him. He excused himself and wandered off with them.

"Is Vlad still training with his father?" Cortes asked.

Nikolai smirked. "Why? You miss your boyfriend?"

Cortes lowered his brows. A distant explosion sounded from a mountain to the west of the valley before the sorcerer could deliver a cutting reply.

A crimson haze rose above the treetops near its base.

"He's a fast learner," Astarte said.

Nikolai made a face. "You can see them from here?"

"No. But I can sense the power of Ilmon's son growing exponentially." She glanced at him slyly. "He could still prove to be competition."

Nikolai wasn't sure if the Goddess was teasing him or not. "Yeah, that's not gonna happen."

Cortes cocked his head at the forge. "So, where are they at?"

Dusk was falling when Armaros finally finished melting Hellreaver. Mae and Brimstone panted beside the demon. They retracted their magic, bodies trembling and cores half drained.

Armaros poured the glistening metal into a stone mold. "Your weapon is a hungry little monster." He frowned at the sight of their pale faces. "Why don't you two go get some rest?"

Mae hesitated, her racing heart finally slowing. "What about you?"

Armaros shrugged. "I'll be fine. It's not like this is the first time I'm going to be up all night making something." Crimson flashed in his pupils. "After all, I *am* the best metalsmith in all of Heaven and Hell."

"Violet said that Artemus guy is just as good as you," Brimstone piped up.

Hellfire exploded on the tips of Armaros's horns. "Oh, did she now?!"

"How about you stop winding him up?!" Mae hissed at the familiar. She worried her lip as she watched Armaros cool Hellreaver's liquefied form in a vat of cold water. "I should stay."

Steam filled the forge.

Armaros scowled at them through the fumes. "You'll only get in the way. Now shoo! Both of you!"

He waved them off dismissively.

Brimstone shifted into his smaller form. Mae picked him up and reluctantly made her way across to where the others sat at a table that Us'gorith had had some servants bring outside. The skeleton key Armaros had fixed hung on Hellreaver's chain around her neck. She hoped she would eventually figure out how to use it in their battle against Vedran.

Some of her weariness lifted when she spotted Vlad and Ilmon. A warm feeling blossomed inside her chest.

Brimstone looked at her curiously. *What is it, my witch?*

"I'm happy for Vlad."

A shrewd gleam appeared in the fox's crimson eyes as he studied the incubus. *He has become stronger.*

Mae blinked. "You can tell too?"

If you mean his sex appeal has bloomed, yes, Brimstone huffed. *You only have to look at the demons ogling him with lustful intent to know his seduction powers are through the roof right now.*

Mae clocked the twitching curtains at the castle windows. Scores of figures were giving Vlad covetous looks, peeking at him from behind the glass. Several hulking demon soldiers were squabbling with one another next to the armory, fighting for pole position to spy on the incubus.

If Vlad noticed, he wasn't showing any sign of it.

"That wasn't what I meant, but you're right." She became conscious of Brimstone's pointed stare. "What?"

Will you be okay? the fox asked in a tone laced with doubt. *Are you feeling a warm stirring in your loins too?*

Mae's mouth flattened into a thin line. "How about you leave my loins out of this conversation?"

Nikolai handed her a drink when they reached the table. "Here."

She accepted it gratefully and took the seat beside him.

"You look like death warmed over," Cortes observed.

"I feel like it." Mae gulped a mouthful of the cold liquid and looked around. "Where did Alicia go?"

"She said she'd sensed something and went to

investigate." Astarte scratched Tarang under the chin. "Who's a good little tiger?"

Tarang made a happy sound.

"Sensed what?" Mae asked warily.

"I'm not sure." The Goddess grimaced. "She has an uncanny sixth sense when it comes to sniffing out trouble."

Mae wrinkled her nose. "Is it okay for her to be out there on her own?"

They all looked at her blankly.

She realized what she'd just said and laughed awkwardly. "Ha ha. Right, she's the Queen of the Soul Reapers."

"Can you stop trying to seduce my familiar?" Vlad muttered at Astarte, who was slipping the tiger her entire platter of meat.

They ate dinner under the stars, Armaros joining them briefly before returning to his forge. Sparks exploded as he patiently pummeled and shaped the magic-infused metal with a hammer that looked like it could smash a mountain, the sounds ringing across the courtyard in a hypnotic cadence.

It was late when Vannog and Vozgan returned from patrolling the neighboring valleys. They had a snack consisting of twenty roasted hellboars each before settling down close to the forge. The heat from the flames soon lulled them to sleep.

"You should go to bed," Mae told Nikolai when the midnight hour approached.

"I'll stay with you."

He dropped down beside her where she leaned her

back against Vozgan's flank, Brimstone in her lap. To Mae's surprise, Astarte and the others chose to stick around too.

"I've always wanted to ask," Cortes mused after some time. He studied the Goddess and Ilmon with a calculated expression. "All that stuff in the Bible. Is any of it true?"

The Incubus king and Astarte shared a wary glance.

"Some of it is," Ilmon acknowledged.

"But a lot of it involves conclusions mankind came to after hearing stories passed down to them by their forefathers," Astarte said drily. "And we all know how information gets twisted when it changes hands."

"The War in Heaven and the Fallen Angels," Vlad said hesitantly. "That really happened though, didn't it?"

"And Artemus Steele truly is the son of the archangel who cast you all to Hell?" Mae added.

Astarte's eye twitched. Ilmon clenched his jaw.

"I think you touched a sore spot," Cortes muttered to Mae.

"It's not that," Astarte ground out. "It's just—"

"—every time we recall that war," Ilmon said between gritted teeth, "we remember—"

"—that asshole's smug face," Astarte finished with an almighty scowl. "At least Uriel and the others had the decency to look remorseful."

"That bastard just smiled." Ilmon's pupils flared scarlet. "Just thinking about him makes me want to punch a wall."

The ground trembled at the demonic energy that

blasted from the Incubus king. Vlad tried to calm his father.

"How about we change the subject?" Mae said hastily when Armaros twisted around and glowered at them.

Vannog stirred in his sleep.

CHAPTER NINETEEN

THEY SPENT THE NIGHT LISTENING TO ASTARTE AND Ilmon's tales of their adventures in the strange new realm they'd found themselves in, all those millennia past. Of how two distinct factions soon formed in the Underworld. The first led by Satanael, the one who had guided them to their downfall, and the second headed initially by Azazel and now by Astarte.

Shock reverberated through Mae when the Goddess revealed that the first hellbeasts who ever walked the Underworld were once divine creatures and humans beloved by the angels who fell from Heaven and were cast into Hell with them.

She couldn't help but glance at Brimstone and wonder if he too had been a divine beast in his past life. The fox stayed quiet, his eyes closed and his tail brushing softly against her arm.

Ilmon described how the fiends and monsters born in the Underworld, those who had never experienced life in Heaven, turned into brutal savages who only knew how to pillage and kill. And why the Leaders of the Grigori and the fallen angels they led decided to educate and take under their wing as many of these demons as they could.

"Every living thing needs a purpose," the Incubus king had said quietly. "We decided ours was to attempt to create a civilization down here. Somewhere those who had fallen victim to our dark fate could build a life for themselves and the new families they created, finding purpose until the time of our final Judgment."

Mae's heart pounded listening to Astarte and Ilmon share stories of the epic battles that had been fought in the Underworld without mankind's knowledge. Of otherworldly disasters that had nearly wiped out the human race on many an occasion. Of wars that would have led to the End of Days so many feared had Azazel and the Leaders of the Grigori not managed to foil them.

It was Uriel's descendants, the Immortals, who had helped mitigate the impact of those catastrophes on Earth. They too had been unaware until recently of the divine hand that had often guided their actions.

Surprise jolted Mae when Astarte revealed how she came to meet the son of the archangel who had commanded the divine army that had banished her and the Grigori to Hell.

"I knew you were enemies but I hadn't realized he was trying to stop you from opening a gate to Hell."

The Goddess made a face. "Yes, well, I'm not exactly proud of that aspect of my history." Her expression turned distant as she gazed at the mist swirling above the distant peaks and forests emerging from the gloom. "Artemus and his friends chose to show me mercy after the contract I made with one of Satanael's henchmen ended and my purpose for standing in their path was as good as gone. I returned to Hell mistress of my own fate once more and sought out Armaros, Ilmon, and the rest to tell them all I had learned while I lived in the shadows of Satanael's council. When one of my spies told me the fallen angel who sired Artemus's twin brother Drake was scheming to drag him to the Underworld, I waited for him to fall to Hell and rescued him before his father could get his hands on him."

"So, that's how Artemus ended up coming here?" Mae mumbled.

"Yes."

Bright spots blinked into life high above as the glowworms roaming the roof and walls of the giant cavern awoke, casting the pale light of what stood for dawn in Hell across the valley. The castle was stirring when Armaros's hammer finally fell silent.

"It is done."

Mae's chest tightened, her unblinking gaze swinging to the anvil he loomed over.

Armaros wiped sweat from his brow and stared proudly at what he had spent the night making. A puzzled expression danced in the demon's eyes. "I must admit, he came together faster than I thought he would."

Mae climbed to her feet and rushed over with Brimstone, Nikolai following. The pentagram pendant lay still on the dark block, metal dull and unmoving.

"Hell?" she whispered, her voice trembling.

Her heart twisted when the weapon failed to respond.

Brimstone whimpered in her arms. Na Ri's anxiety throbbed through her soul.

They couldn't feel anything from the pendant. Not a spark of demonic energy or even a hint of the thousand fiends who inhabited it.

"Don't lose hope yet," Armaros grunted at Mae's distraught expression. "He still needs some finishing touches."

Mae tried not to appear dejected. Nikolai put a comforting hand around her shoulders and led her away. She forced herself to have breakfast with him and the others, her stomach in knots as she stole glances at the forge where Armaros ground, filed, and polished the pendant.

The demon handed her the weapon two hours later.

Her hands shook as she took it, the metal cool against her skin.

"Why don't you try pouring your magic into it?" Armaros suggested.

Mae swallowed. Demonic energy laced with black and white magic bloomed around her as she drew on her cores. She gathered the potent aura into her hands and willed it into the pendant. Brimstone transformed and pressed his brow to her back, his tails vibrating as he lent her his powers.

Despite their efforts, the weapon stayed as inanimate as the tools that had forged it.

Mae's vision swam with tears. Her shoulders slumped.

No, Na Ri mumbled. *This cannot be!*

Armaros scratched his head. "I don't understand. I used the same process the first time I made him."

"Was there something else?" Astarte frowned. "Something Azazel had to do to make him, I don't know," she waved a hand, "—wake up?"

The answer came to Mae and Armaros at the same time.

"Oh!" the demon mumbled.

Mae grabbed a knife from the table, her heart racing. She cut her thumb and squeezed blood on the pendant.

It absorbed the crimson drops with a hungry hiss.

Hope exploded inside Mae, making her dizzy. Na Ri shuddered.

They invoked the name that had inhabited their every dream and waking moment since the fateful night they last fought the Sorcerer King.

"Come, Hellreaver!"

The fire that pulsed inside their cores made Mae gasp. Brimstone stiffened above her when he felt the echo of the weapon's revival.

A crimson light trembled into life around the pendant.

Nikolai tensed. Vlad and Cortes grew wary. Astarte and Ilmon appeared fascinated by what they were witnessing.

A smug smile stretched Armaros's mouth. "Told you guys I could do it."

Mae stared breathlessly at Hellreaver. The power swelling inside her and Na Ri's cores felt stronger than when they'd first experienced the weapon's awakening, in the cemetery in South Ridgewood where Rose's family had laid her empty coffin to rest.

It matched the thickening glow engulfing the pendant.

He is more powerful, Na Ri murmured in a voice full of wonder.

Black and white threads appeared amidst the scarlet energy shivering violently on the metal.

Mae's eyes widened. *Is that because our magic has evolved?!*

Probably.

Hellreaver levitated out of her grasp with a speed that made her suck in air. He transformed, the haze around him shrinking down to an aura of black and crimson static.

"I know I've asked this question before," Cortes said leadenly, "but is he bigger too?"

Mae's heart pounded hard, her stunned gaze riveted to Hellreaver's new form.

He was sixty inches of wicked menace, his metal twice as thick and gleaming ominously despite his inky color, his serrated edges deeper and more jagged where they glinted with magic.

Mae gulped. *He looks like he could cut air molecules by just looking at them!*

Even Armaros seemed shocked by the weapon's appearance.

Everyone startled when Hellreaver yawned and smacked his teeth.

"*Ah. That was a nice, long nap,*" he said drowsily.

The voices of the demons who dwelled within him rumbled faintly across the courtyard.

Mae's eyes bulged.

"Everyone heard that, right?" Vlad said flatly.

Hellreaver tensed when he became aware of his surroundings. "*Where is this? Who—?*" He twisted around, saw Mae, and froze. "*My—my witch?!*" Demonic energy blasted around him, waking Vannog and Vozgan with a start. "*Where is he?!*" The weapon pivoted on himself, his tone murderous. "*Where is that scoundrel Sorcerer King?! I will cut him and bite him and—!*"

"*He broke you.*"

Hellreaver recoiled at Brimstone's quiet words.

The demon fox bent his giant head and nuzzled the weapon affectionately. "*It is good to see you, old friend.*"

"*Br—broke?!*" Hellreaver stammered.

"*You protected me from harm in the battle the three of us fought against the Sorcerer King,*" Brimstone explained. "*He was about to stab me in the heart with a sword made from the soul of his familiar. He thought I was hiding the Book of Light.*"

"You stopped Vedran, but not without taking heavy damage in the process," Mae said in a low voice.

Hellreaver trembled in the fraught silence. "*You mean, I—I was* dead?!"

Mae's eyes welled up as she relived that awful moment all over again.

"Yes." She wiped away her tears with the back of her hand. "We tried to use our magic to revive you but we couldn't. You were too far gone for *Assimilate* to work. So we came to Hell and asked Armaros to fix you."

"*Oh.*"

Hellreaver's quivering got worse. He sagged in midair.

Mae smiled tremulously and opened her arms. "Come here."

Hellreaver shot into her hold. She squeezed him tightly to her chest, her heart swelling with happiness.

"I missed you so much, Hell."

Hellreaver sniveled, the shivers racking him finally abating. It was a while before he spoke.

"*Hmm, my witch, I hate to mention this, what with this being a delicate moment and everything, but have you put on a little weight? It's just your bosom feels a smidgen bigger and your breasts are squishier than—ouch!*" His tone turned offended. "*How could you hit me?! I've just come back to life!*"

"You totally deserved that," Nikolai snapped while Mae scowled and shook her smarting hand.

Brimstone sighed. "*He never learns.*"

"So, he really is just a scumbag, huh?" Vlad observed, his lip curling. "I always suspected he was."

"Can I eat him?" Vozgan asked Vannog hopefully.

"Not unless you want indigestion," his father huffed.

Hellreaver observed the helldragons nervously. He

brightened when he spotted Astarte and Ilmon. *"Oh, it's Astaroth and the Wicked Ravisher."*

Ilmon squinted. Astarte's lips twitched.

Hellreaver's gaze dropped. *"Whoa. Now that bosom right there is as mighty as they—hmmm! Hmmm!"*

Mae had muzzled him. "Have you got a death wish?!"

Astarte tensed. Ilmon's eyes flared. Armaros twitched. Vannog blinked and raised his head.

Their gazes swung as one to the north.

Mae's scalp prickled as she followed their line of sight. She could feel something approaching. A formidable presence that carried an eerily familiar echo of demonic energy.

"What's wrong?" Nikolai asked guardedly.

"I…don't know."

Na Ri stirred.

"Well, I'll be damned." Armaros put his hands on his hips, his expression pleased. "Now *this* is cause for celebration."

"Yes." A fierce light brightened Astarte's face. "He's finally back."

"Who's back?" Cortes said, confused.

Vlad frowned and pointed. "What is that?"

A spot had appeared high above the mountains. It grew rapidly and soon split to form two figures. One was Alicia.

The other was a demon with long, curved horns.

"Someone whose return we have long awaited," Ilmon said softly.

The hairs lifted on the back of Mae's neck. She sensed the newcomer's gaze on her even though she could still not make out his face.

But she didn't have to.

She knew this power. Power that was making her cores tremble and Na Ri quake with joy inside her.

She had felt it once before, standing inside a nexus in Prague.

"Azazel?!" she mumbled.

Nikolai shot her a stunned glance.

Magic surged across the city, rattling the windows of the palace. The air sparkled with crimson flashes that reflected the happiness of the demon who was drawing near. He landed lightly in the courtyard ahead of Alicia, his beautiful eyes on Mae.

"*Master*," Brimstone and Hellreaver mumbled.

The Third Leader of the Grigori and the fallen angel who once wielded the strongest magic in Heaven smiled at them fondly before gazing at Mae. He opened his arms.

"My daughters."

Mae sobbed and rushed into his hold. Azazel closed his arms around her and shuddered, his embrace warm and strong.

I am home, father, Na Ri whispered brokenly.

The demon's heartbeat thrummed steadily in Mae's ears, a soothing sound that calmed her raw nerves. She might not have been born physically of him but there was no doubt in her heart.

Azazel was as much a father to her as her human one had been.

"So, this was the trouble you sniffed out?" Astarte asked Alicia in a mildly exasperated tone. "You could have said before you left."

The Reaper queen frowned. "Azazel was not the one I'd sensed."

CHAPTER TWENTY

Bryony stood staring out of a window overlooking Central Park. Penley sat on the sill in front of her, his tail swinging lazily while he watched the army of aides loading suitcases into the SUVs parked outside the mansion.

The members of the High Council and their entourage were finally returning to their cities.

Though she would never admit it openly, Bryony would miss their presence. Mae's arrival into their lives had not only made all their past squabbles seem like playground spats, it had strengthened their friendships and alliances in a way nothing else could have.

Bryony stroked Penley's head. "I guess having a strong Witch Queen really is the best thing for the world of magic."

The cat closed his eyes and purred.

Bryony's face tightened. *But not just any witch would have done. It's because of Mae Jin that we are now stronger together and finally in a position to face the Sorcerer King, instead of cowering before him like we did for countless years.*

Still, she couldn't help the foreboding gnawing at her insides.

It had been two days since Mae left for Hell with Nikolai, Vlad, and Cortes. There hadn't been any sign of Barquiel or Vedran in that time. Even the bodies of the Dark Council members had stopped turning up.

Bryony wasn't sure if this was because the Sorcerer King was close to achieving his goal, or for another nefarious reason he had yet to reveal. She frowned.

Call me cynical, but things are too quiet for my liking.

"Or maybe I'm just getting old," she told Penley under her breath.

The cat meowed. Green flashed in his eyes. His tail stilled, his alert gaze swinging toward the road.

Bryony stiffened at the sound of tires squealing on 5th Avenue.

An unmarked police sedan with an emergency dash light barreled through the traffic and pulled up sharply at the curb. Jared jumped out just as an SUV braked inches from the bumper of a San Francisco coven's transport. Violet and Miles emerged from it and joined the Immortal.

Abraham and Derrick approached them, Raven, Karin, and Ephra in their wake. A tense exchange followed. Ephra paled. Abraham cursed.

They rushed inside the mansion.

Bryony exited the room at a brisk pace, pulse racing and Penley scampering beside her. She met them in the main foyer.

Jared had stopped to talk to Gerard, Isabelle, and Simon.

"What's wrong?" Bryony said sharply from the main landing of the grand staircase.

A muscle jumped in the Immortal's jawline as he turned to meet her gaze. "Our ally in Chicago just sent a warning."

From Violet and Miles's tight expressions, they too had heard from their Seer friend. Dread knotted Bryony's stomach. Her premonition was coming true.

Let's hope whatever this is, we can handle it without Mae.

"What's going on?" someone said curiously.

Bryony looked over her shoulder.

Roman was coming down the stairs with Marlena and Nadia. His puzzled gaze swung from Bryony to the group below. Marlena slowed when she registered the tension in the air. A wary look dawned on Nadia's face.

Jared glanced at the coven witches and sorcerers watching them from the upstairs galleries and the corridors branching off the entrance hall. "Let's have this conversation somewhere private."

A commotion reached them before they got to Bryony's study. They were passing a drawing room that had been converted into a makeshift office when several horrified shouts rent the air. A witch turned up the volume on her cellphone. Others gathered around her to listen in.

"Looks like it made the news," Jared said darkly.

"What made the news?" Roman asked in a frustrated voice.

It wasn't until they were inside the study and the doors were closed that the Immortal finally spoke. "Vedran is attacking covens around the world."

A buzzing sound filled Bryony's head. She grasped the back of a chair, her legs weak. "What?!"

The Immortal took the remote from the coffee table and switched on the flatscreen TV on the wall.

It took a couple of seconds for Bryony to grasp what they were looking at. Isabelle covered her mouth, horror draining her face of color. Simon swore.

Abraham fisted his hands. "Shit!"

"Is that the London coven?!" Marlena asked hoarsely.

Dread curdled Bryony's blood. There was no mistaking the pale, domed building on the display. It was the headquarters of the biggest coven in Europe. And it was burning with flames that the local fire force was struggling to douse.

Roman sat heavily on the edge of a couch.

"That's Hellfire Magic," he mumbled. "They're not going to be able to put that out!"

Bryony finally registered the female newscaster's voice.

"—sources have informed us that there were more than two hundred people inside the building at the time the blaze broke out. Though it is yet to be confirmed, the authorities suspect no one managed to escape. Some witnesses report hearing screams moments before—"

Jared switched channels. "It's not just England."

Karin recoiled. "Oh God."

Ephra clasped the witch's hand tightly while they watched live feeds of the destruction that had been wrought on several other cities. All the buildings depicted were major coven headquarters.

"The same thing has happened in France, Germany, Italy, Poland," Jared said coldly as he flicked the button. "And not just there. The biggest covens in the Middle East, North Africa, and Asia were hit at the same time."

Nadia drew a sharp breath. She took out her cellphone and speed-dialed a number. Relief had her squeezing her eyes shut when it connected.

"Are they okay?" Roman asked in a strained voice.

"Yes."

The High Priestess rose and went over to the window, her voice low and urgent as she ordered her coven to evacuate their headquarters in Cairo.

Marlena was already on the phone to Prague, her knuckles white where she gripped her cell.

Raven's gaze switched from the anxious witches to the TV. She narrowed her eyes. "It looks like that asshole is attacking covens that don't have Mae's direct protection."

Jared frowned. "What do you mean?"

Bryony swallowed past the lump in her throat. "Mae put *Soul Shield* inside all New York coven members, as well as the covens of all the High Council priests and priestesses in the city right now. It was a safeguard in case something happened in her absence."

"It looks like she was right to be paranoid," Abraham said darkly.

"What is Vedran trying to do?" A muscle jumped in Derrick's cheek. "For what purpose is he—?"

"He's killing them to absorb their cores," Violet said flatly.

Bryony looked at the young witch, her heart pounding.

Wrath lit Violet's eyes with the purple blaze of her magic. "We can only presume he's run out of Dark Council members to slaughter."

"So, he's coming after us," Miles added, standing stiffly beside his cousin.

A fraught hush ensued.

Karin shuddered, her face clearing as if she were waking up from a nightmare. "When was the last attack?"

Jared clenched his jaw. "Eight hours ago."

Horror rounded Gerard's mouth. "What?!"

Derrick squeezed his eyes shut for a moment, his expression pained. "How come we're only hearing about this now?"

"Because that bastard did something to hide what was happening," the Immortal replied in a hard voice. "We think it might have been Illusion Sorcery."

Bryony's insides twisted as she watched Jared's bleak expression. He was no doubt recalling the magic that had turned all of them, including him, against Mae just a few months ago.

Though the Witch Queen had long forgiven them for attacking her while under the influence of Anya's spell, most of them had still not come to terms with their betrayal.

Bryony shivered. *Thank goodness she found a spell to counter it.*

"And the timeline of the attacks?" Nadia asked sharply.

The Sun Magic witch had gotten off her call.

Jared faltered. "We think he struck all of them at the same time."

Bryony swayed. Shocked murmurs broke out.

"What?" Confusion clouded Roman's face. "How is that—?"

"Portals!" someone gasped.

They turned.

Anya was standing in the doorway, face flushed and chest heaving as if she'd run to get there. Her eyes were brimming with tears and her pupils round with fear. She clutched Sable to her chest.

"Nikolai was right. Vedran is sending his army through portals. They just attacked the Caracas coven!"

Ice filled Bryony's veins.

Miles scowled. "So he's going after the South American covens next!"

"Dammit," Abraham ground out.

"No, not—not Valentina!" Ephra mumbled.

Valentina Flores was the High Priestess of the largest coven in Venezuela and a close friend and ally of the High Council.

Anya shook her head. "Valentina is fine. She wasn't at the coven headquarters when it was hit. My father has spoken to her." The witch swallowed heavily. "It's not just Venezuela. He was on the phone to a friend in Buenos Aires when their coven got attacked twenty minutes ago. The sorcerer he was talking to described a heavy aura of corruption and a black gate opening inside the building." Her voice broke. "My—my father said he heard the screams of demons and devils before the connection broke."

Sable crooned anxiously in her mistress's hold. Marlena rose and went to them. Anya allowed the witch to lead her to a couch, her shoulders slumped with grief.

Bryony finally recovered her composure. "What did the Seer say exactly?"

Jared traded a troubled glance with Violet and Miles.

"That the first part of the prophecy concerning the Witch Queen is about to come true," the Immortal said reluctantly.

Simon blanched.

"*On the day the world becomes shrouded in shadows*," Isabelle quoted numbly beside the sorcerer.

Violet's mouth set in a determined line. "She said to get as many magic users as we can to New York in the next twenty-four hours. That the city must not fall."

"And if it does?" Marlena asked in a harrowed voice.

"Then all will be lost." Miles's expression was deadlier than Bryony ever recalled seeing it. "Because it's not just magic users Vedran will slaughter in his attempt to become a God. He will kill every living thing from here to the West Coast."

CHAPTER TWENTY-ONE

A DISTURBANCE OUTSIDE THE OFFICE HAD EVERYONE tensing and drawing on their magic. Jared snatched the switchblade from his ankle strap and unleashed his divine sword.

The door clattered open ahead of a noisy group of witches.

Bryony blinked before sagging at the sight, relief rendering her weak. *She must have called them!*

"Hey, beauty before age!" Regina Nox snapped at Ludmila Vissarion as they hustled one another to get inside the room.

Ludmila shook her cane at Regina. "You want to taste my flames, witch?!"

"*Nana?!*" Roman croaked. He jumped to his feet. "What are you doing here?!"

Ludmila brightened. "Roman." Her expression fell. "What happened to you, my sweetie pie? You look like you've lost weight." She narrowed her eyes at Nadia. "Has that mean witch been mistreating you?!"

Nadia sighed wearily. "Hello to you too, Ludmila."

Regina squinted at Roman. "That is never your great grandkid?! Where'd he get his good looks from?" She glanced suspiciously at Ludmila. "'Cause it sure ain't from your side of the family, hag."

"Oh God," Erik Nox muttered somewhere behind them.

Fire Magic erupted on Ludmila's cane and in her salamander's eyes. Regina's jackrabbit bristled at her feet.

"Let's all calm down," April Blackwood said soothingly.

The Persian cat in her arms meowed softly.

Barbara Nolan appeared behind Regina. She looked like she was giving serious consideration to walloping the Vegas witch.

"Aunt Barbara." Violet rushed over and hugged the older woman. She pulled back and scanned her face anxiously. "I didn't think you'd get here so fast. I," she faltered, "—I thought she might stop you from coming."

"She said she couldn't intervene with more than a warning." Barbara smiled faintly and patted her niece's shoulder. "She saw no reason to prevent us from providing assistance to the New York coven, since this involves the fate of the world of magic."

"Us?" Miles said blankly.

A bevy of Nolans poked their heads around the door.

A man with a gray beard and a friendly parrot on his shoulder greeted them with a dignified expression that was at odds with the jostling happening around him. "Hello."

"Yo," a young woman holding a chihuahua said cheerfully over his shoulder.

"By the way, do you guys know about the giant in your garden?" a guy with a frog on his head said warily. "He's peeing in a flower bed."

Bryony straightened, scowling. "Don't tell me it's my petunias?!"

"It's your roses, actually."

Bryony cut her eyes to Abraham.

The aide sighed. "I'll tell Rambrog off."

"You gave the giant a name?" Jared said leadenly.

"He told Brimstone that's what he was called in Hell," Abraham muttered. "He's quite sweet actually."

A couple of figures squeezed past Frog Guy.

"Mom?!" Miles mumbled at the sight of a woman accompanied by an iguana.

"Oh. Hi, Miles." Miles's mother dug her elbow into the ribs of her companion, a witch with a ginger cat. "*Psst!* Check out those Ming vases!"

The witch with the ginger cat sniffed. "Told you she was loaded."

Frog Guy was studying Nadia with bright-eyed interest.

"Hey, Uncle Floyd?" he said to Parrot Guy out the corner of his mouth. "Do you know that hot chick with the desert fox?"

Nadia narrowed her eyes, Sun Magic glinting dangerously in her pupils.

Barbara met Bryony's gaze steadily over the heads

of the squabbling Regina and Ludmila. "We have a lot of work to do, old friend."

BILE BURNED THE BACK OF OSCAR'S THROAT AS HE watched the Sorcerer King absorb the powers of the men and women he'd had his foul troops massacre.

This was ten times worse than the incident in Philadelphia, when Barquiel had raised an army of ghouls to possess the sorcerers and witches they had kidnapped so as to transmute the *Book of Light's* grimoire into its true form.

Vedran's jaws opened to inhuman proportions as he sucked in the black magic he had ripped from the cores of the corpses amassed before him, the bodies adding to the festering piles of the dead that had accumulated in the days they had been trapped in *Void*. He twitched and jerked, body rigid and expression glazed while the corrupt mist infiltrated his mouth and nose.

Oscar's gaze dropped to his father's cloak. He could see the bulge of the compass. He fisted his hands.

This might be my only chance to get it from him. Maybe he won't find it if I hide it inside one of those bodies!

He hesitated before approaching the Sorcerer King, conscious of the watchful stares of the monstrous army lurking in the shadows.

Black magic washed over him in sickening waves that raised the hairs on his skin. He stopped beside his father. He could smell a stench coming from him.

It evoked old, rotting meat and an evil that could never be purged.

Oscar's hand trembled as he reached for the artifact that would allow his father to become a God. His fingers brushed the cold metal.

Yes! His heart pounded wildly against his ribs. *Almost there!*

Freezing fire scorched his wrist in the next instant. He cried out, the smell of seared flesh filling his nostrils while the excruciating pain of the deadly black magic piercing his body almost rendered him unconscious.

Vedran looked down and met his stricken stare as he swayed in his father's unyielding grip. Terror robbed Oscar of breath.

The Sorcerer King's eyes were black from edge to edge. A vile magic bubbled in his pupils and enveloped him in an inky aura.

"What do you think you're doing?" he asked Oscar icily.

"I—" Oscar's nails sank into his palms. "It looked like it was going to fall."

Vedran's dreadful gaze found the *Book of Light* where it half tilted out of his pocket. He released Oscar.

Oscar stumbled back and clutched his wrist to his chest, the taste of blood on his tongue from where he'd bitten the inside of his cheek to stop himself from screaming.

"I see." Not an ounce of pity showed on Vedran's face when he observed the horrific burns on Oscar's arm. "Let me fix that."

Blood pounded in Oscar's skull. He forced himself to stay still while his father took his arm and cast a healing spell on him, his face a stiff mask that concealed his fear.

He could feel it. No, see it.

The magic trembling around Vedran was testimony to his core being whole once more. But there was more to it than that. He had never sensed this level of power from his father before.

Not only was he stronger, absorbing the cores of the dead had added an even more sinister element to his already sickening magic.

The pain afflicting Oscar faded.

Vedran released him. "Now, let's see if this thing will finally work."

The Sorcerer King removed the *Book of Light* from his cloak and studied it with a zealous expression.

Hellfire Magic burst into life in his father's palm. Oscar recoiled. The dark red sphere whined and sizzled as it spun rapidly on itself, causing the air around it to ripple with intense heat.

Several hellbeasts growled and pulled back. Even the ghouls and devils seemed nervous in the face of the ominous flames.

Vedran shaped the Hellfire into a key, inserted it inside the compass, and twisted. There was a soft click.

A tremor shook *Void*.

Oscar startled. His head jerked, his gaze sweeping the infinite darkness surrounding them.

It came again and again, an escalating pulse that made his eardrums throb and shook his bones. Restless grunts and clicks sounded as Vedran's army retreated farther into the shadows, their pupils bright with fear.

The Sorcerer King never looked away from the *Book of Light*.

Oscar's stomach roiled when he realized the waves of power were coming from the compass.

The fabric of space ripped open a couple of inches in front of the artifact. Glee brightened Vedran's face. A crimson light spilled out of the tear.

Horror drenched Oscar in a cold sweat as it widened, revealing the secret place it had long hidden. The sound of a storm roared through *Void*.

There, spinning within a tempest of demonic energy, was a black book wreathed in shadows.

CHAPTER TWENTY-TWO

ARMAROS FROWNED AT ALICIA. "IT WAS BARQUIEL?"

"Yes." The Reaper queen's knuckles whitened on her drink. "I'm convinced it was his demonic energy. I felt it faintly in Hell Deep, through one of my Reapers. I was making my way there when I crossed paths with Azazel."

Mae's pulse quickened at this news. She'd suspected *Chaos Seal* had imprisoned Barquiel in Hell since that was where Azazel first created the spell, but this was the first time she'd had confirmation of that fact.

"I also detected a trace of his presence." Azazel frowned. "His powers felt...odd. Not at all like those of the demon I recall."

Astarte stared. "What do you mean?"

Azazel hesitated. "It was almost as if I could sense two beings where there used to be one."

Ilmon furrowed his brow.

Mae's stomach knotted. "I—are you sure about that, father?!"

Azazel blinked. A pleased look dawned on his face. "It feels good to be called that after so long, child." The demon sobered. "Yes. The more I think about it, the more I am convinced I could feel another inside Barquiel."

Mae squeezed her eyes shut, hope bringing a lump to her throat. She opened them to find Azazel and everyone else giving her a puzzled look.

"What's wrong?" Nikolai asked guardedly.

"It's Rose." Mae swallowed. "I'm sure of it."

Vlad's eyes widened. Nikolai frowned.

"You mean, your friend who got possessed by Barquiel?" Cortes said, unconvinced.

Mae nodded. "I thought I felt a remnant of Rose's soul when I stabbed Barquiel with Hellreaver in Brooklyn, the second time we fought. I was certain she was still inside him when I used *Chaos Seal* to imprison him."

Armaros and Astarte traded a wary glance.

"*My witch is right,*" Hellreaver piped up. "*Brimstone and I felt it too.*"

The fox huffed in agreement where he'd coiled into a ball on Mae's lap.

Azazel's brow knotted. "Soul Magic." He met Alicia's troubled gaze. "That's the only thing that would make sense."

Surprise jolted Mae. "Soul Magic?"

"Barquiel was cursed when he fell from Heaven," Azazel explained. "He cannot survive in the realm of man in his demon form for long. That is why he must possess another to walk the Earth, so he is able to access his powers outside Hell. Man, woman, demon, beast. It doesn't matter who it is as long as that being possesses a soul that is compatible with his own."

Mae's pulse thumped rapidly as her father's words sank in. *Does that mean Barquiel has a weakness when he's on Earth?!*

We need to remember that when we fight him next, Na Ri said in a steely voice.

A muscle jumped in Nikolai's cheek. "This…Soul Magic is how he does it? How he takes over other people's bodies?"

"Yes," Azazel replied.

"Could he have taught that spell to Vedran?"

Azazel stiffened at the sorcerer's question. "Why do you ask?"

"Because my father killed his familiar and is using his soul to perpetrate his crimes," Nikolai said coldly.

Alastair crooned quietly on his shoulder.

Astarte's eyes widened. Ilmon cursed.

"Nikolai and I caught a glimpse of the Sorcerer King's dead familiar when we last confronted him," Mae confirmed. "He appeared before us a few days ago, after I used *Soul Conjure* on the body of a Dark Council witch Vedran had killed. His familiar was a wolf named Balkin."

Crimson flashed in Alicia's pupils. "How despicable. That magic carries the harshest of penalties. To think Barquiel would even think of teaching it to a human is unbelievable."

"That bastard would do anything to achieve his goal of reviving Ran Soyun," Nikolai ground out.

Azazel froze, his pupils rounding. Demonic energy detonated around him, rattling glass and metal and whipping their hair and clothes into a frenzy.

His enraged roar shook the castle. "*WHAT?!*"

Astarte hung on grimly to her chair in the violent tempest and scowled at Nikolai. "You know, you could have broached that topic more sensitively!"

Mae stood up and closed the distance to her and Na Ri's father, her magic buffering her against the powerful storm shaking Armaros's palace. She knelt before Azazel and clasped his hands, the anger she and Na Ri had felt when they'd first learnt the dark truth of Barquiel's intentions a banked heat simmering in her blood.

"It's okay, Dad."

Azazel shuddered. The fury darkening his face and wreaking havoc on the room abated at her quiet words.

"I—I apologize, child," he mumbled after a moment, his tone haggard.

"The one you should be apologizing to is me," Armaros grumbled.

The demon peeled himself off the mounted hellbear he'd been clinging to.

Azazel grimaced, contrite. "I'm sorry, old friend." He met Mae and Nikolai's gazes, in control of his emotions once more. "Tell me more."

Nikolai related how he had followed Barquiel to a hidden destination in Hell a few weeks back and uncovered a disturbing secret. One which the demon had concealed from the Dark Council.

"Barquiel intends to steal the first Sorcerer King's soul from under Vedran's nose and gift it to Ran Soyun, along with the core in Mae's heart. He believes he can revive her that way." Bitterness underscored Nikolai's voice. "As for my father, not only is he planning to assimilate the first Sorcerer King's soul, but he is likely scheming to kill me so he can consume my white magic." He hesitated. "I overheard a conversation between Barquiel and my father, when I was still under the influence of the Illusion Sorcery spell they put me under. I think Vedran tried to do the same to my mother once but failed."

"There's one more thing," Mae added in a hard voice. "Vedran now possesses the ability to use Hellfire Magic."

Azazel flinched. Armaros swore.

"What?!" Astarte gasped.

"Yeah, I forgot to mention that what with everything going on," Alicia muttered.

"He absorbed it from Nikolai and Alastair's cores," Mae explained. "Dietrich Farago, the Immortal alchemist who was helping the Dark Council, was convinced Fire Magic could open the *Book of Light*." She exchanged a wary glance with Nikolai. "We suspect Hellfire Magic will definitely do it."

Azazel cursed.

Mae's stomach sank. She only had to look at her father's distraught expression to know Farago had been right.

"If he takes Davor's soul, all will be lost," Azazel mumbled distractedly.

Mae chewed her lip. "Was Davor truly that powerful?"

"Yes." Azazel steepled his hands under his chin and scowled at the floor. "He defeated Ran Soyun, after all."

A fraught silence ensued.

Ilmon slapped Azazel heartily on the back. The demon startled.

"I will have less of that glum talk from you, old friend." The Incubus king smiled faintly. "This time, you are not alone." He looked at Mae and her companions. "Your daughters are with you. And those two with her are pretty powerful sorcerers." He beamed at Vlad. "My son, of course, is just awesome."

Tarang made a happy sound, his tail sweeping the floor. Vlad narrowed his eyes.

"I've been meaning to ask you about that, actually," Azazel said. "When exactly did you sire a cambion?" His eyes widened when he got a closer look at Vlad. "Oh. His mother was a very powerful Fire Magic witch."

Ilmon blinked. "You can tell?"

"Of course." Azazel's gaze swung from Mae to the three men who had accompanied her to Hell. "Are they your consorts, child? They all have powerful seeds."

Alicia choked on her beer. Astarte sighed. Armaros smirked.

Mae nearly swallowed her tongue. "What?! *No!* I mean, Nikolai is, but those two aren't!"

"Yeah, I already promised my seeds to someone else," Cortes muttered.

Popo bobbed his head firmly.

Vlad arched an eyebrow at Azazel. "I am trying to convince her to take on a second consort. Maybe you can help."

Nikolai's face darkened. "Over my dead body."

"That can be arranged."

Astarte let them bicker for a minute before calling for silence.

She frowned at Mae. "So, what do you intend to do now?"

Mae met the Goddess's eyes unflinchingly. "We search Hell Deep for the cave where Barquiel hid my mother's body and half her soul. And we stop that bastard demon and Vedran before they can achieve their goals." She turned to Azazel. "There's something else. Something only you can do. Teach me Soul Magic. I want to free Rose from Barquiel's hold."

Azazel's eyes widened.

"But—I'm not sure that's even possible," he protested.

Mae hesitated. "I can already do several *Soul* spells. So, I think—" she fisted her hands, "no, I'm *certain* I can release Rose's soul from her prison."

"Your daughter has achieved quite a few impossible things since coming into her powers," Alicia muttered.

Azazel brightened. "She has?"

The Reaper queen shuddered. "Still, that new *Eclipse* spell gave me the heebie-jeebies."

Armaros frowned. "That's a bold plan and

everything, but this Vedran guy may already have the *Book of Shadows* and the soul of the first Sorcerer King."

Azazel seemed to come to some kind of decision. His eyes glittered strangely as he watched Mae and Nikolai. "There are two things that might still work in our favor if that is indeed the case."

CHAPTER TWENTY-THREE

They emerged from the gloom, sometimes one by one, sometimes in trickles. Though the ghouls and devils kept their distance from him while he traversed the enormous caverns that populated the remotest regions of Hell Deep, Barquiel could tell the creatures were the remnants of the army he had once commanded.

He frowned. *Where are the rest of them?*

It was a while before he came across a ghoul who could converse primitively. The creature stumbled over its words as it told him of a great purge brought about by a mysterious event. Rage shook Barquiel when it described what it had witnessed.

Void?! *That bastard Vedran used* Void *to steal my army?!*

He punched a wall with his fist, causing several monsters to flinch.

Agony seared Barquiel's insides the next instant. He

grunted and clutched his stomach. It was a moment before he could breathe again.

The demon ground his teeth until he tasted blood. *I swear, I will purge that bitch's soul in the fires of Hell when I find someone else I can possess!*

Rose Blake's voice echoed dimly in his ears, the sound mocking.

Barquiel swallowed, pain making his vision swim. He had already examined the souls of the scant troops around him. None of the ghouls or devils who had been drawn to him was a compatible match.

I'll find someone soon enough. But first I must go to Ran Soyun and ensure that my barriers are still holding. A wave of dizziness almost had him swaying as he clung to the wall. *Damn it! I need to recover my strength or I won't last another ten miles.*

The demon straightened with some difficulty and studied his monsters with a calculating look. He raised a hand toward the ones he deemed would satisfy him the fastest.

"Come to me."

The ghouls and devils he'd commanded to step forward crowded around him. They stayed still while he ripped their hearts from their chests and feasted on their flesh and blood, their brethren watching silently.

The demonic life force he consumed coursed through Barquiel, slowly replenishing the reserves that had been depleted by *Chaos Seal*. By the time he'd sated his hunger, half the monsters were dead.

Not enough. The demon wiped gore from his mouth.

I need to devour more powerful beasts if I want to open a rift to draw one of my swords!

He set off toward a dark lake in the distance, the rags of his once powerful army trailing in his steps.

"THE *BOOK OF SHADOWS* ISN'T JUST AN ARTIFACT I devised to hold the soul of Davor Lazar," Azazel said solemnly. "It is a weapon. One that can annihilate what it contains—or used to contain—using the correct triggers."

Mae's pulse raced. "Davor Lazar?"

"That is the full name of the first Sorcerer King. He was a man like any other, except for his soul." A humorless chuckle left the demon, his regret plain to see. "It took me a while to realize that his potential to wield magic was outweighed by his hunger for power and his wicked cruelty." Lines wrinkled Azazel's brow. "The current Sorcerer King reminds me of Davor in many ways. He too killed his familiar when he realized what Soul Magic could do for his powers."

A sick feeling twisted Mae's insides. Her hand automatically found Brimstone where he lay on her lap, just as Nikolai, Vlad, and Cortes touched their own familiars. None of them could fathom ever laying a finger on the creature they had bonded their soul with.

You are not monsters, my witch, Brimstone said quietly.

Hellreaver vibrated against her chest. *He is right.*

"What exactly are the triggers you speak of?" Cortes asked warily.

"First, the *Book of Light* must be opened with that skeleton key." Azazel indicated the item hanging from Hellreaver's chain beside his pendant form. "That is not its true appearance. When it gets close enough to sense the *Book of Shadows*, it will change into its real form, that of a star-shaped device." The demon faltered, his expression growing troubled. "But it is upon incanting Davor Lazar's name and pouring demonic power into that key that it will reveal the *Book of Light's* final form: a dagger of pure magic. It must be stabbed through the *Book of Shadows* to activate its destructive powers."

Shock reverberated through Mae, just as it did everyone else in the room. An ugly truth came upon its heels.

"Ran Soyun's soul is also in that book," Astarte said quietly before Mae could voice her dismay.

Azazel clenched his jaw. "Yes. I sealed half her soul in that book. Which means it too will be destroyed if the artifact is triggered."

"You had no choice, old friend." Ilmon touched Azazel's shoulder. "You were misled by Davor; it was only logical for you to be wary of the next human you gifted your knowledge of magic to."

Azazel's breath shuddered out of him. "Still, I should have released her soul from the book when we wed. I suggested it to Ran but she refused."

Mae grasped the demon's hand, her heart shattering at the pain echoing through her from Na Ri. Azazel gave her a tremulous half-smile before continuing his tale.

"The Inheritance Ceremony Barquiel spoke of is a ritual where a Sorcerer King bestows his powers upon the one who will take his throne. It is a secret art and one I taught Davor and Ran Soyun in the strictest confidence. Unfortunately, the rite also projects the predecessor's ambitions upon his or her successor, which is likely why almost every Sorcerer King who followed Davor turned out so evil." His gaze when he met Mae's eyes was steely. "The skeleton key can still activate the *Book of Shadows* even if Vedran has opened it and absorbed Davor's soul. All it means is that Vedran will also perish. It matters not that Davor's soul is no longer in the book. It will maintain the memory of its presence and destroy Davor's soul wherever it may be."

"But—won't my father be practically invincible once he absorbs Davor's soul?" Apprehension clouded Nikolai's face. "You said yourself that Davor was strong enough to defeat Ran Soyun." He looked at Mae. "We injured him when we last fought, but it was in no way a fatal wound."

Mae's stomach churned. "He's right."

"You're forgetting something," Vlad said.

The incubus was frowning. "Like my father said, this isn't like the time Azazel and Ran Soyun lost the war to Barquiel and Davor. Not only do you have me, Cortes, Roman, and hundreds of powerful magic users at your side...we have you." He blew out a sigh as he studied Nikolai. "And I hate to admit it, but you're the strongest sorcerer on Earth *and* you can wield Hellfire Magic. While Mae is—" He stopped and waved a hand vaguely. "You know."

"Incredibly foolhardy?" Alicia hazarded.

"An idiot who acts before she thinks?" Astarte contributed.

"An all-avenging ignoramus like that Michael?" Armaros grunted.

"That's going too far," Ilmon protested.

"*Well…*" Hellreaver started.

Mae scowled at the weapon. "I don't want to hear that from you!"

"It's freaky how on point they are," Cortes said flatly.

Azazel's lips twitched.

"I was going to say incredibly strong," Vlad muttered.

Gratitude softened Nikolai's face. "Thanks."

Vlad shuddered. "Please. Don't look at me like that."

Nikolai narrowed his eyes at the incubus before addressing Azazel. "You said there are two things that might work in our favor when we face Vedran. What's the second one?"

The demon studied the sorcerer steadily. "He won't be able to absorb your magic. In fact, doing so will likely shatter his core."

CHAPTER TWENTY-FOUR

THE *BOOK OF LIGHT* OPENED YET ANOTHER POINTLESS breach. Vedran scowled.

The first *Book of Shadows* it had led them to had turned out to be a fake, just like the one Nikolai had manifested when he'd used Hellfire Magic on the artifact Dietrich Farago had created.

Damn that Azazel! Vedran clenched his jaw until his teeth ached. The demon had clearly planted dozens of fakes in case anyone ever attempted to use the *Book of Light* in this fashion. His eyes shrank to slits. *I imagine the skeleton key we lost to Mae and the New York coven would be the fastest way to the real tome.* Determination knotted the sorcerer's shoulders. *Still, there are only so many fakes he could have planted. One of these rifts will lead me to the true* Book of Shadows, *I'm certain of it.*

Vedran took a moment to appreciate the magic bubbling through his veins as he tore open doorway after doorway. The power he now harbored in his dark core made his heart race like few things could. Killing off the sorcerers and witches who had been loyal to him and absorbing the magic of the coven members he'd had his hellish army slaughter had been the right call.

He felt pretty invincible right now. But it still wasn't enough.

He would only be satisfied once he had devoured the soul of the first Sorcerer King and the core of the most powerful white magic user on Earth. The treacherous offspring he had sired with the witch he once treasured the most in his harem.

Vedran was dimly aware of Oscar's harrowed gaze on his back. He could practically taste the sorcerer's fear. Logic told him he had no further use for his firstborn son now that the latter's core had been ruined by *Subjugate*. He had already abandoned his plan to gain control of the Witch Queen by bonding her to Oscar via the *Marriage of Magic*; instead, she would die by Vedran's own hand.

The Sorcerer King frowned. *But Oscar might still be of some use. I've kept him alive this long. A few more days won't matter.*

Something distracted him from his reflections. He stiffened.

The *Book of Light* was vibrating in his hand.

He felt the power inside the artifact condense.

The keyhole shifted form.

Vedran stared at the star-shaped opening, his heart in his throat. He manipulated the Hellfire Magic he had stolen from Nikolai and created a matching key, his fingers shaking with excitement.

This is it. This next rift is the one!

He inserted the star-shaped key of flame inside the compass, his mouth going dry. The click of the lock echoed in his ears, a sound that preceded an event even he had not anticipated.

Oscar gasped.

Jubilation brought a mad grin to Vedran's face. *Yes! Finally!*

The crack that had opened in the fabric of space was not so much a rift as it was a doorway. He hesitated but a moment before surrounding himself with a thick aura of black magic and stepping through it.

Vedran paused and blinked on the other side of the threshold. His breath caught. Stars and galaxies flashed all around and above him, so fast they were a blur against the inky firmament.

Is this—another dimension?!

His heart thumping furiously, he took a step onto a dark floor that moved as if it were made of water. Ripples broke out, the wavelets expanding and accelerating before they washed across the base of something that lit up like the sun.

Vedran flinched and covered his face with an arm. He let his eyes adapt to the bright glare before squinting through a gap between his fingers.

It was a moment before he could make out the bright object ahead. It was a dazzling pedestal that glittered and sparkled as if it were made of stars.

A shiver danced down his spine as he gazed at what floated above it.

Levitating within a roaring orb of demonic energy, its pages fluttering lightly in an invisible wind, was a dark book. Black magic crackled and sparked on its cover and spine.

Deep inside him, in the place where Vedran harbored his most wicked secret, his dead familiar Balkin howled.

"You want me to do what?" Edwin McKinney said leadenly.

Bryony met the mayor's gaze steadily. "I want you to evacuate the city."

McKinney turned to Jared. "Is she insane?!"

Abraham bristled next to Bryony. She raised a hand. He settled in his seat, his annoyed gaze shifting to the two somber-faced advisors framing the mayor.

"She is not." Jared frowned at the mayor. "I'm making the same request. I'm still waiting to hear back from the Special Affairs Bureau, but I'm pretty sure they'll agree with our suggestion."

McKinney leaned his elbows on his desk, his expression hard. "I'm afraid I'm going to need more than that before I okay such an asinine plan." He pursed his lips. "Even if I did consent to it, we'd need the National Guard for such a large-scale evacuation. It would take," one of his counselors leaned down and whispered in his ear, "—a couple of days at least before they had boots on the ground."

Bryony clenched her jaw. It had taken her and

Abraham twelve hours to secure an appointment with the mayor, to the point even Barbara had threatened to storm City Hall to speak to the "Goddamn fool in charge of this place!"

We're running out of time. Still, we need his cooperation if we want to save as many human lives as possible.

"We may have had our differences in the past, Edwin," she said in a level voice, "but Jared and I are being deadly serious. New York is facing an imminent attack."

McKinney raised a mocking eyebrow. "From this so-called Sorcerer King you mentioned before? The one responsible for the incident at that hotel?"

Bryony swallowed a sharp retort. "Yes."

"He's also the one behind all those dead bodies showing up," Abraham ground out, the "asshole" unspoken.

McKinney waved a dismissive hand, his expression undeterred. "My advisors believe that was the work of some kind of cult and it's the last we've seen of them."

Abraham drew a sharp breath. Jared stared at McKinney's advisors like they were the dumbest things on two legs he'd ever seen.

"Maybe we should bring Rambrog here," the Immortal suggested flatly to Bryony.

"Don't tempt me," she muttered.

McKinney sneered. "Who the hell is Rambrog?"

Something behind the mayor caught Bryony's gaze before she could utter a reply. She blinked, not quite understanding what she was seeing for a moment. Her eyes widened.

The air trembled on a ripple of sinister magic, making the hairs on the back of her neck rise to attention. Penley's pupils blazed a bright green as he hissed at her feet.

Blood drained from Abraham's face. The aide clenched the armrests of his chair, his gaze riveted to the window. "What is that?!"

Jared cursed when he registered the phenomenon that had captured their attention.

McKinney frowned. He twisted around, his advisors following suit.

"What are you talk—?" The mayor's words ended on a gargled cry.

He swiveled his chair and climbed clumsily to his feet, his thighs hitting the desk and knocking over an ink pot.

"What the devil is that thing?!" McKinney croaked, indicating the sky with a trembling finger.

CHAPTER TWENTY-FIVE

THEY HAD A DIRECT LINE OF SIGHT TO LOWER Manhattan and the Brooklyn Bridge from McKinney's office in City Hall. What was rolling across the sky from the east was not so much a storm as it was a dark pall that would soon engulf the city. Racing ahead of it, an ominous portent that seemed to herald the End of Days, were thousands of birds.

Blood pounded in Bryony's veins as she rose from her chair, Abraham and Jared at her side. *It's the first part of the prophecy!*

"We're too late," she mumbled, half to herself.

Jared's cell buzzed. His shoulders knotted when he saw the number on the screen. He took the call and listened wordlessly, a muscle jumping in his jawline.

"Yes, Ma'am," he said curtly. "Will do."

The Immortal disconnected and eyed a shaken McKinney coldly. "That was the Special Affairs Bureau. They want everyone out of New York ASAP. General

Cooke and his men at the army facility on Staten Island will assist you. Wait for their instructions."

They left the mayor and his two counselors staring fearfully out the window as they exited the office.

"Isn't this too early?" Abraham said tensely when they emerged from the building. He glanced at the sky as they headed to where Jared had parked his sedan. "I thought we had at least another ten hours."

"It's not as if the Seer's visions come with a precise countdown." Bryony shivered. The wind had picked up and was whipping her coat around her legs. "Besides, I can't feel Vedran's presence yet. We'll know when he arrives in the city." Her scalp prickled as she studied the darkening clouds. "I'm afraid this is only a prelude of what is to come."

By the time Jared's car hit Midtown, Manhattan had come to a standstill. The Immortal switched on his dash light and cursed under his breath as he weaved painfully through the stationary traffic.

No one paid attention to him.

Every man, woman, and child was standing on the street and gazing nervously at the menacing sky and the birds streaming silently above their heads.

Bryony had to give credit to the citizens of New York. It was their sheer resilience that meant none of them was running around screaming yet. She wasn't sure how long that state of affairs would last though.

When they pulled up to the mansion, Barbara and Regina were waiting outside with April and Ludmila. Relief flooded Bryony at the sight of the witch and sorcerers beside them.

"Valentina." She stepped out of the vehicle and rushed over to embrace the Caracas coven High Priestess. "I'm glad you're okay!"

Valentina hugged her tightly, her face pale.

Bryony pulled back and acknowledged Sergio Mendes with a nod. "Thank you for coming."

Anya's father gave her a weak smile.

Bryony turned to Felipe Cortes, Enrique's uncle and the current High Priest of the Medellin coven. "I really appreciate you bringing your people here on such short notice. Having powerful Arcane Magic users on our side will come in handy."

Felipe bobbed his head curtly. "This fight is as much ours as it is yours. It belongs to the entire magic community." Anxiety clouded his eyes. "Have you heard from my nephew?"

Bryony hesitated. "Not yet. But I'm sure he's fine. He's with the Witch Queen, after all."

Felipe's shoulders slumped. Sergio touched the sorcerer's back lightly and murmured comforting words.

Cortes had finally made up with the family and coven he'd thought had abandoned him all those years ago, when his aunt broke his core and nearly killed him. Though he had been reluctant to trust them again, Anya's presence in the sorcerer's life had helped ease the difficult reconciliation process.

Eerie magic washed through the city, making everyone stiffen. Even Jared flinched, the divine energy in the switchblade strapped to his ankle flaring briefly in reaction to the corrupt tide.

Bryony's stomach sank as the twilight engulfing New York deepened, blocking out the sun as effectively as an eclipse. The air grew heavy.

"He's close," Barbara warned.

Anya came out of the building with Roman, Violet, Eric, and Miles. The Nolans and the rest of the High Council were close on their heels. Everyone stared at the eldritch clouds roiling above them.

Karin finally dragged her gaze from the forbidding sight. "Did the mayor agree to evacuate the city?"

"Yes." Abraham furrowed his brow. "But we've lost too much time."

A scream rose somewhere in Central Park. Another followed farther down the avenue.

Shimmering shields exploded around everyone. They raised a battery of powerful spell bombs, their familiars on alert and the jewelry they wore shifting into deadly weapons.

"It's not him," Jared said in a hard voice. "I think the people of New York are finally realizing something is amiss."

Gerard swore. Bryony followed his gaze.

A couple of grizzly bears had wandered out of the park. They were followed by several snow leopards and a growing crowd of fast-moving penguins. A snow monkey jumped from a tree and scampered across the road toward a coffee shop, a lemur clinging to its back.

Miles squinted. "Is that a red panda riding a sea lion?"

"Great," Abraham said leadenly as more of the Central Park Zoo animals streamed out onto Fifth

Avenue. "Biblical scenes of the apocalypse are the last thing we need right now."

Bryony turned to Anya, her pulse racing. "It looks like we'll have to go with Plan B."

Anya swallowed and nodded. Sable straightened on her shoulder, the blue flames of their magic sparkling in the eagle's pupils.

Sergio's confused gaze swung between his daughter and Bryony. "What Plan B?"

"This place is about to be gripped by mass panic, which will make evacuating people a nightmare," Bryony explained stiffly. "We suspected as much, so we came up with some ways to deal with all the possibilities we could encounter ahead of this battle."

Anya met her father's wary stare. "I'm going to use an Illusion Sorcery spell on New York. It will persuade non magic users to abandon everything and leave in an orderly manner."

"Anyone that doesn't make it out in time before the Sorcerer King gets here will be guided to the safe zones where we're erecting defensive barriers," Abraham added. "Half the covens gathered in New York are already there, preparing for evacuees."

Valentina's eyes widened. "You planned all that in a day?"

Bryony smiled faintly at Barbara and the others. "I had help."

Felipe fisted his hands. "Is that safe?" He studied Anya with a heavy frown. "You'll be messing with a lot of innocent people's minds."

Bryony registered the dread and anger in the

sorcerer's voice. His family and the Medellin coven had lost his nephew because of an Illusion Sorcery spell after all.

Anya faced the sorcerer squarely. "I promise you. I will not harm them."

"You can trust my daughter, Felipe," Sergio murmured.

Felipe hesitated. His shoulders slumped.

"It's a shame, though," Regina told Bryony. "We could do with someone who can use Illusion Sorcery when we fight Vedran." She squinted at Anya. "She did a number on the Dark Council when they attacked your coven."

"Let's not forget the warehouse incident where she made them believe they were chickens," Eric remarked.

Anya flushed in the face of a battery of impressed stares. "They totally deserved that."

Sergio's expression hardened. "Unfortunately, the few sorcerers and witches we knew of who could use Illusion Sorcery have all disappeared. No doubt, the Sorcerer King went after them when he lost his hold on my daughter."

Abraham rubbed the back of his neck. "We'll have to make do with Anya for—"

A cheerful beep from up the avenue cut out the rest of the sorcerer's words. They turned.

A green Vespa was puttering around the vehicles stuck in the middle of the road. A Chihuahua in a yellow coat sat barking at the sky in the front basket.

Eric's eyes bulged. "Is that Mrs. Son-Ha?!"

"Who's Mrs. Son-Ha?" Valentina asked, puzzled.

"She's a Shaman who's been helping us," Karin explained. "You'll like her."

Mrs. Son-Ha pulled up at the curb. She patted Dexter's head and eyed the churning clouds with a jaundiced stare before meeting their surprised gazes.

"Looks like we got here in time."

Jared drew a sharp breath at the sight of the middle-aged woman in a gypsy outfit sitting on the back seat of the scooter. She was holding a black cat in her lap and studying them warily.

"Gloria?!" the Immortal spluttered.

"What are you doing here?" Violet asked, similarly shocked.

Recognition darted through Bryony. *This must be the witch from the circus! The one who helped Mae find Anya when we were all under the influence of her Illusion Sorcery.*

"Who's Gloria?" Regina hissed as the woman climbed off the scooter behind Mrs. Son-Ha.

"She's a witch who can use Illusion Sorcery," Miles explained excitedly.

Sergio stiffened when the sorcerer explained the circumstances under which he, Violet, and Jared had met her.

Felipe's face darkened. He took a menacing step forward.

"You!" he snarled at Gloria. "You were the one who helped Raya fool us all!"

Gloria eyed the Medellin coven High Priest guardedly. Anya stepped between them.

"Enrique already explained what happened, Felipe," she said steadily. "Gloria was forced to use her magic to protect her daughter, just as I was tortured to use mine. She helped Mae and Enrique save me."

"I'm sorry," Gloria said quietly. "I know it's too little too late, but I truly am."

Felipe fisted his hands. "Why are you here?!"

"To help," Mrs. Son-Ha replied in Gloria's stead. The Shaman walked up to Felipe and furrowed her brows as she tilted her head and looked up at him. "The past is the past, sorcerer. Right now, you need to work together to stop what is to come."

She glanced pointedly at the sky.

Jared sighed and ran a hand through his hair in the fraught hush. "When did Mae give you the keys to Betsy?"

Mrs. Son-Ha flinched. She mumbled something.

"What?"

"I said she didn't," Mrs. Son-Ha said sourly. "I had spare keys made."

Regina sucked in air and clutched her chest. "You stole the Witch Queen's scooter?!"

Mrs. Son-Ha sniffed. "What she doesn't know won't hurt her. She's in Hell, after all."

"Wait," Valentina said to Karin. "Mae rides a Vespa?!"

Karin grimaced. "The coven gave her a car, but apparently she got that many speeding tickets she almost lost her license."

Abraham shook his head. "That woman is a menace behind the wheel of any vehicle."

CHAPTER TWENTY-SIX

"He who wears the mantle of the Sorcerer King cannot wield both black and white magic!" Azazel shouted over his shoulder.

The wind lashed at Mae's hair as she stared at her father. They were flying through Hell Deep on Vozgan. Since the dragon was smaller and faster than his father, they'd requested his help in their search for Ran Soyun's prison.

The young dragon had agreed with an enthusiasm that had worried Vannog and Armaros and had caused Astarte to frown.

"This isn't a fun little adventure, you know," the Goddess had grumbled as they'd prepared to leave Armaros's keep.

"I know," Vozgan had whined.

He'd stood patiently in the courtyard while Us'gorith and Armaros's servants fitted a giant saddle on his back.

"Be careful, my son." Vannog had nuzzled Vozgan's

face lovingly. "And don't just eat anything you fancy," he'd warned sharply, blowing smoke in the dragon's eyes.

Vozgan had flinched and avoided his father's hard stare. "I won't."

"Ten bucks says he's coming with us because of the potential snacks we may come across," Cortes had told Nikolai dully.

I don't trust that dragon as far as I can throw him, my witch, Hellreaver had muttered where he hung around Mae's neck.

"You're one to talk."

Ilmon had hugged Vlad tightly, his eyes bright with a sheen of tears.

"Make sure you come and visit," he'd mumbled. "Just ask Alicia to open a portal for you."

"Hey!" the Reaper queen had protested. "What am I, a revolving door to Hell?!"

Ilmon had ignored her. He'd cradled Vlad's cheeks in his hands and stared into his eyes. "I'm going to miss you, son."

Vlad had gripped the Incubus king's fingers, his face tight with emotion. "Me too," he'd hesitated a beat, "—Father."

Ilmon's pupils had rounded, his expression crumpling. He'd started bawling loud enough for the demons in the castle to run out to see what fresh calamity had afflicted their home.

Azazel had pinched the bridge of his nose while Astarte and Armaros had sneered at the Incubus king.

Vlad had grimaced and gently patted his father's arm. "Now, now, stop that."

A harsh wheeze had left him when Ilmon locked his arms around him, squeezing hard enough to make his spine pop.

"No! I don't wanna let you go!" Ilmon had wailed.

"The Wicked Ravisher sure is an ugly crier, huh?" Hellreaver had mumbled.

Astarte had cracked her knuckles and cut her eyes to Armaros. "You grab Ilmon's arms. I'll punch his lights out."

Nikolai's voice brought Mae back to the present.

"What do you mean?" he yelled at Azazel.

"It's a condition I placed inside the soul of Davor Lazar! A curse that meant he could never simultaneously wield the ultimate magic granted to me by God!" Azazel frowned. "My ability to wield white magic was limited when I fell to Hell, but I could still teach it to Davor and Ran Soyun. Davor had little aptitude for it, but Ran was a natural."

Mae shared a startled look with Nikolai. "That's why Vedran couldn't absorb your mother's magic!"

The sorcerer swallowed and nodded.

They gasped when Vozgan banked. The dragon arrowed toward a narrow pass between two peaks and hurtled through the gap with mere feet to spare on either side. He whooped excitedly as he emerged into a dark valley beyond.

Popo released a panicked screech on Cortes's shoulder as Vozgan swooped in a near-vertical drop.

"Did someone give the damn dragon coffee?!"

Cortes yelled, the parrot wrapping his wings around his face.

"Just shut up and hang on to something!" Vlad shouted, his arms locked on a wide-eyed and green-looking Tarang.

"This is why I hate riding hellbeasts," Alicia grumbled, her scythe humming in the wind while she gripped the saddle with her thighs.

Mae finally asked Azazel the question that had been eating at her to distract herself from the rapidly approaching forest below. "Was Davor's familiar Brimstone's father?"

Brimstone stiffened in her hold.

Azazel met her stare steadily over his shoulder. "How did you know?"

Guilt knotted Mae's belly when she felt the fox's discomfort across their bond.

"I just had a feeling." She squeezed the familiar gently. "I'm sorry, Brim. I didn't mean to bring up bad memories."

The fox sighed. *It's alright, my witch.*

A low whine escaped Hellreaver. Azazel studied Brimstone with a sad expression.

"His name was Akarami," the demon said quietly. "He was a divine beast. And I will forever regret connecting his soul to Davor's." He was silent for a while. "There is something else you must know, daughter."

Apprehension tightened Mae's shoulders. "What is it?"

"You sure you want to talk about this?" Alicia asked Azazel warily.

"It is better that I say it now than never." Azazel hesitated before meeting Mae's anxious stare. "Barquiel, Ran Soyun, and I used to be close friends. Which is why his betrayal stung all the more."

A heavy feeling formed in the pit of Mae's stomach.

"You were friends?" Cortes said, stunned.

Alicia sighed. "This is a bad idea, Zaz."

"Ran Soyun mentioned something similar when I was in the cave, but I wasn't certain if she meant it," Nikolai murmured awkwardly.

"She truly cherished Barquiel," Azazel said.

Anger heated Mae's blood. "Whereas he only coveted her!"

"Your mother was a powerful woman. Many were attracted by her incredible magic."

"Don't defend him!" Mae snapped.

She bit her lip and squeezed her eyes shut for a moment.

"I'm sorry," she mumbled miserably. "But I—all I can see when I think about him are Na Ri's memories of the war he brought to your doorstep and what he did to Rose."

Azazel reached out and clasped her hand. "It is quite alright, child." Sorrow tainted his voice. "I do not expect you to forgive him. I have known Barquiel far longer than you. After all, we were brothers in Heaven before we became enemies in Hell."

Vozgan spoke up in the hush that followed.

"I know you're all having a deep and terribly

meaningful conversation, but would you mind awfully if we went to explore that lake for a minute?" the dragon said sheepishly.

"What lake?" Alicia said suspiciously.

Vozgan shot over the edge of a bluff.

The land dropped vertiginously beneath them. Trees blanketed the flanks of the cliff they had just passed and the distant valley below. A dark body of water occupied the center of the depression.

"That lake," Vozgan said brightly.

Mae's eyes teared up at the speed of their passage as the dragon dove.

"You're not thinking of going for a dip, are you?!" Cortes yelled.

Vozgan flinched guiltily. "Why do you ask?"

"Because we're on top of you, lizard brain!" Vlad snarled.

The dragon looked over his shoulder and huffed out smoke at their frowns. "Jeez. Alright, I'll just dip my toes in for a moment."

He was above the lake in seconds and skimming the surface of the water with a delighted sound, his claws and wing tips leaving white trails in his wake.

Nikolai grabbed Mae's shoulder, startling her.

"I just sensed white magic!" he barked.

Her breath caught.

"*Stop, Vozgan!*" Azazel roared.

The dragon startled and snapped his wings up and forward, his abrupt deceleration almost sending everyone tumbling into the lake. He circled around to the spot he had just passed.

Mae's heart thundered against her ribs as whiteness flared in Nikolai and Alastair's eyes. The sorcerer furrowed his brow, his gaze on the dark waters below.

"There's something down there."

Heat filled Mae's belly and veins. The spell left her lips at the same time Azazel invoked it.

"*Contain!*"

The barrier of magic and demonic energy that bloomed around them and the dragon pulsed with so much power it cast ripples across the surface of the lake and bathed it in a crimson glow.

"Whoa," Vozgan mumbled. "That is so cool."

He extended his neck and sniffed curiously at the shield, only to wrinkle his snout when scarlet static danced across his scales.

Azazel gave Mae a look of admiration. "Your spell is very powerful, daughters."

She smiled faintly. "Na Ri and I learned from the best."

Azazel chuckled before patting Vozgan's neck. "Let's go."

The dragon climbed until he was some two hundred feet above the lake, closed his wings, and dove. Mae hung on to his back grimly as he entered the water inside *Contain,* violent waves exploding around them and surging across the surface.

What little ambient light had illuminated the valley faded rapidly as they sank into the inky depths. Brightness flared around them as Nikolai manifested a sphere of Moon Magic above their heads.

Brimstone shifted in Mae's arms a moment later.

Her head swiveled, her gaze finding the giant, sinewy shapes he was staring at.

Tarang made a worried noise and shuffled closer to Vlad. Popo hugged Cortes's face with his wings, causing the sorcerer to curse. Even Alastair let out an anxious squawk.

"Do not worry," Azazel reassured them. "They cannot get to us."

The water monsters of Hell Deep swam close to *Contain*, the eddies they cast bouncing harmlessly off the barrier. The radiance of Nikolai's magic glinted off dark scales, curious crimson pupils, and rows of jagged teeth that Mae suspected would haunt her dreams for a long time.

"Those are sea serpents," Alicia muttered.

Vozgan licked his chops. "They taste nice salted and grilled."

The dragon's eyes glazed over with longing. Hellreaver drooled a little.

"How about we focus on the mission?" the Reaper queen said hastily.

Nikolai's hands clenched on Mae's waist. "There."

The sorcerer pointed at a spot a hundred feet below them and to the right. White magic erupted on his fingertips. The pale trails danced out of *Contain* and weaved languorously through the water toward an underwater cliff.

Mae's pulse quickened when his magic traced the contour of an opening. Azazel guided Vozgan into the mouth of the giant tunnel.

The dragon flew for what felt like an hour, his

wings beating occasionally as he surfed the currents inside the passage. The shaft twisted, dropped, and rose time and time again, until even Mae started feeling sick.

Redness brightened the darkness below them when they emerged above a precipitous drop.

A chill danced through her at the sight of a river of lava coursing through the bottom of a mile-deep canyon, the eruptions causing hot bubbles to rise toward them. More underwater volcanoes appeared as they navigated cavern after cavern.

Mae suspected they were well beyond the boundaries of the lake and had passed several valleys. She tensed when Nikolai spoke.

"We're close."

An intersection appeared up ahead.

"Which way?!" Azazel shouted.

White magic blazed in Nikolai's pupils. He furrowed his brow.

"Go left."

CHAPTER TWENTY-SEVEN

Void opened inside a bank of low clouds some three thousand feet above New York.

Black magic boiled inside Vedran's veins as he studied the city spread out below his feet through the wispy billows. The once bright metropolis looked dull and dank under the mantle of darkness shrouding it.

It's been a while since I was last here.

His cold gaze found the queues of traffic moving at a snail's pace on the bridges connecting Manhattan to the mainland.

"Look at them," he muttered. "Like insects begging to be killed."

Oscar stayed silent, his face pale and his eyes bright with fear; the sorcerer avoided meeting his eyes.

Vedran could understand his son's reticence. Even the macabre army lurking silently behind them kept their distance from the power making the air tremble around him. The magic surging from his core was so brutal it shook his bones and rattled his teeth.

He took a deep breath and smiled savagely when he tasted the terror in the air.

Davor Lazar's soul was everything he had hoped it would be and more. Dark, twisted, and full of a hunger that matched his own greed. He knew he would now be able to achieve his long-held dream with the first Sorcerer King's spirit inside him.

This is it. This is the day I shall become a god!

Pain stabbed through his belly. He clenched his jaw as Balkin clawed at his insides, his dead familiar's rage a fire that seared his flesh where the creature had slipped through the chains that had bound his soul for hundreds of years. Vedran fisted his hands and reinforced the shackles, his brow furrowing in an almighty scowl.

Curse that witch!

He'd known, ever since retreating inside *Void* after his last battle with the Witch Queen, that her spells had done something to the prison that sealed Balkin's soul. A prison located in the very center of his core and that was now clashing with the other powerful soul that inhabited it.

This wasn't the first time he'd felt Balkin reach through his cage in the short hours since he'd found the *Book of Shadows* and absorbed Davor's spiritual remains. Regret tightened his chest.

It seems I won't be able to hold on to both Balkin and Davor's souls.

Vedran was a little shocked at how conflicted that realization left him. Logic dictated that he abandon Balkin, since the first Sorcerer King would grant him powers beyond those his familiar was capable of. Yet, he found himself strangely unwilling to do so.

A mirthless chuckle left him. *Maybe my heart isn't as dead as I thought it was.*

Balkin snarled inside him, the sound growing faint as he succumbed to the dark fetters binding him.

A flicker below captured Vedran's gaze. The air around the Empire State Building looked different to that in the rest of the city. It was brighter, clearer. As if—

Vedran cursed, detecting the spell emanating from the skyscraper. He realized then that something crucial was missing from the scenario he was observing. He could not discern the screams he'd expected to hear as panic spread throughout New York.

Fury burned his veins, powering up his magic. The spell left his lips like a death sentence.

"*Rot.*"

For a moment, nothing happened.

Black magic detonated silently around the base of the skyscraper and raced up its walls, consuming everything in its path. Inky clouds shrouded the giant structure as it imploded.

Vedran narrowed his eyes when the dark billows faded. Where the uppermost observatory once stood was a shimmering, golden bubble. Floating within it were two witches, a sorcerer, and a man with a blazing broadsword.

Oscar drew a sharp breath at the sight of the blonde with the Harpy Eagle. Vedran cursed.

Blue flames brightened Anya Mendes's eyes and those of her familiar.

She must be the reason the city is so quiet!

It was a moment before he recovered his composure.

"It doesn't matter." Power seared his blood. *"Disperse!"*

Black magic swarmed the golden sphere protecting the witch. It shivered but held.

Rage sent blood roaring in Vedran's ears.

"What is that power?!" he snarled.

Oscar flinched.

Vedran cut his eyes to his son. "You know what it is, don't you?"

Oscar swallowed at his dark stare. Regret darkened the sorcerer's gaze for a moment. Then he did something Vedran never expected him to do.

He stepped out of *Void* and plummeted toward the city.

"No!"

Vedran lunged forward, arm outstretched. His fingers closed on empty space. He scowled and unleashed a net of black magic. The thick threads streamed from his fingers and snaked through the air, wrapping around Oscar's ankle in seconds.

The sorcerer cast *Disperse,* cutting the ties. He fell silently, nary a scream leaving his lips as he plunged through the air.

Vedran stiffened at the glimpse of a glittering object in Oscar's hand. It was the *Book of Light.*

When did he take that?!

He hesitated. He had no further use for the artifact now that he had obtained the *Book of Shadows* and Davor's soul. Still, it rankled him that Oscar had stolen the compass.

He's a pawn that might still come in handy in the days ahead. Besides, I did not give him permission to leave my side.

"Go after him and bring him back," Vedran ordered a regiment of the monstrous troops silently awaiting his command. His eyes shrank to slits. "You can hurt him if he resists, but don't kill him."

The Sorcerer King turned his attention to the city below.

The Hellfire Magic that bloomed around his fingers sent a thrill through him at the same time it made the main body of his army recoil, the sheer power of the flames causing the air to shimmer in a fifty-foot-wide radius around him.

Vedran aimed the devastating spell he had invoked at the bridges spanning the Hudson River. "*Obliterate.*"

A dark smile stretched his mouth.

Hellfire Magic engulfed the overpasses and the vehicles jamming their lanes. Tiny shapes leapt from the structures a moment later, the humans trapped there desperately trying to escape their fate. The flames found them and charred their bodies to black shells before they struck the water.

Bile burned the back of Violet's throat as she watched the burning figures splashing into the river from where she floated above where the Empire State Building once stood.

"Fuck!" Jared snarled.

"Focus!" Violet snapped when the Immortal's concentration wavered for a split second.

Jared swallowed, his knuckles whitening on the handle of his sword. The divine power pouring out of the weapon augmented the barrier she and Miles had erected to protect Anya.

A muffled sob reached Violet's ears.

Sorrow made her belly clench. She looked over her shoulder and saw the tears streaming down Anya's face. The witch could feel the pain of all the people dying at the Sorcerer King's hands.

"Anya," Miles whispered, his tone full of misery.

The witch wiped her nose on the back of her sleeve and took a shaky breath. The magic in her eyes brightened as her face set in hard lines. Sable made an angry sound on her shoulder.

"I want you to tell me where you think his spells are about to strike next," she ground out. "I'll try and get as many people away from there as I can."

Jared's scowling stare stayed locked on the dark portal flickering through the clouds above them. "And if you can't?"

They could just about glimpse Vedran's figure inside *Void*.

Anya's tone grew steely. "Then I will make sure they do not suffer when they die."

Movement in the sky had Violet's head jerking up. Miles sucked in air.

Jared paled. "What the hell are those?!"

Violet's mouth went dry at the sight of the gruesome army descending upon the city from the Sorcerer King's portal. It wasn't just demons, devils, ghouls, and hellbeasts she detected amidst the swarming mass sinking out of the clouds on a wave of black magic.

Outnumbering the fiends were grotesque monsters she couldn't take her eyes off. They looked deformed and disproportioned, as if they had been stitched haphazardly together from mismatched body parts.

Miles gagged. "Oh God!"

Ice filled Violet's veins as she finally made out the details of the creatures. They were the amalgamation of several species that had been mutilated almost beyond recognition and fused together. The upper body of a witch. The trunk of a hellboar. The tail of a devil. The legs of a sorcerer. A ghoul with the head of a hellbear.

Black magic throbbed along the coarse stitches holding the chimeras together, the Sorcerer King's vile power the only thing keeping them alive.

Violet swallowed past the lump in her throat. *Alive is a questionable term!*

Fear knotted her insides as she watched the dreadful army separate into distinct troops that began making their way to locations in Manhattan, the Bronx, and Queens.

CHAPTER TWENTY-EIGHT

BLACK MAGIC MADE THE AIR SHIVER ABOVE YANKEE Stadium. Roman's pulse pounded wildly as he observed the fiendish regiments darkening the sky to the south. One was headed straight for them.

"Here they come!" he shouted at the sorcerers and witches standing on the field with him.

Heat licked Roman's veins and roared through Filomena's core as they prepared to unleash their magic. *"Fire Shield!"*

A wall of flames exploded above the venue. It expanded rapidly to form a veil that dropped around the arena where thousands of New Yorkers who hadn't been able to escape the city huddled silently. The Fire Magic users Ludmila had brought to New York augmented the shield he'd raised, their eyes and those of their familiars reflecting the blaze bathing the stadium in an orange glow.

The first monsters slammed into the barrier a moment later.

Exhilaration shot through Roman. *Yes! The shield is holding!*

Fire Magic engulfed dozens of demons and hellbeasts as they tried to smash through the defensive wall. Their screeches pierced his ears, the sounds making the masses flinch even though they were under the influence of Anya's Illusion Sorcery.

His elation was short-lived. Dread knotted his belly when a scream sounded behind him. Roman twisted on his heels. His eyes rounded.

A monster the like of which he'd never seen before had successfully breached *Fire Shield* and was tearing a man in the upper bleachers from limb to limb.

"What is that?!" a sorcerer gasped.

Roman swallowed and lowered his brows. "It doesn't matter! We need to get rid of it!" Magic warmed his blood. He raised his hand. "*Ignite!*"

The spell engulfed the creature in a blaze of Fire Magic. Still it moved, its claws sparking as it reached for its next victim, seemingly heedless of its burning flesh.

Filomena hissed angrily on Roman's shoulder. He clenched his jaw.

The next spell left his lips on a snarl. "*FROSTFIRE!*"

Flames of ice exploded around the monster, the pale shards piercing its body in dozens of places. It struggled violently before slowly growing limp, the talons clawing the air inches from the face of a dazed woman falling to its side. Its blood coated the ice in dark trails as it grew still.

More shouts punctuated the heavy air inside the stadium.

Roman's core throbbed as he and the Fire Magic users cast spell after spell to kill the monsters who had ripped their way through the shield. Perspiration soon beaded his forehead. A witch swayed beside him.

He gritted his teeth. *Shit! There's no end to these bastards!*

A gargled sound had him looking over his shoulder. A sorcerer was pointing shakily at the sky. Roman followed his horrified stare.

A dark tide was rolling swiftly toward the stadium. He could taste the Sorcerer King's black magic within it.

The wave slammed into *Fire Shield* before any of them could react.

Air locked in Roman's lungs at the violent pressure bearing down on him. His knees nearly buckled. He grunted as he resisted the awful force crushing his body, his nails scoring bloodied lines into his palms.

Dozens of sorcerers and witches fell to the ground around him.

Roman broke out in a cold sweat. He recognized the spell robbing everyone of their strength and magic. He looked up at the inky mantle spreading across the barrier, panic squeezing his heart.

This is Rot!

Terrified yells broke out when the shield protecting the stadium started to disperse, the bright flames hissing into nothingness as they were devoured by the foul mist. A witch in the upper bleachers barely had time to scream before she imploded in a dark cloud, her body and that of her familiar instantly eaten alive by black magic.

Roman shuddered. Determination tightened his jaw.

"Get ready, Filo!"

The chameleon sank her feet into his shoulder as he dropped to one knee and slammed his hands on the grass, her magic blazing brightly across their bond and her anger echoing his own.

Roman's heart slammed against his ribs as he sought out the ley line that ran under the stadium, the Sun Magic spells Nadia had taught him wrapping his and his familiar's cores in a multi-layered, protective barrier. He connected to the dazzling cord of power deep underground, followed it to the nexus under the heart of the city, and grasped the white magic within.

The power that flooded him and Filomena made his insides churn. He gritted his teeth and invoked the spell his great-grandmother had taught him in Prague.

"*INFERNO!*"

White fire bloomed silently above the stadium, the dazzling flames causing many to flinch and cover their eyes. The blaze began combating *Rot.*

Roman tasted blood on his tongue. He kept drawing on the nexus, conscious the magic it contained was the only thing that could counter the Sorcerer King's terrible spell.

He glanced at the witches and sorcerers standing beside him.

"Cast your spells outside the barrier!" he barked. "We mustn't let those monsters get in here!"

They swallowed and nodded.

ABRAHAM'S SPELL BOMB OBLITERATED THE HEAD OF A hellwolf. The sorcerer swung his sword and decapitated a devil before it could leap for the people huddling next to some bushes. Blood splashed across his face. He wiped it dispassionately with the back of a hand and turned to confront his next foe, Shiloh's eyes blazing with magic where the owl clung to his shoulder.

Bryony's heart thumped as she, Barbara, Regina, and April poured their magic into the shield rising above Central Park. The air crackled with magic, bringing with it the smell of ozone.

Half the New York coven was with them. The rest were aiding the High Council and the international covens protecting the humans who had been unable to leave New York. They were gathered in various safe havens they'd hastily created across the five boroughs, including the subways and the tunnels under the East and Hudson Rivers.

Derrick, Raven, Karin, and Felipe were among those assisting Abraham in protecting the witches and sorcerers who'd erected the barrier shielding the two hundred thousand people who'd sought sanctuary in the park.

The Medellin High Priest scowled as he wielded his

whip and cast spell bomb after violent spell bomb, his Arcane Magic cutting down scores of demons.

Raven took care of a devil before it could reach Abraham and incanted *Ice Fortress*. The spell exploded into life some fifty feet away, trapping the demons headed for a group of people hiding under a rocky overhang. She pierced the eye of the hellwolf lunging at her from the right and roundhouse-kicked a hellboar in the jaw, her expression focused.

Rambrog smashed his fists down on the hellbear and helltiger lunging for the young witch, felling the beasts in a single strike.

A hideous scream cut through the noise of the battle.

CHAPTER TWENTY-NINE

Bryony's stomach dropped at the sight of the monsters who had breached the barrier and were emerging from the trees to the north.

"What the hell are those things?!" Regina snarled.

Bryony lowered her brows. She could make out several species within the hideous bodies of the creatures closing in on the gazebo where a hundred or so citizens crouched.

"Chimeras." A muscle jumped in Barbara's cheek. "That bastard fused his monsters together and—" She froze, horror widening her pupils. "Wait. Are those—?!"

"Oh God," April mumbled.

Rage misted Bryony's vision.

Several of the monsters bore human body parts.

"Well, now we know what that bastard did with the missing coven members." She glanced grimly at Barbara. "Can you hold the fort a moment?"

Barbara dipped her chin. "Be careful."

Regina fist-pumped the air enthusiastically. "Go kick some monster ass, Bry-bry!"

Barbara scowled at the grinning witch. "How about you focus on this shield?"

Bryony sighed and unleashed her sword. She and Penley began making their way toward the monsters. The ground shook in their wake.

Bryony stopped and turned.

She eyed Rambrog with a frown. "Stay here and help them."

The giant rumbled something before shuffling his feet awkwardly.

"I'm pretty sure Brimstone ordered him to guard you in case of danger!" Abraham shouted over before cursing and swooping beneath a devil's talons.

Bryony's frown deepened. Rambrog's expression turned decidedly mulish.

Her shoulders slumped. "Alright. Just make sure not to step on any of our friends."

The giant beamed and lumbered after her as she headed for the path that would intercept the chimeras' route. Heat pooled in her belly and warmed her blood when she stepped on the asphalt. Magic shivered into life around her and Penley.

The Sorcerer King's fiendish creations slowed at the sight of the emerald aura brightening the air.

"Are you ready, Pen?"

Her cat meowed and pressed against her leg, his magic strong and steady across their bond.

Motion under the closest tree line had Bryony cursing. A pack of hellbeasts darted out from the shadows under the canopy and bounded for the gazebo.

"Rambrog! Protect those people!"

The giant's brow furrowed. His anxious gaze darted from her to the chimeras.

She smiled faintly. "I'll be okay. Now, go!"

Rambrog hesitated before heading for the hellbeasts. She waited until he'd cleared the area before invoking the spell Mae had taught her before she'd left New York.

"*Wind Fury!*"

A viridescent storm exploded around the chimeras. The currents intensified as Bryony poured her and Penley's power into the spell, the invisible blades slicing the creatures' flesh to shreds.

Most were immobilized by the tempest. Two managed to escape *Wind Fury*.

Bryony gritted her teeth and raised a barrage of spell bombs. She hurled them at the approaching chimeras. Though the blasts took chunks out of the creatures' limbs and trunks and slowed them down a fraction, they kept on coming.

"Get away from there, Bry!" Barbara and Regina shouted shrilly.

"*Bry!*" April screamed.

Horror drained the blood from Abraham's face. "Bryony!"

He began running, desperation making his movements clumsy.

Rambrog roared where he clutched a hellbear and a trio of hellboars in his hands. He flung the monsters across the park and rushed toward her, his feet leaving deep indentations in the grass.

She knew the giant and her aide would not make it in time to help her. Her spine stiffened.

The chimeras' shadows swallowed her and Penley. The cat hissed defiantly at her feet, his fur on end and his eyes bright with magic. She gripped her blade and widened her stance.

We need to take at least one of them down!

Claws glinted when the first chimera swung for her. She ducked, spun, and thrust her sword up as she rose. Something slammed into her chest at the same time her blade pierced one of the monsters.

Bone snapped. Fire lanced through Bryony's body as the blow lifted her off her feet. The world tilted violently around her. She landed hard on the ground, blood bursting from her lips on a guttural rasp.

Penley screeched. The cat jumped on her body and whirled around to face the attacker looming above them, his tiny shape defiant to the bitter end.

"*Nooo!*" Abraham howled.

His scream was drowned out by Rambrog's bellow.

Bryony looked up blearily as a foot descended toward her skull and blocked out the sky. There was movement at the edge of her vision.

"*ROT!*" someone roared.

The spell engulfed the creature about to crush her head in a veil of black magic. Rambrog slammed into the second chimera and took it to the ground. *Rot* swarmed the monster. The giant recoiled.

The chimeras screeched and writhed helplessly,

black magic eating at the coarse stitches keeping their misshapen parts together and consuming their flesh. They convulsed and foamed at the mouth before growing still, the dark light in their mismatched pupils slowly fading as their bodies disintegrated into dark ash.

Heart pounding, Bryony turned her head and saw the sorcerer who had saved her.

Oscar swayed where he clung to a tree. His face was a mess and blood oozed from his various wounds. He swallowed convulsively and made his way unsteadily toward them, one hand clutching the arm hanging limply at his side.

Abraham arrived and stepped between the sorcerer and Bryony, his face dark with anger. Rambrog loomed protectively over them.

The aide prepared to unleash a spell bomb.

Bryony recovered her senses and grabbed his ankle. "No! He just killed those monsters!"

Her breath caught when she registered what Oscar clutched to his chest.

Abraham stiffened. "Is that—?!"

"—the *Book of Light!*" she mumbled.

Abraham pulled Bryony to her feet. Rambrog patted her gently on the back and almost sent her toppling over again. The aide scowled at the sheepish giant.

Bryony winced and clutched her ribs.

"Definitely broke at least one of the damn things," she muttered under her breath.

Penley meowed loudly and scaled her dress in a

flash. He perched on her shoulder and head-bumped her cheek, his chest rumbling with happy purrs.

Abraham cast a worried glance at her before focusing warily on the figure drawing near.

Desperation turned Oscar's expression haggard as he approached. He stumbled and fell to his knees a few feet from them.

"Drabek!" he gasped, looking up with a beseeching expression. He pushed himself up clumsily with a hand and would have fallen again had Bryony not reached out and steadied his elbow. "Is Drabek still alive?!"

"Yes."

Oscar stilled. Tears welled up and trickled down his bloodied cheeks. A shudder shook him.

He squeezed his eyes shut and sagged in Bryony's hold. "Thank God!"

Bryony exchanged a shocked glance with Abraham.

Her chest tightened as she studied Oscar. She could hardly believe the man before them was the sorcerer they had all feared. He looked different. She frowned.

Even his magic no longer feels the same.

She glanced at the vanishing corpses of the monsters he had felled. The black wisps fading into nothingness did not stink of the Sorcerer King's corruption.

Abraham's suspicious gaze never left Oscar. "Why are you here?"

The reply he gave them made Bryony blink.

"To atone for my sins," Oscar whispered, ashen faced. Cold determination filled his eyes when he opened them. "Where's Mae?"

CHAPTER THIRTY

THE AIR RIPPLED WITH HEAT AS VOZGAN FLEW ABOVE A valley riddled with rivers and pits of spitting lava. Mae clung grimly to the dragon's back, her senses on high alert. Tension rolled off Nikolai, Vlad, and Cortes in thick waves where they sat silently behind her. Even Hellreaver and Brimstone had gone quiet, as if they too sensed the strangeness around them.

Azazel and Alicia studied the terrain closely, their sharp gazes sweeping the landscape for signs of Barquiel.

They'd felt the demon's energy signature soon after they'd emerged from the underwater tunnel that had brought them to a part of Hell Deep few knew the existence of.

"There!" Nikolai barked a moment later.

Mae's head snapped around.

He was indicating an area to the far left of the cavern, some quarter of a mile from a mountain pass that would take them out of the valley.

Vozgan cast a worried look at the sorcerer over his shoulder. "There's nothing there but rock."

Nikolai frowned. "And I'm telling you Ran Soyun's magic is strongest in that direction. There must be some kind of barrier that's hiding what's really there."

Mae and Azazel exchanged a startled look. They incanted the spell as one.

"*NEGATE!*"

Vozgan made a startled sound. The wall of the cavern wavered like a mirage under the crimson magic that crashed into it. Mae's pulse quickened when it disappeared. Alicia swore at the sight of the hidden vale and dark peak beyond.

The dragon banked and made rapidly for the distant mountain.

"I can sense Barquiel's army!" the Reaper queen ground out a moment later.

Mae narrowed her eyes. She too could feel the ghouls and devils somewhere up ahead. Sulfur clouds obscured her vision when the dragon flew over a cluster of lava pits. The mountain loomed out of the yellow clouds, a solid black wall of rock that grew until it filled her sight.

Vozgan rose sharply, belly skimming the cliffside and wings beating powerfully to overcome the downdrafts dragging at his body. Mae's stomach lurched.

White magic raised the hairs on her nape when the dragon shot past a breach in the rock face.

"*Stop!*" she and Nikolai yelled at the same time.

Vozgan pulled up abruptly, causing Vlad and Cortes to curse.

"There!" Mae pointed beneath them, her heart racing. "That opening!"

She glanced at Nikolai. He swallowed and nodded.

Azazel's anxious gaze remained locked on the crevice while the dragon hovered down next to it.

Vozgan studied the slit-like passage with a dubious expression. "I won't get through that."

"Then we'll have to go alone from here," Azazel said in a strained voice.

His face was tight with a mixture of apprehension, anticipation, and bone-deep longing.

Mae's chest tightened, the same emotions coursing through her from Na Ri. Hellreaver and Brimstone whined.

Vozgan sagged. "Drat. I was looking forward to a good fight." His voice dropped to a low mumble. "And maybe a snack or two."

"Told you so," Cortes muttered darkly to Vlad and Nikolai.

Azazel smiled faintly and patted the dragon's neck. "There might still be some fighting left for you to do, my young friend."

Vozgan brightened.

Mae invoked *Levitate* and erected *Contain* around herself, Nikolai, Vlad, Cortes, and their familiars. They followed Azazel and Alicia inside the chasm.

"Good luck!" Vozgan called out anxiously in their wake.

Acrid fumes danced around *Contain* as they

navigated the narrow corridor, the walls at times brushing against the solid barrier of magic. The outlook opened out some two hundred feet later.

A cliff rose at the end of a gully lit by the glow of dozens of bubbling firepits. Mae's breath caught.

She could feel Ran Soyun's magic pulsing from it. From the way Azazel and Nikolai tensed, so could they.

"There's a cave at the bottom of that bluff," the sorcerer said with a jerk of his head. "Barquiel erected barriers to hide the entrance. It leads to Ran Soyun's prison."

Alicia's eyes shrank to slits. She accelerated, her scythe extending into its deadliest form.

"Wait!" Azazel warned. He scanned the shadowy cliffs rising around them. "You don't know what traps he may have—!"

Demonic energy saturated the air without warning.

Alicia grunted, black lightning striking her flank. She twisted and deflected the next deadly bolt with her scythe, the jagged hole in her robe fluttering around the wound the attack had inflicted.

Mae's heart pounded in her throat as her gaze found the demon standing on a ridge high up to their right. Hellreaver growled and transformed.

Barquiel glared at them. The broadsword in his hand was different from the one she had last seen him wield, its serrated blades resembling Hellreaver's teeth. Black lightning crackled on the weapon and sparked inside the dark clouds swirling above his head.

Mae clenched her jaw. "I'd hoped he could only do that on Earth."

Brimstone shifted into his nine-tailed demon form, *Contain* enlarging to accommodate him. *"It is a power that transcends dimensions, my witch."*

"Brimstone is right." Azazel frowned at Barquiel. "It has been a long time, my friend."

"Friend?!" Barquiel spat. "Don't make me laugh! You stole the woman I loved from under my nose!" His pupils flared crimson with loathing. "You are nothing but a traitor!"

Fury hardened Mae's stomach.

Azazel's face darkened. "She was never yours to claim."

Mae blinked at the formidable aura of demonic energy and magic that detonated around her father and shook the gully. A rift opened beside Azazel. The demon extracted a dark spear crackling with crimson magic from within it.

"Ran Soyun and I trusted you, Barquiel," Azazel said in a hard voice. He spun the spear slickly in his hands before adopting a battle stance Mae was certain he had taken thousands of times before. "We trusted that you would watch our backs when Davor first made his intentions clear. But you betrayed us." His eyes flashed with anger as he glanced at her. "And you hurt our daughters." He snapped his wings and rose, his voice dropping to a low growl. "I hope you're ready for the ass-kicking coming your way, old friend!"

Barquiel dove from the bluff on an enraged snarl.

The sound their weapons made when they clashed arms had Mae's ears ringing and the others flinching. She stared wide-eyed at the near invisible battle taking place above them, the echoes of the clash reverberating loudly against the cliffs.

It was only thanks to her powers that she could make out the two demons' figures where they blurred in midair, sword and spear sparking as metal met metal.

They're so fast!

Alicia regrouped with them. "Come, let's get to that cave while your father has him distracted!"

They headed swiftly through the sulfurous clouds toward the cliff, Barquiel roaring angrily as Azazel blocked his path again and again.

Dark shapes loomed out of the shadows when they dropped to the ground some hundred feet from the bluff. Brimstone's lips curled back on an unholy sound. Hellreaver snapped his teeth, his blades thick with crimson and black static.

Mae ended *Contain* and narrowed her eyes at the ghouls and devils standing in their path. She called forth *Devour*, the spheres hissing and rotating furiously as they formed above her palms, the crimson light they emitted reflecting in the monsters' pupils.

White magic brightened Nikolai and Alastair's eyes. Cortes unleashed his sword and whip, Popo's wings blazing with the golden light of their Arcane Magic. Tarang growled as Vlad manifested a thick aura of incubus energy from their cores.

Alicia flinched. Her head snapped up, her orbits blooming scarlet. She stared blindly at the distant ceiling.

Fresh tension knotted Mae's shoulders at her glazed expression. "What's wrong?"

The Reaper queen was silent for a moment.

"My Reapers tell me there is a sudden harvest of souls happening on Earth," she mumbled.

She shuddered and blinked, awareness returning to her face. The look she gave Mae curdled her blood.

"Vedran is in New York," Alicia said with a haunted expression. "He has Davor Lazar's soul."

CHAPTER THIRTY-ONE

Dread formed a cold pit in the bottom of Nikolai's stomach.

"Vedran is in New York?!" Mae said hoarsely.

Brimstone lowered his head on an angry sound, drool dripping thickly from his exposed fangs. Hellreaver hummed furiously where he hovered in midair.

"He has already slaughtered thousands of people." The Reaper queen's voice shook with rage, her knuckles white where she gripped her scythe. Her expression grew conflicted as she studied Mae. "I know this is the last thing you want to hear right now, but you must return to Earth."

Mae's eyes widened incredulously. Her gaze swung toward the invisible opening to Ran Soyun's prison.

"But I—I can't leave now! I *have* to see this through!"

Vlad touched her shoulder. "Alicia is right, Mae." A muscle jumped in the incubus's jawline. "Only you can save New York from Vedran."

Cortes bobbed his head in agreement, his face tight with dread.

Azazel landed a short distance away. The shield he raised around them impeded Barquiel as the demon tried to attack. He turned his back on the crimson barrier and joined them, his brow furrowed.

"What's wrong?"

Alicia updated him on what her Reapers had told her.

Azazel cursed. He scowled at the ground for a moment before meeting Mae's harrowed stare.

"Alicia is right, Mae. You should return to New York." The demon cut his eyes to Vlad and Cortes. "Take them with you. Nikolai will help us free Ran Soyun."

Mae turned haggard. Tears filled her eyes. Hellreaver whined and pressed against her side.

"Na Ri." She swallowed convulsively and clutched her belly, her voice trembling. "Na Ri needs to see her mother!"

Azazel's expression softened. "And she will. You both will. I promise you this on my life."

Mae flinched. "Don't say that! I refuse to have you die on us!"

"Mae," Azazel murmured, chagrined.

Nikolai's pulse thumped heavily. He took a shaky breath. He knew he was the only one who could convince her to go.

"You need to leave, Mae."

She recoiled, shock and hurt flaring on her face.

He closed the distance to her, grasped her cheeks,

and took her mouth in a kiss full of love, despair, and a searing promise. Mae froze before clinging to him, her fingers digging into his back like she never wanted to let go.

Nikolai ended the kiss and pressed their feverish foreheads together.

"Azazel, Alicia, and I will save Ran Soyun. And you *will* see her." He smiled tremulously. "Trust me."

Mae closed her eyes and shuddered, her shoulders slumping. She bit her lip and nodded.

Nikolai looked past her to Vlad. "Watch her back."

The incubus arched an eyebrow. "You don't need to ask me twice." He hesitated before coming over and patting Nikolai's shoulder awkwardly. "Don't die."

"Give him a kiss," Popo suggested salaciously. "Go on, you know you—"

Cortes muffled the parrot under Vlad and Nikolai's glares.

Azazel sighed and hugged Mae to his chest. "Look after yourself, my kind, wonderful daughters."

Loud banging reached them. Barquiel raged as he slammed his demonic sword repeatedly on the barrier, trying to smash it apart.

Azazel narrowed his eyes at his nemesis before giving Mae a final, solemn look. "Remember what I taught you."

He pressed a kiss to her brow.

Mae clenched her jaw and nodded. Her gaze lingered on Nikolai while Cortes prepared the spell that would take them to New York.

"See you soon," she whispered.

The sense of loss Nikolai experienced when *Distort* magicked her away made his throat thicken. Alastair crooned comfortingly and nudged his cheek with a wing. He touched the crow.

"I know. We'll see them again."

A sound drew his gaze to the barrier. Barquiel was almost through.

Determination knotted Nikolai's shoulders. Heat flowed through his belly and filled his veins as he invoked a spell that would augment Azazel's shield, Alastair strengthening his magic with an angry squawk.

"*Shield!*"

The wall that blossomed into view crackled with a light that blinded the ghouls and devils crowded at the base of the bluff and caused them to fall back to a safe distance.

Azazel's eyes widened. He shot a dazed glance at Nikolai.

"You managed to fuse white magic with Moon Magic?!"

"Yes."

"That won't hold Barquiel off for long," Alicia said bitterly. "He knows how to overcome white magic. That's how he's succeeded in keeping Ran Soyun down here for thousands of years."

Nikolai's voice hardened. "That's not the only trick I've got up my sleeve."

❄

Dampness soaked into Mae's skin and hair when they emerged under an ominous sky outside the temporary headquarters of the New York coven.

Vlad swore. "What the hell?!"

Mae's scalp prickled. She stared at the black clouds roiling above them. A light rain was falling across the city. It did nothing to mask the stench of magic and ozone imbuing the air, nor the suffocating pall of terror hanging over the deathly silent metropolis.

"What on Earth happened while we were away?" Cortes said numbly. "We were only gone for a couple of days!"

Na Ri's anger flooded Mae's insides. *I can feel Davor's soul. He's close!*

Mae dug her nails into her palms. "Vedran brought death to our doorstep."

Her gaze found the shimmering dome rising above Central Park. She detected Bryony and Abraham's cores and those of their allies inside the barrier.

They were fighting hordes of monsters.

Surprise jolted Mae when she clocked Gloria Espenoza's core and the Illusion Sorcery she was wielding against the enemy.

More monsters approached across the sky from the east and south.

She narrowed her eyes. "Let's go!"

The magic vibrating off Brimstone's tails warmed her cold body as they headed across the road, just as Hellreaver's newly awakened core filled her with a power that made her blood sing.

She just hoped it would be enough to fight Vedran.

"Hell."

"*On it, my witch.*"

Her bond with the weapon grew so hot Mae was surprised it didn't scald her insides. A thick, crimson aura laced with black magic whooshed into life around Hellreaver. He moved, his jagged blades slicing a doorway into the shield with an effortlessness that made Vlad and Cortes pause.

Mae closed the opening behind them and extended her magic to form a secondary shield outside the original barrier. A savage smile stretched her mouth when she felt dozens of monsters bounce off it, their attempt to enter the western boundary of the park thwarted.

They moved swiftly toward the sounds of a battle.

Vlad and Cortes cursed at the sight that met them when they emerged from under the trees. Mae clenched her jaw.

There were thousands of people inside the park. Non magic users clueless about the supernatural war that had been fought in their city for hundreds of years. Even now, their expressions were glazed and they appeared oblivious to the bloodied conflict taking place around them as the New York coven and the allies who had come to aid the city maintained a thin line of defense against the hellish creatures trying to claim their lives.

Mae frowned. She tasted a familiar magic around the subdued citizens.

"I can sense Anya's Illusion Sorcery," she told Vlad

and Cortes. "She must have used her powers to calm them so they would not panic."

And I suspect to help evacuation efforts.

Her gaze swiveled to where the Empire State Building once stood. Gold glinted high up in the sky.

Tension tightened Cortes's jaw. "Is that where Anya is?!"

Mae nodded. "She's safe. Violet, Miles, and Jared are with her." She cracked her neck and knuckles and scanned the battleground with a calculated stare. "How about we wrap things up here?"

Arcane Magic bloomed around Cortes and Popo. "I'd thought you'd never ask."

"Let's go kill some monsters, Tarang," Vlad said in a hard voice.

The tiger growled. The incubus energy that flowed from them had Mae and Cortes staring.

"What?"

"I think you're gonna charm the pants off those ghouls," Cortes told the incubus bluntly.

"Yeah," Mae muttered.

Vlad curled a lip. "Like I want to see that shit."

Tarang huffed.

The ground shook up ahead.

Spheres of power blossomed around their fists at the sight of the horde of hellish creatures charging toward them.

CHAPTER THIRTY-TWO

A BLAZE IGNITED MAE'S STOMACH, STARTLING HER.

Her gaze jerked to Brimstone.

The demon fox's chest swelled a second before he opened his jaws and released *Wrath*. The orb flashed through the air with a high-pitched whine, blasted most of the incoming enemy to smithereens, and took a chunk out of an iconic bridge in the distance.

Mae, Vlad, and Cortes gave Brimstone a pointed look as debris rained down into the lake below.

"That was an acceptable loss under the circumstances," the fox said, unabashed.

Hellreaver zoomed after the remaining creatures with an evil cackle.

Mae's hair fluttered around her shoulders as magic unfurled from her cores and roared through her bloodstream. She levitated to some hundred feet above the ground.

From that height, she had a better impression of

where her allies, and the foes they were dealing with, were located. She unleashed her first spells.

"*Soul Guard! Augment!*"

Startled cries rose from the sorcerers and witches clashing with Vedran's monstrous army as her magic reinforced the *Soul Shield* she had placed inside them. A few spotted her and pointed, excitement lighting up their faces.

Mae was about to focus her magic into her next spells when movement below drew her gaze and made her pause.

Hellreaver tore seamlessly through entire packs of beasts, his blades carving his targets in half before they even sensed his presence.

Brimstone invoked *Wrath* again and again as he decimated the fast-moving devils trying to attack him, the power of the spell undiminished even though he unleashed it repeatedly.

Arcane Magic burned dozens of ghouls as Cortes wielded his blade and whip with deadly efficiency, his eyes and those of his familiar blazing with incandescent brightness.

But it was the indomitable power Vlad demonstrated that made Mae's pulse quicken. The incubus brought entire troops of hideous monsters to their knees with his sheer demonic will before finishing them off with his blades and the energy bombs Ilmon had taught him to use, Tarang delivering the death blow to many with his claws and fangs.

Mae swallowed. *Damn. We would never have gotten this strong had we not gone to Hell.*

I don't know about that, my witch. Brimstone stopped and gazed at her, his crimson eyes bright with affection even across the distance. *You could even give Azazel a run for his money right now.*

Mae blinked. *Really?!*

Really, Brimstone huffed. *Now, how about you show these fools the power of the Witch Queen?*

Mae smiled faintly. She took a shallow breath and guided the magic bubbling inside her veins into her next spells. The power she unleashed detonated across the park with a force that made her allies cry out in surprise and the monsters attacking them scream.

"Negate! Purge! Decimate!"

The first two spells robbed the ghouls and devils of the demonic energy powering their bodies and the black magic controlling their minds. *Decimate* crackled violently above her head as it sent out deadly currents next, the black and crimson arcs snaking through the air to reduce the enemy to ash. It took a moment for her to make out those still standing in the aftermath of her devastating attack.

Mae lowered her brows.

The only creatures who'd resisted her spells were the abominations Vedran had put together from the dead bodies of the humans, fiends, and hellbeasts he had killed.

Her frown deepened when she detected the dark cores inside them. The soul orbs throbbed with malevolence, powering the creatures with a continuous supply of black magic faster than *Purge* could consume it.

Looks like he put those things inside them to counter my magic.

"Shame you didn't know about this spell, asshole," she muttered darkly.

Magic whipped her clothes and hair into a frenzy as she voiced the first incantation Azazel had taught her and Na Ri.

"DECAY!"

The air thickened, the sharp rise in pressure driving many to clutch their heads and drop to their knees.

Mae's heart thudded wildly against her ribs at the crimson light that bloomed into life around her and rolled across the landscape. Laced with black and white magic, the tide uprooted bushes, bowed trees, and made water surge violently across the lakes and ponds in the park.

The chimeras screeched, the spell destroying their cores and the vile stitches keeping their bodies together. *Decay* consumed their dead flesh until all that was left were wispy, black clouds that faded into nothingness.

The end came so suddenly that even Mae blinked. A deafening silence fell across Central Park in the wake of the enemy's downfall. Her chest shuddered, not so much because she was out of breath as because the magic she had just wielded defied the laws of this world.

Mae's pulse was still racing when she floated to the ground. Vlad and Cortes joined her.

The incubus's eyes glittered.

"That was pretty incredible," he said quietly.

"Yeah, remind me never to piss you off," Cortes grunted.

Mae smiled faintly. "You guys weren't so bad yourselves."

"Mae!" someone shouted.

They turned.

Abraham was running across the park, Bryony following in Rambrog's arms. Mae's eyes widened at the sight of the sorcerer behind them.

"Oscar!" Vlad hissed.

His knuckles blanched on his demonic blades.

Mae couldn't take her eyes off the black magic sorcerer. He looked…different. She startled when she realized what it was about him that had changed.

Oh, Na Ri murmured. *His core.*

Mae stared dazedly at the source of Oscar's power before exchanging a shocked look with Brimstone.

The fox nodded. *"It seems he no longer carries the Sorcerer King's corruption inside his body, just like Drabek."*

Vlad furrowed his brow.

"What do you mean?" Cortes asked uneasily.

Abraham arrived before Mae could reply. "Where have you been?!"

"Hmm, in Hell?" Mae grimaced and scratched her cheek. "You were there when we left."

The aide scowled.

Her stomach knotted queasily. "My family?"

"They're safe. Noah took them to a haven in Brooklyn. Nadia and Sergio are guarding it with their covens."

Relief had Mae blowing out a heavy breath.

Cortes's gaze swung between Bryony and Rambrog. "He your new ride?"

The giant lumbered to a stop next to them. The High Priestess sniffed while Rambrog carefully put her down.

"He insisted on carrying me. Apparently, some fox told him to be my bodyguard." She squinted at Brimstone. "Wait. Are you bigger?"

"He definitely is," Abraham said leadenly, head tilting to take in the demon fox's new form.

Mae chewed her lip. It was only now she was realizing her familiar had kept the size he'd manifested in Hell, this despite the fact that they'd returned to Earth.

"*It's because my witch is stronger now,*" Brimstone huffed. He cocked his head toward the open park. "*That one's second awakening had something to do with it too.*"

Hellreaver reappeared on cue, serrated blades coated with blood.

"*Man, that was fun!*" he enthused.

Abraham and Bryony's eyes bulged. Even Rambrog looked uneasy at the sight of the sentient weapon.

"He can talk now?" the New York coven High Priestess said warily.

"You'll get used to it." Mae's gaze locked on the man watching them silently from a distance. "Why are you here, Oscar?" She scanned his wounds with a neutral expression. "And why does it look like you've been fighting on our side?"

Oscar's face tightened with resolve as he met her

stare. "The spell Nikolai cast on me back at that castle broke the hold my father had on me."

Mae swallowed. *So, we were right!*

She felt happy for Nikolai then. Even though he'd never said anything out loud, she knew he'd been thinking about Oscar ever since they'd seen what *Subjugate* had done to Drabek.

Vlad took a threatening step forward.

"So what?! Are you saying we should forgive you for all the horrible crimes you've committed over the years? That we should feel *sympathy* for you?!" The incubus's pupils burned with a crimson radiance that sought to scorch the man he glared at. "Don't make me laugh!"

Cortes similarly glowered at Oscar. The Dark Council had assisted Raya in killing his first familiar and removing him from his destined role as the next High Priest of the Medellin coven.

Oscar sighed. "No. That's not what I'm saying at all. I will never be able to make amends for all the evil acts I've perpetrated and the people whose lives I've taken. I will never—" His voice broke, his shoulders slumping. He took a shuddering breath before meeting their gazes unflinchingly. "I will never receive my brother's forgiveness for what I did to him and our kin. But I do regret everything I have ever done to you and yours. That's why I left my father's side at the earliest opportunity. So I could bring you this."

He removed something from his pocket, walked over, and placed it in Mae's hands. Her breath caught at the sight of the *Book of Light*.

A shudder shook Hellreaver. He coughed and spat out the skeleton key she'd given him for safekeeping.

Mae snatched the artifact out of the air. Her pulse spiked.

It was vibrating.

The *Book of Light* trembled in her other hand, matching the key's resonance. It could only mean one thing.

We need to find it, Mae! Na Ri urged.

Blood thrummed in Mae's veins.

She met Oscar's steady gaze. "Where's the *Book of Shadows?*"

CHAPTER THIRTY-THREE

Alicia's scythe sliced a group of ghouls neatly in two. Nikolai blasted the devils dropping down on him with *Hell Flare*. The spell obliterated the monsters and scorched the air inside the tunnel, painting its walls with a bright glow.

The light sparked off Azazel's spear where he clashed with Barquiel farther down the passage, his expression focused and his movements confident as he delayed his archenemy's advance.

With Barquiel's army nowhere near as large as they'd expected it to be, they were more than halfway to the location where the demon had hidden Ran Soyun's soul and her mortal remains.

Nikolai could see Barquiel's desperation growing with every step they made toward their final destination.

We need to hurry!

Alastair crouched on his shoulder, the crow's power

amplifying his own as he cast spell after blinding spell, obliterating the enemy even faster than the Reaper queen's blade. White magic was the one weapon few in Hell could overcome and the reason why Ran Soyun had been so powerful down here.

Soon, the last ghouls and devils fell, clearing the path ahead.

Alicia flew back to where Azazel fought Barquiel. "Go, Zaz!"

Crimson brightened the Reaper queen's orbits. She moved in front of the demon and slammed her scythe on the ground. Her blade expanded in a flash of light, forming a glinting, metal lattice that blocked the passage with a thin wall sharp enough to cut the air. Darkness swarmed Alicia as her form grew, her cloak billowing and casting long shadows all around them.

"I will keep this bastard here," she growled. "Take Nikolai and free Ran Soyun!"

An unholy sound left Barquiel. He slammed his broadsword into Alicia's barrier.

It held.

Azazel whirled around, shot toward Nikolai, and grabbed his wrist. Nikolai's stomach lurched as his feet left the ground.

The demon flew rapidly, his wings skimming the walls of the tunnel whenever he swerved inside one of its many branches, his face brightening with every bifurcation and chasm they crossed.

They could both feel Ran Soyun's magic growing ahead of them.

A faint light finally glimmered in the distance.

Azazel's breath caught. "Ran!"

The demon accelerated, his speed bringing tears to Nikolai's eyes and causing Alastair to crouch even lower where he sank his claws in his shoulder.

They rounded the corner of the widening passage and came upon the cave holding the first Witch Queen's prison.

Azazel landed lightly on the ground and folded his wings. He let go of Nikolai, his eyes glinting with unshed tears as he marched toward the dome of demonic energy trapping the brilliance of his wife's incredible magic.

Ran Soyun's eyes rounded where she floated above her sarcophagus. "Az?!"

A wretched sound left Azazel. His knees buckled. He fell before Ran Soyun and bowed his head, tears rolling down his face and darkening the floor where they landed.

"I'm sorry. I'm sorry it's taken me so long to get here, my love!"

Ran Soyun's chin trembled as she drifted down to where her husband crouched. "Don't, Az. It wasn't your fault."

They reached for one another, only to flinch when Barquiel's powers sparked against their fingers. Azazel scowled and cast *Negate*. It barely did anything to the barrier.

The demon turned to Nikolai, desperation darkening his crimson gaze. "Your magic! It might work on—!"

"It won't," Ran Soyun interrupted miserably. "I've already used all the spells I've mastered."

Nikolai's pulse quickened. "Then, it's time to try something else."

Azazel and Ran Soyun gave him a confused look.

The sound of distant fighting made them stiffen.

Barquiel was drawing closer.

Nikolai's heart thundered in his chest. He closed the distance to the dome and crouched before Barquiel's barrier. The suspicion that had been growing inside him ever since Vozgan flew over the lake that had brought them here solidified into a shocking certainty when he put his hands on the ground. He squeezed his eyes shut, relief lightening his chest.

Yes! I was right!

"Nikolai?" Azazel said.

He opened his eyes and gave the puzzled demon and first Witch Queen a hard smile. "Did you know Hell has a nexus?"

Azazel and Ran Soyun startled.

"What?!" Ran Soyun mumbled.

"I believe it's under the lake we had to cross to get here," Nikolai told a stunned Azazel. "It was resonating with Ran Soyun's magic, which is why I picked up on it. The only reason I'm sure of it now is that there's a ley line under this mountain and it connects to that nexus." His pulse raced as his gaze shifted to Ran Soyun. "I'm sorry I wasn't in a fit state to make that out the first time I came here. I think the reason you can't sense it is because you've been trapped inside that barrier for so long." He paused. "Azazel had never been to this part of Hell before, so I gather neither had you."

Ran Soyun hesitated before nodding. "You're right. When my soul was roused after the war, I was already here." She faltered. "I retain the faintest connection to the nexuses on Earth, which is how I've been able to communicate with Mae. I never imagined Hell would have one too."

Alicia's curses echoed dimly in the corridor outside the cave. Azazel rose, spear in hand and face set in grim lines.

"Do what you need to do," he told Nikolai harshly. "I will make sure Barquiel doesn't stop you!"

Nikolai's stomach tightened. "You ready, Al?"

Alastair clicked his beak.

Nikolai took a deep breath before reaching for the bright cord dancing far beneath the ground. He knew he was risking his and Alastair's cores by tapping into what was effectively a demonic ley line. But it wasn't as if there was an alternative option. He frowned.

Besides, we harbor a power that can hopefully protect us from harm.

He unleashed an aura of Hellfire Magic around them before grasping the ley line and following it to Hell's nexus. Fire filled his blood as he drew upon the incandescent power within it.

It burned his veins. Scorched his mind. Blinded his vision.

A tortured grunt left Nikolai's throat as his body struggled to keep up with the dazzling blaze. Alastair trembled and swayed on his shoulder.

Ran Soyun's voice reached him dimly through the ringing in his ears. "*Stop!* It's going to kill you!"

Sweat poured down Nikolai's face. He clenched his jaw.

"It won't," he ground out. "I won't let it!" He bared his teeth. "Besides, I made a promise to your daughter. I told her I would see her again. And I meant it, with every breath I have in me and every inch of my heart!"

Ran Soyun's eyes flared.

The spell he had been working on ever since he returned to New York grew in power, fiery runes searing his consciousness. It left his lips on a roar that rose from his and Alastair's very souls.

"*HELL STORM!*"

Flames exploded on Barquiel's barrier, their power and potency making the air inside the cave tremble and robbing Nikolai of breath. The fire grew, an invincible tempest that swarmed the demon's defensive wall and consumed it in a violent flash.

Azazel gasped behind Nikolai.

The brightness sparking the air around Ran Soyun expanded to fill the entire cave as she was finally freed from her prison. The first Witch Queen shuddered.

Nikolai's heart swelled. Her white magic washed over and through him, replenishing his and Alastair's cores.

"Thank you, child." Ran Soyun floated down to him and caressed his cheek. Though he could not perceive her ghostly touch, he felt her magic where she stroked his skin. "Thank you for believing in yourself and for saving me." She hugged him and kissed his brow before moving past him to embrace the demon who had waited thousands of years to take her in his arms. "Az."

"Ran!" Azazel sobbed.

Alicia backed into the cave behind the demon, her scythe sparking as she strained valiantly against Barquiel's sword. Her robe was in tatters and her bones bore scratches where the demon's blade had made contact.

Barquiel faltered at the sight of the ethereal figure in his rival's arms. Horror widened his eyes. His face crumpled.

"*Nooooo!*"

Ran Soyun's eyes glittered with a mixture of emotions as she observed the demon who had helped the first Sorcerer King destroy the kingdom she had built with her husband. The demon who had killed her and her daughter. Her face hardened. Magic brightened her pupils.

"*Reverse.*"

Barquiel grunted and bent over. His nails scored his stomach, like he was trying to rid himself of a fire no one could see. His legs buckled.

"My daughters created that spell to defeat you," Ran Soyun said calmly as the demon fell to his knees with a tortured groan. "You should not have angered them, Barquiel. Because they are a greater Witch Queen than I could ever be." She looked lovingly at Azazel. "In that sense, they are truly their father's daughters."

Azazel smiled tremulously.

The scream of rage and pain that left Barquiel made Nikolai flinch.

"*Curse you!* You belong to *me!*" Crimson boiled in his pupils, jealousy and rage distorting his features in a hideous mask. "I will make you mine if it's the last thing I do, Ran Soyun! I swear upon my dark soul!"

The demon tore open a portal with his bare hands and escaped inside it. Alicia's scythe missed his back by a hairbreadth as it closed. She cursed, frustration tightening her face.

Ran Soyun turned to Azazel and Nikolai. "He will go after Davor's soul and Mae's core. You must hurry and stop him!"

Dread knotted Nikolai's stomach.

Azazel stared at his wife, his expression torn. "What of you?"

Ran Soyun indicated the sarcophagus on the plinth. "I cannot leave my remains unguarded here. Alicia can help me take them to a safe place. Besides, I need to free the soul of my familiar. I can sense where he is, now that I am outside Barquiel's barrier."

Nikolai blinked. *Her familiar?!*

"We will follow you afterward, I promise." She kissed Azazel's cheek. "Hurry, my love!"

"But—!" Azazel protested.

Ran Soyun pressed a spectral finger to his lips. "Hush. You know I'm right." She looked at Nikolai and smiled faintly. "Besides, now that I know there's a ley line in Hell, I'll be practically invincible."

Azazel's expression turned rueful. "It's incredible

how much of your stubbornness our daughters have inherited."

Nikolai made a face. "He's right."

"Yeah," Alicia muttered.

Ran Soyun wrinkled her nose.

Her expression turned serious. "There is something I must tell you before you leave."

CHAPTER THIRTY-FOUR

"ARE YOU SURE THIS IS A GOOD IDEA?" BRYONY ASKED Mae with a pinched expression.

"Not really, but I can't see what other choice we have."

The wind blowing in from Upper Bay made her hair dance around her face as it washed over the west end of the pedestrian promenade on the Brooklyn Bridge.

"Wait for my signal," Mae told Bryony and Abraham.

She headed out onto the walkway toward the first stone tower with Brimstone and Hellreaver. Cortes, Vlad, and Oscar followed in her steps.

A chill danced down Mae's spine when they entered the shadows of the Neo-Gothic construction, the cables above them gleaming with a sinister light under the cloud-laden sky.

Hellreaver hovered closer to her. *"This is creepy."*

Even Brimstone looked uneasy as he scanned the area.

They emerged from under the tower and walked another two hundred feet. Mae stopped and brought forth a single crimson sphere. She cast it into the sky.

Magic bloomed around the bridge at the sight of her sign, the New York coven and their allies raising a massive barrier from the east and west banks of the river. The shield made the water sizzle as it closed around the structure on four sides.

Mae reinforced it with her own *Shield* and prayed it would be enough to prevent the city's destruction. Tension knotted her shoulders.

She'd wanted to take this war out over the waters of Upper Bay, or even all the way out across the Atlantic. But she didn't do so for one reason and one reason alone.

She and Na Ri could not win this fight on their own.

"Remember the plan," Mae told the men beside her. "This is going to go down fast, so keep your wits about you. We have two goals. Separate Vedran from the *Book of Shadows*. And buy me time to destroy that artifact."

The two sorcerers and the incubus exchanged a guarded glance.

"First things first." Mae walked over to Oscar and pressed a hand to his stomach.

He stiffened, his eyes rounding. "What are you—?!"

Heat surged through Mae. "*Purge.*"

Her magic flowed through Oscar, reversing the

Subjugate spell that had weakened him. Vlad cursed. Cortes scowled.

Color slowly returned to Oscar's face, his core freed from the shackles that had bound it. He gave Mae a dazed look.

"Why?! You didn't have to—!"

"Mae!" Vlad said angrily.

"I did," Mae said firmly. She glanced at Vlad. "He won't betray us. And I can't have Drabek's sorcerer dying on me. Not after everything I've done to keep her alive."

Oscar's eyes glowed with gratitude.

"Besides, Nikolai wants to see his brother," Mae added quietly. "And that is one wish I will do my utmost to grant." She fished inside her jacket and passed Oscar a vial. "I'm sorry we didn't have time to get a healer to treat your wounds. Mrs. Son-Ha gave me this potion. She said it would help."

Oscar stared. "Who's Mrs. Son-Ha?"

"A Shaman."

Oscar hesitated before uncorking the bottle and taking a careful sniff. He grimaced. "You sure this is a healing potion? It smells like old socks."

"Just drink the damn potion, Oscar," Mae snapped.

He swallowed the contents of the bottle and managed to only gag once.

Mae waited until his wounds had mostly healed before studying the sky above the city.

Vedran's *Void* was no longer visible, the Sorcerer King having gone to ground the moment she'd arrived in New York. Mae wanted to believe it was because he was scared, but she knew better. She frowned.

He's probably regrouping to figure out his next move, now that we've annihilated over half his army and are close to ridding the city of the rest.

Na Ri spoke. *Still, Vedran is an army all on his own with Davor's soul inside him.*

Mae pursed her lips. Her gaze shifted to Oscar. "You ready?"

Oscar nodded. He took a deep breath and steeled himself when she took up position in front of him.

Power seared her cores and danced through her bond with Brimstone and Hellreaver. An aura of crimson, black, and white blanketed the three of them, the static sparking off the demon fox's fur and the weapon's blades.

Mae touched Oscar's stomach and conjured *Reveal*.

Her breath stuttered. The spell instantly linked him to Vedran's location. Images flashed before her vision. Her head snapped up.

There you are!

Fire filled her veins. She raised a hand to the sky over Upper Bay.

"*DECAY!*"

The sound of the air shearing above Governors Island put her teeth on edge. *Void* appeared, a black stain against the firmament.

The next spell left Mae's lips on a growl.

"*ICE FORTRESS!*"

A glittering white cage bloomed around *Void*.

"Rambrog, *now!*"

The bubble of magic hiding the giant materialized where she'd guided it straight above Vedran's prison. A roar left Rambrog as he smashed his fists down on *Ice Fortress* and sent it hurtling toward the bridge.

It took but seconds for the prison of ice to crash onto the promenade. Debris filled the air, an explosion of pale crystals amidst a thick, white mist.

Vedran emerged from it like a dark god.

Black magic filled the Sorcerer King's eyes from edge to edge, the corruption bubbling around him so foul it brought bile to the back of Mae's throat. He arrowed straight toward her, the inky sword made of his familiar's soul aimed at her heart, his face a mask of sheer, evil determination.

Mae scowled. *"PURGE!"*

The spell slammed into Vedran and slowed him a fraction.

A scarlet storm erupted around Brimstone. He stepped forward, his tails vibrating with a force that made the bridge tremble. He chomped down on the Sorcerer King's shoulder with a snarl and cast him violently aside.

Vedran smashed into one of the trusses supporting the eastbound roadway. Metal caved. He grunted and sagged, blood spraying from his lips.

Cortes's whip wrapped around the Sorcerer King's right wrist, dispersing some of his black magic and immobilizing his sword.

A barrage of incubus spell bombs crashed into Vedran next. The deck shuddered under the explosions, the cables above them whining as they moved under the dark sky.

"*ROT!*" Oscar barked before the dust cleared.

The black magic around Vedran wavered even more. The cloak he wore fluttered open, revealing their target.

Mae's pulse spiked. "Hell!"

Hellreaver disappeared in a burst of black and crimson. He slipped underneath Vedran's clothes, snatched the *Book of Shadows*, and zoomed back toward her.

A sense of wrongness prickled her scalp.

Mae! Na Ri warned.

Mae's mouth went dry. Magic was racing across Vedran's flesh, a map of dark lines that turned his skin to sinister parchment. The smile he gave her made her stomach twist. His gaze shifted. So did hers.

Her eyes widened. *No!*

"*Brim!*" Mae screamed. Fear brought forth the only incantations she could think of to protect her familiar. "*SHIELD! REVERSE!*"

The Sorcerer King's attack smashed through her spells like they were made of air.

Rambrog blocked Vedran's spell bomb before it could strike the demon fox where he'd moved to cover Hellreaver's retreat. The giant grunted, toes scorching deep grooves into the asphalt as he skidded backward some hundred feet. He clutched his flank and fell to his knee with a groan, blood pooling around his fingers.

Relief rendered Mae weak. Though the attack had

taken a chunk of flesh out of Rambrog, it had spared the giant's life.

I'm glad I reinforced his body with magic!

She only had a moment's warning before her instincts told her everything was about to go very wrong.

No, Na Ri mumbled.

Mae's head snapped around. Her stomach dropped.

CHAPTER THIRTY-FIVE

Cortes and Vlad were leaping toward the Sorcerer King, Arcane Magic and incubus energy brightening their eyes and those of their familiars.

Time slowed.

Oscar's head shifted like he was moving in treacle, horror draining his face of color as he met Mae's gaze. He too had registered the spine-chilling magic thickening the air.

Power detonated around them, the destructive incantations they wished to cast at the Sorcerer King forming on their lips.

The spell that froze them and everything inside the barrier manifested with a suddenness that robbed Mae of breath.

This is—this is a wordless incantation! Na Ri gasped.

Mae swallowed, heart thundering and limbs rooted where she stood. She couldn't move. Couldn't speak.

Movement captured her gaze.

Vedran straightened from where he'd crouched

next to the metal truss he'd indented with his back. He wiped the blood from his lips, patted down his clothes, and ran his fingers through his hair. Amusement brightened his mad gaze.

Mae shuddered. She knew then that they had been fools to believe they could take on both Vedran and Davor Lazar at the same time.

"Ah." A gleeful smirk stretched Vedran's mouth, etching satisfaction across his face. "That little subterfuge was worth it just to see your expressions." Darkness burned his pupils when he locked eyes with Mae. "Did you really think you could take me on, little girl?" His lips twisted, his smile turning mocking. "Just the five of you?!"

He indicated the motionless figures around her with a dismissive wave of his hand.

Despair thickened Mae's throat. *Shit. He was taking us for a ride all along!*

Na Ri's fury scorched her insides. *Don't give up, Mae.*

She is right, my witch, Brimstone growled.

That guy hasn't seen what we can do yet! Hellraiser snarled.

Mae's shoulders knotted.

Vedran was approaching Cortes. He gazed at the sorcerer where he floated, frozen in midair, jaw clenched and face tight with fury. Fear chilled her to the bone at the look in the Sorcerer King's eyes.

She could tell there was not a single drop of humanity left in him.

Cortes's gasp made her stomach clench.

Vedran had pressed the tip of a finger to his chest.

"The name of the spell that currently has you in its grip, the spell that will bring about your demise, is *Vortex*," the Sorcerer King told Mae casually. "No one who has borne witness to it has lived past its incantation to tell the tale."

Horror rounded Mae's eyes. Black magic was spreading across Cortes's skin, turning it into a macabre map. The dark lines sliced into his flesh and stained his shirt with blood. Popo trembled on his shoulder, his feathers growing dull as Vedran's vile power invaded his and his sorcerer's cores, the golden light in his pupils quivering brightly before dying out. They fell unconscious, chests barely moving with their breaths.

Tears distorted Mae's vision. *No. This isn't happening!*

Vedran moved to Vlad.

Blood pounded loudly in Mae's ears. The Sorcerer King touched the incubus. Tendons corded in Vlad's neck as black magic seared his flesh. His face flushed a bright red.

The scream lodged in his throat never left his lips.

Vlad ground his teeth, crimson lines blooming on his skin, his blood steaming where it dripped heavily and struck the asphalt. Brimstone roared silently inside Mae's mind when Tarang went limp beside the near senseless incubus.

Mae's breath shuddered out of her. Her next inhale brought with it a torrent of rage that seared her soul and obliterated all trace of fear.

She had to stop Vedran and Davor Lazar.

We cannot let them walk off this bridge alive. Her face hardened as she sought the strength of the ones who stood with her. *Together!*

The power of four roared through Mae, raising all the hairs on her body. Na Ri warmed her ice-cold flesh as she poured all her magic into their cores. Brimstone and Hellreaver directed their demonic energy into their bond.

Heat flowed sluggishly through Mae's veins.

Soul Guard! Augment!

She panted, the effort of manifesting the wordless spells rendering her so weak she would have fallen to her knees had her limbs not been immobilized by the Sorcerer King's dark magic. Mae clenched her jaw until she tasted blood and invoked the third and fourth incantations.

Assimilate! Absorb!

Vedran stilled. The black lines mapping Cortes and Vlad's faces vanished with a hiss of crimson. He scowled.

Mae knew he'd just realized she'd shielded the two men's souls and those of their familiars.

Vlad and Cortes's wounds started to heal. The incubus's eyelids fluttered slightly. He mumbled her name. Cortes groaned.

The Sorcerer King cut his eyes to Mae. "What have you done, little girl?!"

His pupils widened at the sight of the blood soaking her T-shirt.

My witch, Brimstone whimpered.

Hellreaver made a wretched sound.

It's okay. Mae ignored the fire scorching her flesh where she'd just assimilated dozens of cuts. *I'm okay!*

She glowered at Vedran, the dark power he had unleashed seeping into her body through her pores and mouth and nose as the rest of Cortes and Vlad's injuries were transferred to her. Her white magic purified the Sorcerer King's power of the corruption that tainted it before it entered her cores.

She felt her strength return.

Mae began consuming *Vortex* next, her wounds healing as magic flowed freely through her veins once more. Air started moving on the bridge.

Vedran took a threatening step toward her.

Oscar's fingers twitched. His lips trembled. *"Dis... perse."*

The Sorcerer King recoiled, eyes widening in disbelief as the spell accelerated *Vortex's* destruction. He whirled around with an enraged snarl and stormed over to Oscar, grabbing him by the throat and lifting him into the air. The sorcerer gasped.

Vedran's lips curled back on a hideous grimace. He squeezed.

The handful of seconds Oscar had bought Mae was all she needed to gather her magic so she could incant her next spell. Her lungs expanded as she took a deep breath.

"ABSORB!"

The barrier protecting the bridge wavered as she consumed it. The New York coven and their allies replenished it instantly.

Mae found she could move again. Brimstone

snarled and shook himself out. Hellreaver hummed, black and red static coming to life around him. Magic churned the air around them, their auras so powerful it created ripples in the river far below and caused the bridge cables to sway.

Mae lifted a hand.

"*SUBJUGATE!*" she and Na Ri roared.

Vedran grunted and almost doubled over, shock flaring across his face as he clutched his stomach.

They headed for the Sorcerer King.

ELATION LIGHTENED ROSE'S CHEST AS SHE TORE AT THE darkness enclosing her soul fragment. She had witnessed the moment Ran Soyun used her magic on the demon who had possessed her body and she knew her every movement must be filling him with agony.

A faint groan echoed through the void surrounding her.

Rose smiled savagely.

Ran Soyun's spell had granted her the advantage she needed, just as she'd promised it would. All Rose needed to do was hang on a little longer until Barquiel confronted Mae. Her heart swelled.

I'm coming, Mae! Wait for me!

BARQUIEL GROUND HIS TEETH AS HE BOUNCED INSIDE

the portal taking him to Earth, his movements all over the place.

Although the effect of Ran Soyun's magic had faded once he'd entered the rift, it had weakened him considerably in the seconds he had been in contact with it.

How could she? How could she leave me for that bastard?! His talons scored deep cuts into his palms as he recalled the sickening image of the woman he loved in his archenemy's arms. *I swear, I will kill Azazel with my own two hands and give Ran Soyun his bloodied, beating heart!*

Light appeared at the end of the portal.

A tint of corruption filled his nostrils.

Barquiel scowled. *Vedran!*

VEDRAN'S FINGERS LOOSENED AROUND HIS SON'S NECK AS *Subjugate* scorched his insides. Oscar scowled, grabbed Vedran's wrist, and tried to peel his fingers from his flesh, legs kicking out as he struggled to free himself.

Vedran cursed, nearly losing his grip on the sorcerer. He clenched his jaw and called forth the dark sword made of his familiar's soul. It appeared in his right hand, the blade solid despite the debilitating spell afflicting him.

The weapon wavered as he aimed it at Oscar's heart, Balkin roaring within it.

CHAPTER THIRTY-SIX

Heat surged through Mae's veins. She and Na Ri invoked the second spell Azazel had taught them.

"*Soul Unchain!*"

A sound of disbelief and agony left Vedran, his hold on Balkin shattering. The blade dissolved into a black mist before it could reach Oscar.

The power of Hell washed over the bridge and Mae's back, startling her. She turned and cursed at the sight of the demon emerging from a portal with a vengeful expression.

"*VEDRAN!*" Barquiel roared.

Mae scowled. "I really don't have time for this shit!"

She was about to call Hellreaver to her when a figure loomed behind the demon archduke and snatched him in a double-armed grip, trapping his wings and body. An outraged sound left Barquiel as Rambrog grunted and squeezed him.

"You foul giant! *How dare you?!*"

"Good job, Rambrog," Vlad called out.

Incubus energy rolled off him and Tarang as they closed in on Barquiel.

Cortes and Popo accompanied them, the parrot's eyes and wings blazing with the Arcane Magic dancing on the sorcerer's sword and whip.

Vlad looked at Mae. "We've got this."

She nodded and turned.

Surprise jolted her. The wisps of Balkin's soul had coalesced to form the specter of the black wolf. He landed lightly on the bridge, his ethereal shape fluttering at the edges.

Vedran blanched and retreated a couple of steps, his jaw sagging open at the sight of the ghostly apparition.

"Bal—*Balkin?!*"

Balkin scowled at the man who had chained him in death for hundreds of years.

"*Do not say my name, sorcerer.*"

The wolf walked past Vedran.

Mae's chest tightened when the noble wolf stopped and bowed his head.

"*Thank you for freeing me, Witch Queen,*" Balkin said calmly. His eyes gleamed as he met her stare. "*May we meet again, in another life.*"

The familiar's form faded, his soul finally heading to the place he had long been denied.

Vedran fell to his knees. "Ah."

Mae startled at the tears streaming down the Sorcerer King's face.

Fear brightened Oscar's pupils. He shook his head at her in warning and backed away from his father, like he knew what was coming next.

The air locked in Mae's throat. Rage was filling Vedran's eyes with a darkness that threatened to scorch the world.

The corruption that detonated around the Sorcerer King made the bridge quake and brought with it the stench of the wicked soul he'd stolen from the *Book of Shadows*.

He turned his livid gaze on Oscar, his expression inhuman. "Where do you think you're going?"

Oscar stumbled and fell on his ass with a choked sound. He backpedaled along the deck.

"I should have killed you when the thought first came to me, you ingrate!" Vedran hissed.

"Run, Oscar!" Mae shouted.

The sorcerer twisted around and scrambled to his feet.

Black magic shot out of Vedran's hand and wrapped around his ankle. Oscar grunted as Vedran tugged on the dark cord and brought him to the ground.

Mae started running, a spell falling from her lips on a desperate shout as the Sorcerer King's intentions became horrifyingly clear.

"*NEGATE!*"

Vedran did not waver an inch. He yanked Oscar to him, straddled his body, and punched his hand straight through his stomach to his core.

Oscar went rigid, his gaze locking blindly on his father's face. His spine bowed off the asphalt as the man who had sired him tried to rip his soul from his body.

Brimstone reached the Sorcerer King first and

smashed into his black magic aura. The fox snarled when he bounced off it and skidded some fifty feet.

A high-pitched ululation left Hellreaver as he attempted to slice Vedran's corruption apart. He might as well have tried to punch through water for all the difference he made.

Mae's heart slammed violently against her ribs.

"PURGE! CHAOS SEAL!"

The spells brushed off Vedran.

Shit! Bile burned the back of her throat as she tried to think what would work against him. *We need Nikolai.*

Oscar moved his head a fraction and met her frantic gaze as she closed in on Vedran. His mouth curved on a small smile even as his eyes glistened with sadness.

"Look—after Drabek!" he gasped.

His eyelids fluttered closed and his body went limp.

A crimson portal blasted into life to Mae's right.

Azazel shot out of it, Nikolai right behind him.

Brightness flooded the bridge, the white magic sorcerer landing on it with a thud. His power dispersed Vedran's corruption on a wave that made the air breathable again.

Nikolai snarled and spun the spear in his grip, the weapon crackling with the dazzling light of white and Moon Magic. "Not this time, asshole!"

He brought it down and sliced Vedran's hand off at the wrist. The Sorcerer King froze, eyes rounding in incomprehension.

Nikolai made the most of his father's shock and kicked him violently in the chest. He snatched the corrupt appendage still buried in Oscar's stomach and destroyed it with a burst of pale magic, the foul power it contained hissing and bubbling as it vanished between his fingers.

Azazel alighted next to Mae. "Daughter, are you okay?!"

"Yes!" Mae shuddered as the demon took her in his arms and squeezed her to his chest. She pulled back and searched her father's face. "Ran Soyun?!"

Azazel smiled. "She'll be here soon."

Mae's jaw tightened, her relief short-lived. "This isn't over yet."

Nikolai's voice had her head jerking around.

"Oscar!"

The sorcerer had dropped to his knees and was pressing his fingers to the wound in his brother's belly, his hands shaking. He lowered an ear to Oscar's lips. Relief had his shoulders sagging. He met Mae's eyes as he straightened, his lips stretching in a trembling smile.

Vlad cursed as Barquiel broke free of the hold he, Cortes, and Rambrog had on him. The demon flashed toward Mae.

Azazel blocked his nemesis's sword with his spear before he could reach her.

"Not today!" he snapped. "You're not touching a single hair on my daughter's head!"

Mae's scalp prickled. The sky darkened, eldritch clouds forming above the bridge, their spinning motion reminding her of *Eclipse*.

Her pulse accelerated when she looked over at Vedran.

The Sorcerer King had risen to his feet and was moving toward his sons in a black cloud of corruption. The asphalt melted under his steps. Metal corroded when he brushed against a truss.

"Brim! Hell!" Mae barked.

The demon fox and the weapon regrouped around Nikolai.

Brightness filled the sorcerer and his crow's eyes.

He widened his stance and shot a warning look at Mae. "Brace!"

Confusion fluttered through her. The bridge shuddered violently. She gasped.

Vlad swore. Cortes cursed. Rambrog almost stumbled off the deck.

The Sorcerer King seemed oblivious to what was happening, his attention focused on Nikolai.

"Give me your core, you wretch!" Vedran spat. "You do not deserve that magic!"

Nikolai lowered his brows. "Fuck you, asshole."

The waters below Brooklyn Bridge turned a dazzling white as he drew on the nexus beneath New York, static crackling around him in an ever-growing cloud.

Mae almost swallowed her tongue when a stream of dazzling magic rose from the East River and slammed into the deck straight beneath Nikolai's feet. Alastair opened his wings wide and screeched, his feathers running pale with magic.

"*HELL STORM!*" the sorcerer roared.

The flames that erupted across Brooklyn Bridge

swarmed its stonework and trusses, and brightened its cables with white fire.

Vedran choked and fell to his knees, hands rising to clutch his throat.

"Now, Mae!" Nikolai yelled.

Her heart pounded in her throat as she removed the skeleton key from her jeans. It had already assumed the star-shaped form Azazel had warned her about. Mae removed the *Book of Light* from her jacket and swallowed.

There was movement in the magic streaming from the New York nexus.

Her breath froze. An ethereal figure emerged from the bright beam rising from the river. Na Ri shuddered inside her.

The woman who floated down in front of Mae had long, black hair and a face that was nearly identical to her own. A beautiful, white Korean dragon danced sinuously in the air above her, his wise eyes observing Mae kindly.

"Hello," Ran Soyun murmured. "It's nice to finally meet you in the flesh, Mae."

Her face blurred as tears swarmed Mae's vision.

"Mother!"

She rushed into Ran Soyun's arms, only for her to stumble through her ghostly shape. A wretched sound left her throat.

"We cannot touch right now, my daughters," the first Witch Queen said in a voice tinged with sadness. "But we will, one day."

Mae squeezed her eyes shut when Ran Soyun

caressed her face, her magic warming her skin. Na Ri sobbed inside her.

"Now, do what must be done, daughters." Ran Soyun's voice hardened. "Destroy the *Book of Shadows*."

Agony scorched Mae and Na Ri's souls. They knew it was the right thing to do. Yet, they could not bear the thought of shattering their mother's soul too.

"I died a long time ago, Mae, Na Ri." Ran Soyun hugged Mae then, her spectral arms hovering close to her body, her warmth soothing the iciness gripping Mae's flesh. "My soul must return to the cycle of life and death so I can come back."

Her words jolted Mae.

Ran Soyun pulled back and smiled. "This is not a final farewell. This is simply a 'goodbye and see you next time.'" Her gaze shifted to where Azazel and Barquiel were locked in battle. "Besides, someone needs to keep your father on the straight and narrow."

A hysterical chuckle left Mae at that.

"Mae!" Nikolai yelled.

Alarm squeezed her chest. Vedran was climbing to his feet, black magic blanketing his body once more.

There was no more time left.

CHAPTER THIRTY-SEVEN

Demonic magic filled Mae's veins and shook her bones on a tidal wave that drenched the bridge in a scarlet light. She focused it into the skeleton key, jammed it inside the *Book of Light,* and incanted the name of the first Sorcerer King.

"*DAVOR LAZAR!*"

The artifact trembled and whined before shifting shape with a blinding flash.

Mae squinted. Her vision cleared.

A dagger filled with all the colors of magic had appeared in her hand, metal warming her skin.

"*NOOOO!*" Vedran screeched.

The Sorcerer King twisted around and started running toward her.

"*Hellreaver!*" Mae barked.

Hellreaver spat out the *Book of Shadows,* spun on himself, and lobbed it at her.

Vedran jumped, his arm rising desperately to catch the artifact. The tome sailed inches above his fingers on a wave of white magic that came from both Nikolai and Ran Soyun.

The sound of rage that left the Sorcerer King made Mae's ears throb. She snatched the *Book of Shadows* out of the air and stabbed it with the dagger the *Book of Light* had become.

Her hair and clothes levitated around her as a silent detonation shook the bridge and spread across the city.

The clouds parted when the invisible blast of power reached them. They rolled out in every direction, exposing the bright, blue sky they had shrouded.

Vedran screamed and clawed at his throat and stomach. He choked, knees buckling. Black magic poured out of his mouth and eyes and nose as he struck the deck.

Motion out the corner of Mae's eye had her head turning.

Waves were surging across Upper Bay.

Shudders shook the Brooklyn Bridge. She gritted her teeth and widened her stance, clinging grimly to the artifacts quaking violently in her hands.

Brimstone appeared at her left flank and pressed against her. Hellreaver whooshed into view and supported her right side.

Mae swallowed. "Thanks, guys!"

Of course, my witch, they rumbled, pleased.

A spectral shape whooshed out of Vedran's body. Mae's pulse quickened at the glimpse of a dark face full of menace before it vanished under the effect of the magic drenching the air.

"Was that—Davor?!"

Yes, Na Ri said.

Vedran twisted onto his back and convulsed, dark foam bubbling from his mouth. His hair turned white. His flesh shriveled. His body contorted and shrank.

Ran Soyun looked away from the awful sight and met Mae's gaze steadily. "Goodbye for now, my daughters."

Mae's throat constricted. "Goodbye, Mother."

I love you, Mother, Na Ri murmured brokenly.

Ran Soyun's magic danced across Mae's forehead as she kissed her brow.

"RAN SOYUN!" Barquiel roared. "*Don't you dare leave meeee!*"

Rambrog muzzled the demon.

"Come back to me, Ran!" Azazel's eyes were dark with grief where he, Vlad, and Cortes blocked Barquiel's path. "You promised you would!"

Ran Soyun smiled at her husband. "And I always keep my promises, my love."

The flow of time seemed to stop when she looked at Mae. Their gazes stayed locked as the souls of the first Witch Queen and her familiar shivered and broke apart in pale threads that vanished with sparks of dazzling white magic.

Grief tightened Mae's chest until she could barely breathe, Na Ri's sobs rocking her soul.

By the time the *Book of Shadows* stopped quaking, all that was left of the Sorcerer King was a skeletal husk that began crumbling to dust.

An enraged shout sounded behind Mae. She spun around.

"*Mae!*" Azazel yelled, fear raising the pitch of his voice.

Her father was chasing after Barquiel, blood pouring from the deep cut his archenemy had inflicted on his shoulder.

Barquiel raced ahead of him, mouth open on a silent snarl.

Wrath seared his right wing off.

The demon reeled, shock flaring in his crimson eyes. His dazed gaze swung to the cauterized stub of his pinion, his motions jerky.

The voices of the fiends inhabiting Hellreaver shook the air on a deafening roar as he flashed toward Barquiel. The demon cursed and parried his attack with his sword.

The blade snapped, Hellreaver chomping neatly through it.

Magic ignited Mae's cores. She marched toward Barquiel in a dazzling haze of crimson, black, and white, her brow furrowed in a heavy scowl. The spell left her lips on a hiss of rage.

"*SOUL UNCHAIN!*"

Barquiel shuddered. His form shifted.

Light filled Rose's world. She blinked and nearly stumbled, her feet touching solid ground for the first time in months. She looked dazedly at the broken sword in her hand before dropping it and staring at her shaking fingers, conscious of a burning sensation on her right shoulder blade.

"Rose?!"

Rose's head snapped up.

Heat spread through her cold flesh and made her heart swell at the sight of the woman taking hesitant steps toward her, her large, black eyes round with shock and swimming with tears, her beautiful face crumpling.

"Mae!"

Rose rushed into her best friend's arms.

"Rose!" Mae sobbed.

She squeezed her tightly, like she never intended to let her go.

Rose took a moment to bask in the warmth of the woman she had long considered her sister. She pulled back, conscious there wasn't much time left.

"You must bind my soul to this body and kill me, Mae! It's the only way to get rid of that demon!"

The color drained from Mae's face. "What?!"

"Rose is right, Mae."

Rose recognized the man who appeared at Mae's shoulder. He was the one who had stood by her side since the very beginning. From that dark night when her and Mae's world changed forever more. And now, at the end. His magic brightened his gaze even as regret and sorrow carved deep lines in his handsome face.

"Ran Soyun told me and Azazel before we left Hell that this is the only way to truly free Rose and stop Barquiel," he murmured.

A demon with large, curved horns approached, his

face full of kindness as he willed his strength upon his daughter. "Nikolai is right."

"I can't." Mae looked blindly at her father and the sorcerer before staring at Rose. She swallowed and shook her head, panic quickening her breaths. "I can't kill you, Rose! That's—!"

Pain tore through Rose's stomach. She winced and clenched her jaw. She could feel Barquiel trying to regain control of her body.

Rose scowled and grasped Mae's face. "It has to be you, Mae! Because you know me! Because you *love* me! That's why you must be the one who sends me to my eternal rest."

Mae clasped her fingers, sobs shaking her frame.

Tears choked Rose's breath.

"This body is but a shell, Mae." She hugged the trembling witch. "I died a long time ago. The only thing that remains of me is a fragment of my soul. A fragment Barquiel imprisoned so he could use this body. So let me go, Mae. I beg of you." Her voice broke. "Let me return to the cycle of life and death."

Heat pierced Rose's body. She looked down at the dagger of dazzling magic Mae had embedded in her flesh.

MAE'S HEART SHATTERED INTO A MILLION PIECES WHEN Rose slowly lifted her head and met her unblinking gaze. Her best friend smiled, her hauntingly beautiful eyes dazzling her as they filled with happiness and relief.

Mae's heart thudded dully inside her chest. She whispered the third spell Azazel had taught her. The one Vedran had used to imprison Balkin's soul.

"*Soul Bind.*"

Rose shuddered and closed her eyes briefly.

Barquiel's demonic presence faded from Mae's awareness.

"Thank you, Mae." Rose closed her arms around her, bleeding out from the fatal wound Mae had inflicted in her abdomen. "I love you, sister of...my... heart..."

Mae's world stopped when Rose went limp, her arms sliding to her sides.

Brimstone and Hellreaver pressed against her back and Nikolai and Azazel embraced her as she raised her face to the sky and screamed out her agony and sorrow, her magic filling the air with a red haze that made the city tremble and turned the waters beneath them crimson.

CHAPTER THIRTY-EIGHT

THE CALAMITY THAT BEFELL NEW YORK THAT DAY WAS put down to a freak weather phenomenon. It was a reality seared into the citizens' memories by Anya's Illusion Sorcery and bolstered by Gloria's magic to such a degree that most could describe in accurate detail the fluke lightning storm that had smashed the Empire State Building to smithereens, with the winds carrying the debris into the Hudson River.

As for the Brooklyn Bridge, a rogue typhoon became the prime culprit for the damage done to its deck and cables.

It helped that the Immortals and the Special Affairs Bureau had blacked out the satellites orbiting above the East Coast that day and shut down all media communication, courtesy of Jared and the Chicago Seer's forward planning.

The only ones who retained an awareness of the real reason behind the disaster were the mayor and his closest advisors. Mae would have preferred it if Anya had used her Illusion Sorcery to make them forget what they had witnessed prior to the magic war breaking out, but Bryony and Jared had insisted that would be a bad idea.

The Immortals, their allies in Chicago, and the magic community needed to work together with humans to prevent the End of Days. Mae had grudgingly arrived at the same conclusion.

Which was why they were currently sitting across from the mayor and his advisors at City Hall. The meeting began cordially enough with McKinney welcoming Mae and acknowledging everything she and the magic community had done to protect the city.

Things got awkward after one of McKinney's counselors presented them with a document.

Abraham frowned when the advisor handed him the file. "What's this?"

"A bill for damages," McKinney said coolly.

Jared arched an eyebrow. Bryony's mouth flattened into a thin line.

Abraham paled as he leafed through the paperwork. His eyes bulged when he got to the final figure. Mae leaned over and sucked in air when she saw the number.

Abraham regained his voice. He stared wide-eyed at McKinney.

"Five—five billion?!" the aide spluttered.

Bryony's knuckles whitened on the armrests of her chair. "What?!"

"We're willing to provide the New York coven with a generous repayment plan," one of the counselors, whom Mae had named Tweedle Dee, said with a thin smile. "It's on the next page."

Abraham flipped the document. He swore.

Mae looked at the proposal and narrowed her eyes at the mayor. "Thirty-five percent interest? What are you guys, loan sharks?"

McKinney's advisors bristled.

The second guy, Tweedle Dum, sneered at Mae. "You might be the Witch Queen, but you shall address Mayor McKinney with the respect he deserves!"

Hellreaver quivered a little on Mae's chest. *This guy is begging for an ass-kicking, my witch!*

Bryony, Abraham, and Jared cut their eyes anxiously to the weapon. Mae willed an incensed Hellreaver to calm down.

"Look," she told McKinney and his clowns once she'd promised the weapon steak for dinner, "at the end of the day, this city would have been flattened and you'd all be mindless, drooling slaves serving a Sorcerer King who enjoys nothing more than ripping your limbs from your body and feeding them to his monsters. Considering the final outcome of this war, *you* should be offering us a reward."

McKinney's face darkened. The Tweedle twins glared at Mae.

"How dare you?!" Tweedle Dum snapped.

Crimson static sparked around Hellreaver.

"Shit," Mae mumbled.

"He's gone and done it now," Abraham said flatly.

Hellreaver transformed. Mae winced. Jared groaned.

Bryony pinched the bridge of her nose and muttered, "This isn't happening," under her breath like it would make all of this go away.

McKinney and his counselors backpedaled hastily from the desk when Hellreaver hurtled threateningly toward them, teeth snapping.

"*How dare* you, *you little shits?!*"

Brimstone emerged from concealment. *Now, now, Hell, we must not threaten the humans.*

Tweedle Dee sucked in air. "Is that—is that a *fox?*" He flushed, shoulders quaking. "You brought a wild animal in here?!"

Brimstone curled a lip on a low growl. *Hey, the only wild thing in here is your hairstyle.*

Mae swallowed a snort and avoided Bryony's glare.

Tweedle Dum, whom she was starting to suspect possessed the survival instinct of an amoeba, pointed a shaky finger at the demon fox.

"His eyes are red! Has he," the counselor swallowed and recoiled, "—has he got the *mange?!*"

"Oh boy," Mae murmured.

Brimstone morphed into his nine-tailed form with an angry sound. The ceiling creaked as his head pressed against it.

"*The mange?!*" His roar rattled the windows. "*I'll have you know that I am a divine beast, you festering piles of excrement!*"

The fox stamped a giant paw on the floor, causing it

to crack. Abraham chewed his lip, eyeing the fresh damage to New York public property.

"*Now, bow to me and my Queen, you scum!*" Brimstone demanded haughtily.

"*And me!*" Hellreaver whined.

"*And the demonic weapon with the short fuse,*" Brimstone added charitably.

"*Hey!*" Hellreaver protested.

Bryony's eyes gleamed with an unhealthy shine.

She looked at Jared. "Maybe we could get Anya to do something about this."

She indicated the cowering mayor and his counselors. They shrank back from her finger. Jared dropped his face in his hands and groaned louder.

"Why don't we leave?" Mae suggested hastily.

They emerged from the building a moment later.

"All things considered, that could have been worse," Mae said encouragingly.

Bryony squinted. Abraham's eyes closed. Jared scowled.

"Wow," Mae murmured. "You guys were completely in sync there."

Abraham grumbled all the way back to the mansion on Fifth Avenue. Mae kept half an ear on his scolding, her gaze sweeping the city outside the SUV.

Two weeks had gone by since the day the prophecy concerning the Witch Queen had come to pass. The end of Anya's Illusion Sorcery had seen the citizens' lives slowly return to normal, the fake events they recalled of that day sinking into their subconscious like a bad dream.

The city still mourned the passing of those who had died and was planning to hold an official ceremony centered around the unveiling of a monument where the names of the dead had been engraved.

Violet had said they should put a statue of Mae next to it.

Mae shuddered. *I'm pretty sure she was only half-joking.*

It is no more than you deserve, my witch, Brimstone said firmly.

Yeah, Hellreaver enthused.

Mae rolled her eyes. *Like I need that headache.*

Just as it did every hour of every day since the awful events on the Brooklyn Bridge, a pang of sorrow squeezed her heart. Brimstone and Hellreaver pressed closer to her when they sensed her grief.

Saying goodbye to Ran Soyun and Rose still stung and would do for a long time to come. Though Mae had wanted nothing more than to shut out the world and wallow in her misery, those around her would not let her sink into depression.

To that end, Azazel had stayed in New York for a week after the war ended. He had met her human family and had even had dinner with them on a couple of occasions. For once, Ye-Seul had surprised everyone by refraining from her usual shocking dinner revelations. Mae suspected her mother and grandmother had been pretty much in awe of the demon.

When she'd asked Azazel what he intended to do upon returning to Hell, his answer had surprised her.

"I will revive the kingdom Ran Soyun and I once called home," he'd said with a smile. "It is time I restored it to its former glory. Besides, Ran will return one day so I must make sure our palace is ready for its queen."

Mae had glanced at Nikolai. "We can help."

Azazel had nodded solemnly. "I would like that dearly."

Abraham pulled up outside the mansion on 5th Avenue. The sounds of a commotion greeted them when they entered the foyer. Mae stared in the direction of the ballroom. The hall outside it was packed.

Violet emerged from the crowd.

"What's going on?" Abraham asked with a frown.

The witch sighed. "Alicia's here to take Rambrog home. The coven members don't want him to leave."

Mae wrinkled her nose. "Ah."

Bryony led the way to the ballroom.

Alicia wore a harassed expression where she stood surrounded by the Rambrog fan club, a group of witches and sorcerers the giant had saved during the battle in Central Park.

"You can't take him," a sorcerer protested.

Mae stared at the banner on the guy's chest. It depicted Rambrog leaning curiously toward the camera's viewfinder.

"Where'd they get that?"

"Miles had them printed in China Town," Violet muttered.

Her cousin stood amidst those campaigning for Rambrog to stay.

"Yeah, let him stay!" Miles said mutinously, waving a flag stamped with the same picture of Rambrog.

Abraham furrowed his brow. "He wasn't even in Central Park."

Bryony glowered at a figure in bright yellow pantaloons and a T-shirt emblazoned with the words: *Freedom for the Giant!* "What *is* she doing?"

Regina was going "Ra! Ra!" under her breath and utterly ignoring Barbara and Karin, who were scowling at her from the other side of the ballroom.

"Look," Alicia said in a voice that indicated her patience was wearing thin. "He's a giant from *Hell*, get it? That's where he belongs and that's where he's going back to!"

She pointed toward the windows. Everyone followed the direction she indicated.

Rambrog sat quietly on the lawn, his eyes crossed as he stared at the pretty butterfly perched on the tip of his nose, his expression one of awe and admiration.

"You gotta admit, he's kinda cute," Abraham mumbled.

Alicia cut her eyes to the aide. "Not you too!"

There was motion outside. Rambrog was rising to his feet.

He ripped some flowers out of a patch of soil and presented them shyly to the butterfly dancing around his head.

"Not—not my *dahlias!*" Bryony wailed.

Mae caught the witch as she swayed.

"Brim," she snapped.

On it, my witch.

Brimstone nudged Alicia out into the garden with his snout and had her open a portal. He shifted into his nine-tailed form, grabbed Rambrog by the back of his neck, and flung him unceremoniously inside it, dahlias and all.

Horrified objections rose from the Rambrog fan club. The protests died in the face of Bryony's glare. Miles put down his flag, shoulders drooping.

"Thanks," Alicia told the demon fox. She discarded her human appearance and dove inside the portal. "I'll visit soon!"

The Reaper queen was headed for Azazel's kingdom, where Rambrog intended to settle.

Mae waited for the brouhaha to die down before going in search of Nikolai. She found him in Oscar's room.

To everyone's surprise, Bryony had provided the sorcerer with temporary accommodation in her home. She was also the one who, along with Mae and Nikolai, had persuaded the High Council not to take action against Oscar and convict him of the crimes he'd committed under the aegis of the Dark Council.

It had become clear to everyone after seeing the dramatic difference in the sorcerer's personality and witnessing his actions in the war that the awful acts perpetrated by those who had worked for Vedran had been heavily, if not completely, influenced by the dark magic he had forced into their souls.

That some might have been innately evil was not a possibility Mae, Nikolai, and Bryony ever denied.

But Oscar was the sole survivor of the Dark Council. And they would not have won the war against the Sorcerer King had he not betrayed Vedran.

Oscar was closing a backpack when she knocked and entered the room. Mae's heart sank at the sight of the duffel bag by his feet.

CHAPTER THIRTY-NINE

Oscar smiled at her faintly. "I think most people in the New York coven would appreciate it if I did not prolong my stay further."

Drabek jumped off the bed and came over to greet Mae. She bumped heads gently with Brimstone, her chest rumbling with happy purrs. The fox licked her face.

Mae's chest lightened at the bond that thrummed brightly between the lynx and her sorcerer. Their cores were devoid of any aftereffects *Subjugate* might have left, something she knew Nikolai had been worried about.

A muscle jumped in Nikolai's jaw. "Promise you'll visit from time to time."

Oscar stiffened.

"I...don't think that's such a great idea," he said awkwardly.

He looked at Mae, seeking her help.

"He wants you to be the best man at our wedding if we ever tie the knot," Mae said quietly.

Oscar's eyes rounded. His gaze swung between them. "You guys are getting married?!"

Warmth flooded Mae's chest as she and Nikolai traded a secretive glance.

"We've talked about it," Nikolai said.

"But—what about the incubus?" Oscar said, confused. "I thought you would ask him if it ever came to—"

"Are you joking?" Nikolai scowled. "That asshole still wants to get in Mae's pants!"

She sighed. "No, he doesn't."

Nikolai pursed his lips. "He said as much last week."

"And I'm telling you he was yanking your chain."

Oscar finished packing and got ready to leave. Mae, Nikolai, and Bryony accompanied him and his lynx to the entrance of the mansion.

Bryony studied Oscar with a conflicted expression. "I wish you'd stay longer."

"Thank you. But I should go on this trip." He stroked Drabek's head. "It will be good for us."

The sorcerer intended to travel across North America for a few months before returning to Europe and dismantling what remained of the businesses run by the Dark Council.

Nikolai's eyes darkened as he studied his brother.

Their reconciliation had not been an easy process. Still, Mae knew the sorcerer no longer harbored a grudge toward the man who had ended his mother's life.

"Don't be a stranger." A tremulous smile danced across Nikolai's lips. "You're family."

He hugged Oscar.

Oscar squeezed him hard, his chin quivering.

Mae's throat tightened as the brothers pulled back and gazed warmly at each other.

Abraham came down the stairs. "Hey, anyone know about the crack in the pink Ming vase in Bryony's study?"

Drabek flinched. Oscar's shoulders knotted. Bryony narrowed her eyes suspiciously.

"It was an accident, honestly," Oscar protested. "She didn't mean to knock it over."

Bryony scowled. "Do you even know how much that vase is worth?!"

"Half a million," Oscar said promptly. "I checked." He grimaced. "I'll pay you back."

Magic flashed in Bryony's eyes.

Oscar paled. Nikolai and Abraham did their best to calm the High Priestess, to no avail.

"Run for it!" Mae urged the sorcerer and his lynx as Bryony unleashed her sword.

Oscar and Drabek bolted out of the door.

IT WAS LATE BY THE TIME NIKOLAI PARKED HIS SUV outside their apartment. They'd finally vacated Vlad's place and returned to the quaint, two-bed unit above the cinema in Ridgewood.

"Man, that was a long day," Mae muttered.

Nikolai closed the front door and dropped the keys on the console table. "Wanna have a nightcap before we go to bed?"

Mae shook her head. "I'm kinda pooped, to be honest. I think I'm gonna hit the sack."

"Oh," the sorcerer murmured. "Okay."

He stood and watched while Mae headed to her room, a strange expression on his face.

It was when she was stepping out of the shower some fifteen minutes later that Mae froze and blinked. "Wait a minute!"

Brimstone appeared in the bathroom doorway, a hot dog in his mouth. *What is it, my witch?*

Mae squinted. "Why is that in your mouth?"

It's a late-night snack. What's troubling you?

"Oh." Mae gripped the towel to her chest. "I just realized something. Nikolai and I haven't, you know," she shuffled her feet and bit her lip awkwardly, her voice dropping to a low mumble, "—had sex yet."

Brimstone choked on the hot dog.

Hellreaver woke up with a snort where he'd been dozing on the sink. The pair of them stared at her like she had grown a second head.

It took you this long to realize? Brimstone said pityingly.

That poor sorcerer has the patience of a saint, is all I'm saying, Hellreaver mumbled.

Mae pursed her lips. "Let me get dressed first. I feel uncomfortable having this conversation naked."

Fear not, my witch, Brimstone huffed. *Your pale, plump flesh does not excite us.*

Mae scowled. Five minutes later saw her dressed in her pajamas and her hair dried. She started pacing the floor.

"I mean, it'll be kinda awkward if I just walk up to him and say—"

Would you like to proceed with an amorous congress? Brimstone suggested.

Do you wish to do the deed of darkness? Hellreaver said salaciously.

How about we engage in some horizontal—? Brimstone began with a smirk.

"Alright, that's enough out of you two," Mae snapped.

She plopped down on the edge of her bed and put her head in her hands. "I don't know what to do."

Brimstone and Hellreaver exchanged a glance.

The weapon quivered. *There are books about the mechanics of intercourse if that's—*

"That's not what I meant, Hell!" Mae snarled.

Alright. Sheesh.

Determination tightened Mae's jaw. "I'm just going to walk over to his bedroom and seduce him."

She stood up.

Brimstone squinted at her pajamas. *Maybe you should change into that lingerie the incubus gave you. I sense your consort may not find your bunnies arousing enough.*

Mae studied her reflection in the mirror and chewed her lip. "You're right." She hesitated. "No, Vlad's gifts are too dangerous. They might give Nikolai a coronary."

Brimstone rolled his eyes. *He's a white magic sorcerer. He's as healthy as—*

A helldragon, Hellreaver interrupted excitedly, getting into the spirit of things. *A lustful one whose fiery loins have been curtailed for far too—*

Mae threw a pillow at him and marched out of the bedroom.

She bumped into Nikolai in the hallway. "Oh!"

He steadied her with a hand behind her back. "Hey."

Mae sucked in air when she found herself standing close to the sorcerer. His hair was damp and he smelled of vetiver shampoo.

"What," she gulped, "—what are you doing?"

"I was coming to find you," he said huskily.

Her breath caught at the look in his eyes.

They glittered with a banked heat, like he wanted to devour her whole.

A shiver danced down Mae's spine, her blood heating up to match the fire in his gaze. "Oh, hell."

She clasped his neck and yanked him down for a kiss.

Nikolai hesitated a fraction of a second before molding their mouths on a groan of pure desire. He grabbed her thighs and hitched her up his chest. She wrapped her legs around his waist and clung on for dear life, her fingers kneading his back.

Nikolai broke their kiss.

"Your room or mine?!" he gasped.

"Mine's closer."

Mae clutched his face and claimed his lips again. He headed for her bedroom, his hands hot where he clasped her thighs, his tongue clashing with hers in a way that was making her lose her mind.

Mae moaned when he put her down next to her bed, ending the kiss. Nikolai yanked his T-shirt off and dropped it on the floor.

Mae bit her lip as she scanned his six-pack and the alluring treasure trail arrowing past the waistline of his lounge pants. She hastily undid the knot in them. He chuckled, his fingers finding the buttons of her pajamas.

A snigger pulled them up short. Their heads swiveled.

Brimstone sat by the door. The fox was grinning.

Don't mind us, my witch.

Alastair perched on his head, the crow staring unblinkingly at Mae and his master in wide-eyed innocence.

Mae marched over, snatched up the fox and the bird, and deposited them outside the bedroom before slamming the door shut in their faces.

Oh, come on! Brimstone protested through the wood. A muffled snort followed. *Things were just getting interesting.* The fox paused. *The crow has questions, my witch. It would be better if he got a visual.*

"What's he saying?" Nikolai asked at Mae's pinched expression.

"Nothing you want to know. Now, where were we?"

Nikolai fiddled with the second button of her pajama top. "I was about to get ravished by a very hungry witch."

His lips curved in a devastating smile. Mae cursed

and pushed him down on the bed, lust making her feverish.

Nikolai laughed as he bounced. His expression sobered when Mae climbed on top of him. His hands found her hips. She parted her lips and lowered her head to claim his mouth, her hair falling in a silken curtain that brushed his flushed cheeks.

They froze when something hummed quietly in the room.

You guys know I'm still here, right? Hellreaver said.

EPILOGUE

"Six giant meatball subs and four pastrami cheesesteaks with extra bacon!"

Mae finished texting Nikolai and raised her hand. "Here!"

She slipped through the crowd packing the diner and took her order from the deli guy. He smiled as he handed her a couple of large carry bags.

"You're looking a bit peaky, doc. Everything okay?"

"Yeah. I just finished a nightshift." Mae arched an eyebrow. "And you know what they say about those."

Almost the entire diner roared, "Nightshifts suck!"

Mae laughed and waved at familiar faces as she made her way to the exit. A blustery wind cooled her cheeks when she stepped outside. Autumn had come to New York.

When do we eat, my witch? Hellreaver whined where he hung around her neck.

"When we get home," Mae said firmly.

Brimstone huffed beside her as they crossed the road. *He is nothing but a glutton, my witch.*

Mae glanced at Hellreaver. "You think he's gotten chunkier too?"

Hellreaver flinched.

Mae bit back a smile and headed for the garage where she'd left Betsy. She stopped at a red light for the ambulances that were reversing into bays next to the emergency department, her thoughts turning to the future.

With the end of her surgical residency at Grandview in sight, she needed to think about what she intended to do in the coming years.

You can always just be the Witch Queen, Na Ri said quietly. *It's not too early to start training the army we will need at the End of Days.*

Mae wrinkled her nose. *We have decades left before that happens.*

An army does not get strong overnight.

Mae sighed and stepped off the curb. *Alright, I'll think about—*

A panicked shout made her stiffen.

"*Rose, no!*" a woman yelled.

Movement opposite drew Mae's eyes.

A black ball of fur bolted across the road toward her. A little girl dressed in pink followed on its heels, heedless of the ambulance about to turn the corner.

Magic sparked through Mae's veins as she and

Brimstone dashed toward the girl standing in the path of the oncoming vehicle with the puppy she'd just picked up.

"*Shield!*"

The ambulance slammed into the invisible wall of magic she'd raised ten feet to her left. The eyes of the paramedic driving it rounded as the rear tires rose off the ground. The vehicle smashed back down on the asphalt, suspension groaning.

Mae stooped, snatched the little girl up in her arms, and reached the sidewalk where a woman stood shaking, her trembling hands covering her mouth.

Mae carefully handed the girl to her mother.

The woman reprimanded her daughter sharply before shuddering and squeezing her tightly to her chest, the puppy yipping between them.

Mae stared. "Samantha?"

The woman startled. Recognition flared on her face. "Mae?!"

Mae smiled. Samantha Bale used to be Steve Hodge's assistant. They'd been friends when they'd worked together in the autopsy labs.

"I haven't seen you since you went on maternity leave."

Samantha slowly relaxed. A weak smile stretched her lips. "I got pregnant again straight after, so there wasn't much point coming back." Her eyes twinkled as she glanced at the surgical scrubs under Mae's coat. "I'm glad to see you're back where you belong."

Mae returned her smile. She became aware of an inquisitive stare. She looked down at Samantha's daughter. Her breath caught when she registered the little girl's features for the first time.

Gray eyes the color of a summer storm sparkled brightly as they studied her from under a pink, fluffy hood that framed a pretty, chubby face.

Mae's chest tightened. "Rose?!"

Samantha's expression turned sad. "Sorry. I ended up naming her Rose after all."

Mae blinked and looked at Samantha jerkily, conscious she'd misunderstood her. "Oh. Yes, of course."

Samantha stood the little girl on the sidewalk. "Say hello to my friend, Rose. Her name is Mae."

Mae squatted, her pulse racing as her gaze roamed Rose's face.

The little girl beamed. "Mae!"

Emotion clogged Mae's throat. She blinked.

It's Rose!

Yes, my witch, Brimstone said softly. *And that is not just a puppy.*

Mae startled, her gaze finding the dog in Rose's arms.

The creature panting and beaming at them wore the eyes of a familiar they had last seen on Brooklyn Bridge, four years ago.

"Balkin," Mae breathed.

Rose grinned toothily. "Baki!"

She presented the puppy to Mae proudly.

Balkin's small, pink tongue darted out to lick Mae's nose, his kiss full of the gratitude of the noble wolf reincarnated inside him.

Mae laughed. Her breath hitched. Tears blurred her vision.

Thank you! Thank you for bringing them back to me so soon!

"Mae?" Samantha said worriedly. "Are you okay?"

"Yeah." Mae smiled and wiped the tears from her eyes. "I'm more than okay."

She unclasped the pink sapphire bracelet on her left arm and tied it around Rose's wrist.

Samantha blinked. "Isn't that—?!"

"It's alright. I want her to have it." Mae took the little girl's hands. "This used to belong to a friend of mine. Her name was Rose. Will you accept it?"

Little Rose watched her solemnly for a moment. Something flared in her pupils.

Mae, Na Ri whispered.

My witch, Brimstone murmured in a voice equally full of wonder.

Hellreaver trembled on her chest. *They have magic!*

Mae's mouth went dry when she detected the tiny cores inside Rose and the puppy, and the bright bond that tied them. "Oh."

She almost fell back when Rose slammed into her. Her arms closed automatically around the little girl.

"Rose, be careful!" Samantha warned.

The little girl ignored her mother, her chubby arms locked tightly around Mae's neck.

"Mae!" she whispered tremulously.

Mae squeezed her eyes shut, the familiar warmth of the soul belonging to the woman she had long considered her sister filling her with peace.

When Rose let her go, she looked like a little girl again, and Balkin a mischievous puppy.

Mae watched the mother and daughter leave after they parted ways, confident this would not be the last she would see of Rose and Balkin.

A man approached as she stood lost in thought, the carry bags she had dropped in her haste in his hands. "Here, I believe these are yours."

"Oh." Mae took the bags and smiled. "Thanks."

"Did you see what happened to that ambulance?" The guy scratched his head. "It was the weirdest thing, wasn't it?"

"I totally missed that, I'm afraid," Mae lied.

She thanked him again and resumed her walk to the garage, her pulse still racing and her chest light.

Wait till I tell Nikolai and the others about this!

Mae's stomach grumbled a moment later, reminding her that it was well past her breakfast time. A grimace twisted her mouth when she peered inside the carry bags.

Their contents were slightly flattened and had started to grow soggy.

"We better eat these the minute we get home," Mae muttered. Her hand froze. She stopped abruptly. "There are four giant meatball subs in here. Where'd the other two go?"

A gulping sound had her and Brimstone's gazes switching suspiciously to Hellreaver.

The weapon quivered innocently against her chest. *It's a Christmas mystery, my witch!*

Mae scowled. "Okay, first off, it's not Christmas yet.

Second, you should wipe that cheese off your teeth before you tell a barefaced lie, you sandwich thief!"

Hellreaver vibrated self-consciously. *Dammit!*

THE END

Thank you for being part of the final journey in the Seventeen Universe. It has been an incredible privilege to bring these stories to life for you. All good things must come to an end, so that new adventures can begin. A brand new A.D. Starrling series begins this year! It's funny. It's snarky. It features one of the most hilarious animal sidekicks I've ever written and a cast of characters that will leave you howling. Literally.

Make sure to sign up to my store newsletter for new release alerts and special deals on my books. Or you can sign up to my author newsletter to get upcoming release notifications, sneak peeks, and giveaways.

Don't forget to check out Seventeen and Legion, the first two series in the Seventeen Universe.

ACKNOWLEDGMENTS

To my friends and family. I couldn't do this without you.

To my readers. Thank you for reading Witch Queen. If you enjoyed my book, please consider leaving a review on Goodreads or on the store where you purchased it. Reviews help readers like you find my books and I truly appreciate your honest opinions about my stories.

BOOKS BY A.D. STARRLING

SEVENTEEN NOVELS

Hunted

Warrior

Empire

Legacy

Origins

Destiny

SEVENTEEN SHORT STORIES

First Death

Dancing Blades

The Meeting

The Warrior Monk

The Hunger

The Bank Job

LEGION

Blood and Bones

Fire and Earth

Awakening

Forsaken

Hallowed Ground

Heir

Legion

ABOUT A.D. STARRLING

Visit Shop AD Starrling and buy all of AD's ebooks, paperbacks, hardbacks, audiobooks, and exclusive special edition print books direct.

Want to know about AD Starrling's upcoming releases? Sign up to her author newsletter for new release alerts, sneak peeks, giveaways, and more.

Follow AD Starrling on Amazon.

Join AD's reader group on Facebook
The Seventeen Club.

Check out this link to find out more about A.D. Starrling
Linktr.ee/AD_Starrling.

www.ingramcontent.com/pod-product-compliance
Lightning Source LLC
Chambersburg PA
CBHW051240210726

48287CB00002B/336